PRIMAL
EXODUS

JACK SILKSTONE

VINCI
BOOKS

By Jack Silkstone

The **PRIMAL** Series

This book is dedicated to the PRIMAL fans. You've been with me through the good times and the bad. This one is for you.

Vinci Books

vinci-books.com

Published by Vinci Books Ltd in 2025

1

Chapter One

LIFEBRIGHT FOUNDATION FACILITY, RWANDA

THE TRUCK CAME to a shuddering halt with a hiss of brakes and a belch of diesel fumes, slamming the twenty teenage girls crammed into the back against each other. Not a single one of the Somali schoolgirls cried out or complained. Shackled at the neck they sat quietly, dressed in filthy school uniforms as the tailgate dropped with a clang.

A girl, her friends called her Jamilah, turned as the canvas cover was lifted revealing the angry face of a white man dressed in a dark green uniform.

"Get out of the truck!" he bellowed.

As the girls filed from the vehicle Jamilah glanced sideways at another man who was standing with other Caucasian green-uniformed guards. He looked like a soldier, barrel-chested, thick-necked, with tattoos covering muscular forearms.

The girl in front of her stumbled. One of the guards caught her arm and effortlessly hoisted her upright. It was at that moment Jamilah noticed that these men didn't look at the girls like the rebel soldiers had. There was no lust on their faces, no leering or ogling as they shuffled across smooth concrete under powerful lights. No, these men paid scant attention to them. It sent a shiver up her spine as she recognized the look on the men's faces. She'd seen it before on the face of their village butcher as he selected cattle for slaughter.

As the girls shuffled under a roller door they were met by a team of masked medical staff and unshackled. From here Jamilah and the others were ordered to strip and forced to shower in open stalls. The water smelled of chemicals but at least it was warm. When they'd toweled themselves dry they were handed baggy blue smocks and pants.

Showered and clothed the confused teenagers were shepherded through double doors by the guards, into a rabbit warren of sterile corridors. Jamilah had lost all sense of direction when she was finally shoved into a tiny room with another girl and the door was locked.

Their cell was half the size of the hut where she lived with her mother and sister. It contained two hard-looking beds and a tiny alcove that housed a toilet and sink. As she inspected the amenities her cellmate, a girl from her class at school, slumped onto one of the beds and wept.

Jamilah sat alongside and wrapped an arm around her. "It's OK. Everything is going to be alright."

"How?" the girl blubbered. "We're miles from home and no one knows where we are."

"People will be looking for us, and they will find us."

"You don't know that," she said between gasps.

She was right. Jamilah had no way of knowing if anyone from their village was looking for them. A savage militia had taken her and her friends from their school.

Over a hundred of them, including her younger sister, had been snatched and transported to rebel camps across the border in Kenya. She'd last seen her sister in one of those squalid camps, before she'd been dragged away and loaded into a truck. Tears ran down her ebony cheeks as she remembered the fear on her sister's face and her terrified screams.

"Someone will come for us," she managed as she held her friend.

Little did Jamilah know that they were being watched. In his office Doctor Dennis Morrison was gazing at a screen that displayed the feed from hidden cameras in all fifteen of the facility's cells. Behind the elderly geneticist the head of security, Elias, stood with his muscled tattooed arms folded across his dark green uniform. Around his waist he wore a battle belt bristling with the tools of his trade: radio, pistol, magazines, a baton and handcuffs. Alongside him, dressed in a khaki shirt and slacks stood a middle-aged white man with a smooth bald head, Ross Krenich.

"How many more do you need?" asked Krenich, a Rhodesian-born smuggler.

Dr. Morrison turned from the monitors. "Quantity is not the issue. I'm concerned with the quality. Over half of the last shipment was diseased or infertile."

Krenich shrugged. "This is Africa, Doc. You get what the Lord intends."

"Then you're not going to get paid until all of the subjects have been screened."

"I've delivered twenty girls. I get paid for twenty girls," snapped Krenich.

"I'll pay double for healthy specimens."

"I selected the ones that looked good."

"Looks can be deceiving." The Doctor gestured to a low

table stacked with lunchbox-sized containers wrapped in shiny metal foil. "These are test kits. You can use them to check the girls' blood."

Krenich took one of the packages from the bench and examined it. "Easy to use?"

The Doctor nodded. "The instructions are simple. You take samples and then send them to me. My people will load them into your truck."

The smuggler tossed the kit back on the bench. "We test them and bring the healthy ones. Then you pay double?"

"Yes."

"Sounds like a deal. I'll see you in a week." Krenich gave the head of security a nod and departed the room.

The Doctor took a seat at his desk and unlocked his computer. "Are we going to have any problems disposing of the waste?" he asked as Elias made to leave.

"No, we'll incinerate them on site and ship the barrels out later. There will be no evidence."

"And the woman that's been sniffing around?"

"I'll take care of her."

"Good, now if you don't mind, I have a call to make."

The Doctor waited until his hulking head of security had left before he opened his Skype account. Checking the clock on the corner of the screen he confirmed it was time for his weekly update with the Proteus Program Director. On cue, a call request appeared from Marnisha Copeland, his boss. He accepted the call, and her elfin features appeared on the screen.

"Doctor Morrison, how are you this evening?" she asked.

"Very good, we've made some important progress this week."

Marnisha's perfectly sculpted brow rose and she canted her head to one side. "Excellent."

Morrison swallowed, he found the senior geneticist's looks particularly disconcerting. Her long auburn hair, elegant neck and striking green eyes left him feeling flustered.

"Are you going to share the details?"

"Yes of course. We've had a breakthrough regarding the life-support system required to keep a womb alive outside of a body. I'm confident that within the next six months we will be able to birth one of your subjects without a host body."

Marnisha smiled, flashing near-perfect teeth. "That is exciting news. Well done, Dennis. Are you still having problems with the quality of your test subjects?"

"I'm confident that they will be improving in the short term."

"Excellent."

Doctor Morrison managed a nervous smile. "Is there any chance of an increase in funding? Acquiring optimal test specimens is getting expensive."

"With any luck. Now, talk me through the details of how you've managed to halt the deterioration of the host cells."

As the Doctor outlined the details of his procedure he gave the screen showing the cells a cursory glance. The medical staff had commenced testing of the new subjects. With any luck, one of them would provide the womb that would allow the next evolution in artificial birthing.

NYAGATARE, RWANDA

Less than thirty miles from the facility where Jamilah was imprisoned, in the town of Nyagatare, Bianca Paquet strolled through the city's only upmarket hotel and positioned herself at the bar. The CityBlue hotel was a recent addition to the town; sleek, modern and utterly soulless. She had no intention of spending any more time there than required.

Athletic with short blonde hair and defined angular features, the thirty-two-year-old immediately drew the attention of every man in the venue, much to the chagrin of the hookers on the lookout for clients. Leaning over the polished bar she cocked one long tanned leg up from under her floral print summer dress revealing a Converse sneaker.

"What are you having?" the waist-jacketed bartender asked.

"What beer do you have?"

"Primus or Skol."

Bianca, a French Canadian, had been in Rwanda for over a month and was familiar with the local brews. "I'll have a Primus, please."

He took a beer from a fridge, flicked off the cap and slid it across the bar. She took a few greasy US dollars from in her bra and left them on the counter before turning and surveying the room. Her grey eyes swept from left to right evaluating everyone sitting at the low tables and then the few men standing at the black marble bar. The man she wanted to speak to was sitting alone at the corner, studying his phone. He was a security guard at a local medical facility.

Taking a swig from her beer she swept her hand through her short blonde hair and moved along the bar. A

6

moment later the guard looked up from his phone and she flashed him a smile. He grinned back as he slipped the device into a pocket of his jacket and approached.

"Hello," he said with a South African accent. "I haven't seen you here before."

The man was tall with ebony skin and a chiseled jaw. Bianca guessed his age at early thirties, and probably, like her, ex-military. However, he'd taken a different path post-service, choosing to work for a corporation, whereas she was in Africa to teach children.

"I'm new in town."

His eyes narrowed. "Are you French?"

She shook her head and she sipped her beer. "No, I'm from Canada."

"Ah, yes. And what brings you to Nyagatare? No, let me guess. You're a doctor working with the WHO?"

"Close, I do work for the UN."

"So you are a doctor?"

"No, I work in logistics. I'm here to help non-profit organizations move more resources into the area." She paused. "What do you do?"

"Me, I'm in security. It's boring, but it pays the bills. By the way, my name is David."

"I'm Bianca, a pleasure to meet you, David."

"Are you staying here?" he asked.

"I should be so lucky. No, they've put me up in a dump across town. Where do you live?" Bianca continued the small talk, looking for any angle to pry into the guard's role at the medical facility and what he may have seen or heard. Twenty minutes and another drink later she'd made no progress and was doubtful about the rumors of kidnapped children. Politely excusing herself she left the bar.

Bianca sighed as she exited the hotel. The reality was

that her time in Rwanda was coming to an end. Her job teaching children had been satisfying but the non-profit had closed, funding drying up. Reluctant to return to Canada, she'd decided to investigate rumors of kidnapped children but that too seemed to be a dead end.

Flagging a cab she rode it through the dusty streets in the direction of her hotel. Nyagatare was a surprisingly clean township considering it was home to a population of fifty-two thousand Rwandans, most living well below the poverty line. The buildings were low slung and built primarily of mud brick with tin roofs that sweltered under the African sun.

She frowned as the cab slowed and the driver pulled over to the side of the road. "Why are you stopping?"

"I don't want any trouble," the driver said as he glanced up at the rearview mirror.

Bianca checked over her shoulder and saw a black four-wheel drive parked a distance behind them. "Keep driving."

"I don't want any trouble."

"I'll give you trouble," she hissed as she slid a thin fighting knife from a sheath fastened high on the inside of her thigh.

The driver took one look at the blade and jumped out of the vehicle.

"Son-of-a-bitch."

Bianca glanced over her shoulder and saw that two men had left the four-wheel drive and were approaching. She checked the front of the cab. The driver had taken the keys and she didn't have enough time to hotwire it. Instead, she chose to leave the cab and confront the men with her knife hidden behind her wrist.

"Can I help you?" she asked as the two men stopped a short distance from her. They were both black and dressed in cargo pants with khaki shirts worn loose over T-shirts. They had the same bearing as David, who'd no doubt tipped them off.

"Boss wants to talk to you."

Bianca smiled as she took a business card from her bra and flicked it at the man. "Well, then he can contact my office in Kigali."

The man opened his shirt enough that Bianca could see his pistol in its holster.

She grimaced. "Fine, lead the way."

They directed her to the rear seats of a black Toyota Landcruiser. One of them opened a door and she looked inside. A thick-necked white guy with tattooed forearms sat in the back.

"Get in."

"I'm good here."

One of the men placed a hand on her shoulder and she twisted out from under it and struck him in the throat with her palm. He doubled over, coughing. The other man pulled his pistol and aimed it at her head.

"You going to use that?" Bianca asked as she let her knife slide down into her hand.

The boss in the four-wheel drive shook his head and the man holstered his gun.

"So what's this about?" she asked.

"I was hoping you could tell me," said the guy inside.

Bianca shot him a look implying she had no idea what he was talking about.

"Rwanda isn't a safe place for a pretty blonde. Keep sticking your nose in where it's not wanted and you're going to find out first hand." He waved his men into their vehicle and drove away, leaving Bianca with the abandoned cab.

Intimidation was something that she had lived with her

entire life. She'd faced bullies throughout her childhood and into her military career, never being dissuaded her from her goals. Plus, whoever the guy was in the four-wheel drive, he'd just confirmed there was definitely something worth investigating at the medical facility.

She sheathed her knife as she strode back to the cab. As she reached the driver's door there was a shout from her left and the cabbie appeared from behind some bushes. "The meter is still running," he announced cheerfully.

"Only in Africa," she mumbled as she climbed into the back seat.

BORDER REGION, SOMALIA

A cricket chirped as Kurtz crouched in a thicket waiting for a signal from his forward scouts. The tall German was dressed from head to toe in A-TACS arid camouflage. Across his chest he wore body armor with pouches stuffed with magazines. In his gloved hands he held a heavily modified and suppressed AK-104 painted in the same camouflage pattern. His angular face was daubed in earthy hues, rendering him almost invisible in the soft light of an African dawn.

To his right knelt Kruger, a broad-shouldered South African dressed in similar garb except for his choice in weapon, a suppressed PKP-SP. The compact machine gun resembled a standard assault rifle in the massive arms of the former special ops soldier.

Kurtz and Kruger, or Team K2 as they called themselves were members of a vigilante organization waging a global war on injustice. Their current mission was the recovery of a hundred schoolgirls kidnapped by Al-Shabaab in Somalia. Over the last few weeks they'd been tracking the girls from camp to camp, leading to this location on the Somali-Ethiopia border. Now they were waiting for their scouts to confirm the base was occupied before making their assault.

"This is taking too long," whispered Kruger. "Booyah should have reported in by now. It's going to be too light soon."

"Patience." As Kurtz replied, there was a crackle in his earpiece.

"Jack Hammer," transmitted Booyah.

"Finally," said Kruger as he rose to his feet and readied his weapon.

The pair advanced in perfect synchronization. Each man covered his allocated space as they moved between thick thorn bushes on their way to the camp. Booyah had marked them a trail of broken sticks, and they followed them, eyes peeled for any enemy.

A hundred yards into the scrub they spotted rubbish among the bushes; plastic bottles and wrappers. At the very edge of the camp they found Booyah and one of his men. Two sentries lay at their feet, blood staining the earth.

The Somali scouts were dressed in ragtag uniforms designed to allow them to blend among the Islamist militants as well as the harsh African landscape. Only the condition of their AKs, supplied by Kurtz, differentiated them from their quarry.

"About fifteen men," Booyah whispered. "We can't see the girls, but there is a prison in the ground. They may have been here."

"How long ago?" asked Kurtz, his voice laced with desperation.

"I can't tell."

"We'll need a prisoner," said Kurtz.

Kruger sighed. "Fine." The South African wasn't one for showing any quarter to the fanatical Islamists.

Kurtz led the small patrol toward the camp with Kruger off his right shoulder and the two scouts bringing up the rear. His keen eyes spotted a brush hut among the bushes and he raised his weapon. Four men were crouched around a fire warming their hands and brewing coffee. Their guns were stacked a short distance away. He moved forward silently, the red dot of his sight balanced on an Al-Shabaab fighter's head.

He was less than a dozen yards away when a stick cracked under his boot. The fighter glanced up, spotted him and reached for his weapon. He had barely moved when Kurtz's bullet split his head like a melon and he toppled sideways.

The others died in a hail of gunfire as Kruger hosed them down with the PKP. His weapon sounded like sharp thunderclaps in the still morning air, despite its suppressor. The camp came alive with yelling as the other fighters spread the alarm. Kruger's belt-fed machine gun continued to stammer as he engaged a pair of men who appeared on their flank. They jerked like puppets as 7.62mm rounds sliced through them, cutting their fanatical charge short.

Somewhere deeper in the camp an AK barked followed by another as the Al-Shabaab fired at shadows.

Kurtz gestured to his left and they moved swiftly around a large tin shack. Another fighter appeared, weapon ready. Kurtz squeezed the trigger and he fell backward into the dust with a steaming third eye. Three more men appeared only to be cut down by Kruger.

As the noise from their shots faded a deathly silence

descended over the bush camp. The battle-hardened Al-Shabaab fighters were laying low, listening.

Kurtz knelt alongside a tree stump. The others found cover and aimed their weapons outward.

The enemy's probe came from their right. Kurtz caught a glimpse of movement among the mud huts and makeshift shelters. A moment later he saw a combatant creeping forward. A thumb down and a pointed AK barrel indicated his target to the others and they oriented themselves, lying prone.

Their camouflage gave them the advantage. The gunmen moved forward cautiously but didn't spot Kurtz's team until it was too late. Kruger's machine gun, supported by the others, cut them down in a hail of lead and steel. Kurtz spotted another target and aimed for his knee. He squeezed off a single shot and a bearded fighter lurched over with a cry.

With the enemy decimated the team swept forward dispatching wounded men with single shots.

Kurtz made a beeline for the man he'd downed, his sights aligned for a kill shot. His prey was trying to crawl into thick bushes. The tall German checked Kruger was covering him and grabbed the man's leg, dragging him into a clearing. A savage punch to the face ensured he wouldn't resist before securing his hands with plasticuffs.

As the team cleared the rest of the camp Kurtz spotted an empty hole with wooden bars over it.

"That's where they kept the girls," said Booyah.

Emotion washed over Kurtz as he imagined their scared dirty faces looking up from the pit. Rage boiled inside him and he stormed back to their wounded prisoner.

"Booyah, ask him where the girls are."

The scout questioned the wounded man in his native tongue with Kurtz standing menacingly beside him.

After a short conversation, Booyah translated. "He says there were no girls here. I told him not to lie to the green devils or they will cut out his stomach and leave him for the baboons."

Kurtz slid his combat knife from his rig and held it in his left hand to reinforce the point. The man's eyes went wide with fear and words flowed from his mouth like a machine gun.

"They were here, but word came that the green devils would come for them. He said his chief took them across the border to El Leh to sell them," translated the scout.

"To who?"

Booyah asked the man then looked back. "He doesn't know the man's name. He's a white mercenary."

Kurtz's eyes narrowed as Kruger joined them. "Rest of the camp's clear. No sign of the girls. This guy know anything?"

"*Ja*, we're looking for a white people smuggler in El Leh." Kurtz sheathed his knife.

The Al-Shabaab fighter exhaled.

Kurtz raised his rifle and shot the extremist through the head. Then he thumbed the mike of his radio. "Toppie, we need a pickup."

Chapter Two

TEL AVIV, ISRAEL

KEILA BACHMAN SWIPED an access card and entered her office deep within Mossad Headquarters. Striding into the open workspace she shared with her *Kidon* team she placed a tray of coffees on a conference table and lowered herself into a chair. "Sorry I'm late. Mega queue in the cafeteria."

The veteran Mossad agent was dressed in a pencil skirt with a white blouse. It wasn't her usual attire. An avid athlete her daily dress was usually leggings with a T-shirt. Broad-shouldered with a short ponytail and green eyes she was pretty in an unconventional way.

Her team left their desks and rolled their chairs across to the table. Keila's *Kidon*, or operations team, consisted of six members, including her.

Abel, a lanky mid-thirties graduate, was her lead analyst. He worked with Jacinta, a middle-aged motherly type and Fahim, a bespectacled twenty-five-year-old male with a fair complexion and flaming red hair. The other two members, operatives Dan and James, were on leave for the next month. James was still recovering from wounds while Dan was recently married and enjoying some well deserved down time with his wife.

"How did your meeting go with the director?" asked Abel as he reached for his latte.

"Positive. I outlined the potential in working with Bishop and his team and he agreed to provide additional funding and compartment the project. I'll report directly to him, and we'll be the only ones with the complete picture."

"That's good news. It will definitely help keep the dogs at bay," he said, referring to the poaching of intelligence sources that regularly occurred within the agency.

"And, with additional resources, we'll be able to capitalize on the success we've already had." Keila's team had recently captured a High Value Target with the assistance of a shadowy group of mercenaries operating out of the Emirates.

"Jacinta, any progress on identifying other members of Bishop's team?"

The mother-of-three's facial expression told Keila that she hadn't had a breakthrough yet. "None of the other Lascar employees have turned up a lead. According to social media he's a bit of a loner."

"Except for Saneh?" Keila referred to Bishop's partner and lover, a beautiful woman of Middle Eastern descent with superb espionage skills.

"Yeah, and all we know is that somewhere in Mossad there's a sealed file on her," added Abel. "Did you ask the Director about that?"

"No. I think it's best we give him the impression that we're focused on Bishop and Priority Movements Airlift. I'm not sure if he's aware of the file on Saneh."

"And bringing it to his attention might get the whole project taken off us," said Abel.

"Exactly. Now, how are we tracking on Priority Movements assets?"

"There are a half dozen specialist aircraft listed in their holdings including a LM-100 Hercules, Ilyushin-76 and a Gulfstream ER650," said Jacinta.

"And crew?"

"From what I can ascertain they use Lascar pilots with specialist security from inside Priority Movements."

"That's where Bishop fits in," added Keila. "Where are we with 8200's penetration of their communications network?" she asked between sips of her caramel latte.

Abel was her man when it came to liaison with the Israeli signals intelligence agency. "Making some good progress. They're focused on mapping the network to identify potential weak points they can penetrate."

"They've been unable to break the encryption?" Keila asked.

"Correct, Asher, the lead analyst, doesn't want to trip their defenses. They're going to sneak in through the back door," said Abel.

"Good, the last thing we want to do is jeopardize our relationship with Bishop. His access and capability is critical."

"Asher also asked if you're single," added Abel with a wink.

Keila blushed into her coffee.

"First, a hot Aussie and now a charming SIGINT Captain, you're in demand," said Jacinta.

"OK, let's keep this work focused."

"When it rains it pours," said Fahim.

She shook her head. "Abel, did they give a likely time frame on penetration of the network?"

"A week, possibly two. However, they have got some initial reflections that indicate a possible operation running on the Somali Ethiopian border."

"That's interesting."

"Yes, I got them to break it off under a separate task number. Didn't want to put all our eggs in one basket."

"Good call." She clapped her hands. "I'm excited. Once we've got access to their communications we'll be able to truly understand their capacity and put Bishop and his team to work."

ABU DHABI, UAE

Aden Bishop relaxed on a couch in the living room of his penthouse apartment in Abu Dhabi. The former Australian Army intelligence officer wore a headset and was sipping from a Coopers Pale Ale as he stared at his laptop. His Border Collie, Daisy, was curled up alongside him.

Dark-haired with a crooked nose and almost black eyes, Bishop looked like he'd been around the block a few times. The man on the other end of the video call, Mitch Freeman, sported a heavy beard and shaved head. Bishop and Mitch were members of PRIMAL, an elite private vigilante organization. Bishop was a field operative while Mitch was the team's quartermaster and lead pilot. With the organization currently on hiatus, both men had time to work on projects of their own.

"Mitch, where are you at the moment?" asked Bishop.

"New Zealand, South Island," replied Mitch in his crisp British accent.

"You get down to Queenstown?"

"I flew into QT and drove out to Central Otago to check out some property for Vance."

"The old man looking to retire in the wine country?"

"Something like that. He bought this old pub a few years back and wanted me to check out the renovations and add a few features. I'd never been to NZ, so I jumped at the opportunity."

"Great part of the world, Saneh and I love it."

At the sound of her name Bishop's partner, Afsaneh Ebadi, Saneh to her friends, appeared from the master bedroom dressed in tights, sports bra, and a loose-fitting singlet. The former Iranian operative had long black hair and exotic Middle Eastern features with almond-shaped eyes. Despite being in her late thirties she had a taut, athletic figure. Bishop's eyes tracked her as she crossed the room. Eight years of emotional turmoil had done little to dampen the feelings he had for her.

"You guys have fun, I'm off to the gym," she said, grabbing a sports bag and heading out the door.

"Things OK with you guys?" asked Mitch, once she had left.

Bishop shrugged. "I think so. She seems a bit distracted at the moment."

"That's to be expected. It's a tough time for everyone."

Bishop stroked Daisy's ears. "Tell me about it."

"You heard from Mirza?"

"Yeah, he's studying law part-time and assisting Sonia on domestic violence and immigration cases. I'd be surprised if they don't tie the knot soon." Mirza Mansoor, a former Indian soldier, had been Bishop's offsider within

PRIMAL. When the organization had stood down, he'd moved to London with his partner, Sonia.

"Good stuff. I'll have to drop by when I'm next in Blighty. Oh, by the way, I got an update from the shipyard in Siros. Your boat is almost finished. They're making some final adjustments to the rigging."

Bishop grinned. "Sweet, once it's ready Saneh and I are going to sail it through the Suez and berth it down at the marina. When it's time to move on we simply up-anchor and the world's our oyster."

"Well, you're going to be pretty comfortable on a fully automated 112-foot ketch. She's got all the bells and whistles, and a few extras on the side." Mitch winked. The former British Ministry of Defence scientist was a master of covert technologies.

"You ramped up the gym, didn't you?"

Mitch shrugged his muscular shoulders and shot Bishop a cheesy grin. "Maybe!"

"I better not get to Greece and find you've turned my baby into a floating fitness center."

The Brit laughed. "No, Bish. She meets all your specs and more."

"So, when are we going to see you back in the Emirates?" asked Bishop as he finished his beer.

"End of the month. I've got to shoot over to California to check on a few things at the workshop." Mitch had purchased a private airfield an hour north of Los Angeles. He was in the process of turning the former desert military outpost into a Special Effects facility.

"Mate, that's the best retirement plan ever."

"Hey, I've gotta be able to blow stuff up otherwise I'm going to go insane. Right, I've got to love you and leave you, brother. I've got a dozen contractors working on Vance's place and they're currently unsupervised."

"Roger, I'll catch you soon." Bishop terminated the call and rose from the couch. Daisy followed his lead and tailed him across to the floor-to-ceiling windows that overlooked the ultra-modern city of Abu Dhabi. From the apartment he could see down to the marina where his ship was soon to be berthed.

PRIMAL had relocated to the city a little over two years earlier and Bishop hated it. Sleek buildings and shiny malls hid a dark underbelly of greed and waste. It was a city of consumption and Bishop longed to escape it with Saneh, the love of his life. He felt Daisy lean up against his leg and knelt to stroke her ears. "Oh, you're coming too little lady."

———

EL LEH, ETHIOPIA

The engine of a battered, but well-equipped Nissan Patrol labored as it clambered up a slope through thick red mud. Cresting a rise it turned a bend that snaked through dense jungle and emerged into a clearing. The four-wheel drive slid to a halt in front of a grubby concrete-walled building. What had once been a school was now in disrepair. The driver's side door opened and a heavily muscled Ugandan emerged cradling a compact AK. He eyeballed the ragtag group of rebels standing around the dilapidated structure. "Where are the girls?"

"Inside," one of them responded. "With da boss."

He nodded and opened the passenger door.

Ross Krenich stepped out wearing his usual khaki shirt and slacks. "Mukisa, get the kits."

The Rhodesian people smuggler waited for his man to pull a rucksack from the rear of the vehicle then followed him into the building. As his eyes adjusted to the gloom he spotted a cluster of scared schoolgirls in one corner of the large room. There were at least twenty of them hunkered together like livestock, rope linking their necks. At the opposite end of the trash and rubble-strewn room a man was sitting on a rusted barrel, smoking a cigarette. Krenich recognized the figure as Dula, the militia leader who'd supplied his previous merchandise. Slight, with a dark scraggly beard and narrow features, he looked like a weasel.

"Ah, Mr. Ross, back for more of my finest products," said Dula in heavily accented English.

"If the last lot were your finest…" He gestured to the women in the corner. "Are these the scraps?"

Dula dropped off the barrel and flicked his cigarette toward the girls. "We kidnap hundreds. They're all good."

"You'd know."

He smirked. "I've tried a few."

Krenich waved Mukisa forward. "I need to test their blood."

"What?"

"The girls, I need to test their blood. The buyers will only pay for healthy ones."

His bodyguard opened the rucksack and removed the foil-covered packages provided by the doctor. He handed one to Krenich who tore it open and pulled out the test kit. "I'll pay double for them. You can sell the others to someone else."

Dula considered the offer as he knocked a cigarette from a packet and lit it. "How long will it take?"

"A day or two."

"The price will be triple."

"Too much."

The militiaman took a deep drag of his cigarette. "Do you know what *Ibliisku* are?"

"It's Somali for devil."

"Yes. The *Ibliisku* have been raiding our camps. They've been chasing the girls. The price is triple because we need to move them every day."

Krenich held out his hand for a cigarette. "Tell me more about the *Ibliisku.*"

Dula lit a second cigarette with the ember of his own and passed it to him. "We don't know much. They've hit three camps and killed dozens of warriors."

"They're after the girls?"

He nodded. "We think so. They've only raided the camps with girls from Mogadishu."

"OK, I'll pay triple. We'll take samples now and test them." He took a deep suck on his cigarette. "Meet us here with the girls day after tomorrow. We'll take the ones that pass. You keep the rest."

"Agreed. Payment will be in diamonds."

"As you wish." Krenich finished the cigarette and stubbed out the butt on the side of Duma's barrel before sliding it into a plastic bag in his pocket. "Can you get your men to line them up? We'll take the samples and get going."

Once the girls were lined up Krenich and his bodyguard moved along them using the sampler extractors to take blood. They marked the cylinders then scribbled a matching number on each girl. As he pressed an extractor against the last girl's arm she looked up at him with sad eyes. She looked remarkably like one from the previous shipment. Perhaps they were sisters. Pushing the thought from his mind he slid the tube of thick red blood into a foam safety box. "Dula, we'll see you back here at the school in two days."

The militia boss grinned. "Bring lots of diamonds. I think all of these ones will be good."

———

MADIINO, SOMALIA

Kurtz finished cleaning his AK and snapped the receiver cover in place with fingers black with carbon and oil. Maintaining the weapon was a cathartic process that he conducted at the end of every mission. Not only was it good practice, but it also allowed him to gather his thoughts and process the often-traumatic events that occurred during a PRIMAL operation.

The mission to recover the girls had become intensely personal for Kurtz. He and Kruger had met with the families of the girls who'd been kidnapped, to gather intel. One look at their grief-stricken faces was all he'd needed to dedicate himself to finding them. A former German Counter-Terrorist policeman, Kurtz was utterly committed to making the world a better place.

Kruger was already inside the buried shipping container that served as their armory. The broad-shouldered South African was servicing his own equipment under the supervision of his dog, Princess. The burly Ridgeback Mastiff-cross turned and ambled across to greet Kurtz as he placed his AK on a rack.

"Debrief in five?" asked Kurtz as he patted the dog.

"*Ja*," replied Kruger.

He left the shipping container and crossed the twenty yards of junkyard that separated the buried shipping containers from a rusted hangar. The odd assortment of buildings was part of a complex that belonged to Toppie, a colleague from Kruger's Recce days. The eccentric bush pilot and smuggler had built what resembled a cross between a military scrapyard and an apocalyptic fortress. It was the perfect base of operations for their hunt for the girls.

Shoving open a side door to the hangar Kurtz was greeted by aggressive barks. Five of Princess's brothers and sisters swarmed him with wet noses and slobbery tongues. "OK, OK." Kurtz shoved his way through the excited animals to a Mi-17 helicopter. Originally a transport helicopter, Toppie had recently upgraded it into a formidable gunship. Soviet-era rocket and cannon pods hung from four hardpoints under stub wings, purchased with a recent injection of funds from PRIMAL.

"Just a minute!" Toppie said before rolling out from beneath one of the rocket pods and climbing to his feet. Squat and rotund with a heavy beard that reached the center of his chest, Toppie looked more outlaw biker than arms dealing, pilot mercenary.

"How's it, bro?" he asked Kurtz when he was closer.

"*Gut, ja.* Kruger and I are going to conduct a debrief with Booyah if you're free."

Toppie wiped his hands on a rag as he turned from the helicopter and made eye contact with Kurtz. "For sure." He paused. "Don't be so hard on yourself, eh. We're going to find those girls. All in good time."

"*Ja*, of course," Kurtz said half-heartedly. He turned, ducked under a drooping helicopter blade and navigated through the piles of helicopter parts that cluttered the side of the hangar. Exiting through a side door he stepped into the operations center that Toppie had constructed for them.

It consisted of two shipping containers welded together side by side. The walls inside had been removed and the exterior paneled with wood. A pair of air conditioners kept the temperature at a pleasant level.

Their Somali scout, Booyah, was already inside, standing in front of a large map of Somalia and surrounding countries. He was studying the red pins that Kurtz had placed at the locations of camps they had raided.

On hearing Kurtz enter the lean-faced former pirate turned and shot him a nod. "Kurtz, I've got good news."

"What is it?" he asked, sitting at the central table.

The oil-stained wood was strewn with maps and print-outs of aerial surveillance photos of their potential targets. More imagery was plastered across the walls, including a poster with photos of the seventy teenage girls who remained missing. From their school photos they stared out at the men who had dedicated themselves to finding them. For Kurtz, it was a daily reminder that so far they had only rescued thirty.

"We think we've found another camp across the border in Ethiopia." Booyah was the team's leading source of intelligence. Formerly a pirate, he'd worked for the man who had hired Kurtz and Kruger to find the kidnapped girls. That man's name was Al-Mumit, the self-proclaimed Pirate King of Somalia and he was single-handedly funding the operation.

"Who's your source?" asked Kurtz as Toppie and Kruger entered the room.

"A family link. They said that the local militia leader's name is Dula. He's a smuggler with ties to Al-Shabaab and ONLF based in Omorate," he explained, referring to the two Islamist militant groups most active in Somalia and surrounds. "My contact says he's been throwing a lot of cash around."

"So he might be the one selling the girls to the white smuggler?" asked Kruger as he joined Kurtz at the table. Toppie helped himself to a soda from a bar fridge.

"What else do we know about this Dula?" asked Kurtz.

"He's got several camps." Booyah directed their attention to the map. "Moves around a lot to avoid the authorities."

"Which is going to make it hard to pin him down."

"Yes, but he's in an area with lots of people. It will be easy to infiltrate and work out exactly where he is. Then you fly in with the helicopter and rescue the girls," said Booyah.

"Good plan, *ja*," added Toppie. "Maybe this time I can use some rockets to shake things up a little."

Kruger snorted. "You and your damn rockets."

"Hey, you get to shoot these bastards all the time," said Toppie.

"It's not a competition!" snapped Kurtz. "We've been hunting for two months, and so far we've only found thirty *schülerin*."

The comment plunged the room into silence. Booyah, Kruger and Toppie all stared at Kurtz, solemnly.

"We need to step up our operations or they're going to be dead."

The trill of Kurtz's phone broke the tomb-like atmosphere of the room. He pulled the device from his pocket and checked the number. It was Al-Mumit. The Pirate King would be looking for an update on the hunt. Kurtz slid the phone back into his pants. He'd call their employer back later. "This Dula looks promising. Let's put together a plan and get after him."

Chapter Three

THE SANDPIT, ABU DHABI

JAMES CASTLE, or Ice as his colleagues knew him, spun his massive shoulder as he extended his arm and shoved a floor-to-ceiling punching bag with his palm. At the same time, he sidestepped as he snatched his pistol from its concealed holster inside his belt-line and fired two plastic ball bearings into a man-shaped paper target. Holstering the airsoft gun he inspected the target. His pellets had punched two neat holes through the bridge of the zombie terrorist's nose.

Ice flexed his artificial left hand as he stepped back to repeat the drill. The former CIA operative had lost his hand when he'd been severely injured in Afghanistan. The blast that had destroyed his limb had also left his face heavily scarred. Mitch had designed him a state-of-the-art prosthetic that worked as well, if not better than the original. The joke among the **PRIMAL** team was that Mitch was slowly turning the six foot seven blue-eyed blonde operative into the *Terminator*.

"Nice shooting," said a gravely voice from the doorway of the three-bay garage that served as their gym. He nodded and turned to the bald African American. Vance, the Director of Operations for PRIMAL, was dressed with his usual flair: a garish Hawaiian shirt, linen pants and leather slip-on sandals. The outfit accented his barrel chest and bulging biceps.

"Yeah, when you gonna put me in, coach?"

Vance chuckled. "You know as well as I do that the whole team's been benched."

"Except for Kurtz and Kruger. They've got a mission."

"Well technically, it's not a PRIMAL mission."

"Yeah, well at least they're making a difference."

Ice walked across to a workbench in the corner of the garage, unloaded his pistol, and removed his holster and belt. "Coffee?"

"Right on."

The two men entered the luxury beachfront villa that contained what remained of PRIMAL's command element. The organization had previously numbered nearly a hundred operatives and had been based at a hidden island facility in the South West Pacific. However, compromise by the CIA had resulted in a significant downsizing, relocation and ultimately, hiatus.

Now, the Sandpit was merely a monitoring site, PRIMAL's arsenal of weaponry and equipment nowhere to be seen. The closest thing to a firearm was the replica pistol Ice used for training. Weapons were not something anyone wanted to get caught with in a country that regularly enforced the death penalty.

Ice and Vance had initially started the vigilante organization together. Disgruntled CIA operatives, they were given a unique opportunity from the son of a wealthy

Emirati extremist. Decisive action had resulted in their retirement from government work and the establishment of the world's only truly independent covert operations team.

Chen Chua, the Chief of Intelligence, was already in the kitchen firing up the espresso machine.

"Long black and a chai latte please, barista," barked Vance as he and Ice sat at a sleek marble breakfast bar.

"Do I look like a hipster?" he shot back.

"You've got skinny little hipster arms," Ice said, with a grin. "Must be all that *CrossFit*."

There was a good-natured rivalry between the three men that stemmed from their differences in exercise methodologies. Ice and Vance were both powerlifters and had solid builds. Chua, an American of Chinese descent, had a lean wiry frame that favored high intensity over power.

"Yeah, well all that bulk's gonna catch you out big man," said Chua. "Too much weights and not enough speed work," he continued in his best New Zealand accent.

"Once Were Warriors," added Vance, identifying the source of the quote.

"On the money," confirmed Chua as he poured two espresso shots and commenced steaming milk for the latte.

As the machine squealed Ice gazed out of the floor to ceiling windows, over the pool and past the beach to the Arabian Gulf. In the distance he could see a tanker cruising out to the Gulf of Oman. The 'Sandpit', as the team called the residence, was a great place to live but it wasn't for Ice. Nearing fifty, the battle-scarred operative still longed to get out into the field and do what he did best, track down bad guys and serve out justice.

"So, Chua and I have been discussing a new operational concept," Vance said interrupting his thoughts.

Ice's focus was snapped back to the kitchen. "Yeah?"

Vance chuckled. "Thought that might get your attention."

"What are you thinking?"

"Small and nimble," said Chua as he placed their coffees on the countertop. "Operatives, or pairs of operatives, linked in with trusted agents inside government agencies."

"So no centralized command. No more Sandpit?" asked Ice.

"A smaller C2 element that's mobile with less infrastructure," said Vance. "We get our missions from our interaction with other agencies. We pick and choose what we go after."

"Doesn't that increase our risk?"

Chua shook his head. "No, only a single operative, or at worst a pair, will have contact with the agency person. Think Al-Qaeda or a US Special Forces model. If our link with an agency goes sour, our people cut contact and disappear."

"And if they get wrapped up they can only compromise one layer back. Which will ultimately be a cutout."

Ice sipped from his coffee.

"However, Chua and I also think we're going to need a contingency element. A heavy hitter who can augment the pairs when and if required." Vance paused. "That sound like something you'd be interested in?"

He lowered his cup, nodding. "Hell yeah, get me in the game coach."

———

TEL AVIV, ISRAEL

Manfred Lisker strolled into Mossad's headquarters wearing a well-cut navy suit with a leather briefcase under his arm. Balding with glasses and an academic build a casual observer may have assumed he was one of the bean counters, an accountant responsible for keeping the spy agency's books in order. The reality was very different. Lisker ran Mossad's Special Operations Department. That meant that all paramilitary and military action sponsored by the agency came under his authority. He literally decided who lived and who died.

The heavily armed guards at the building's access control point nodded respectfully as Lisker swiped through inch thick blast doors into the foyer of Mossad HQ. The gaggle of staff clustered around the elevators parted as he approached, their conversation dying to a whisper.

They left him to ride the elevator alone and he selected floor twelve. When it opened he swiped through another door and turned right into a long corridor. At the end he arrived at the Director of Mossad's office.

A secretary spotted him as he entered and leaped to the door. "He's waiting for you, sir."

As he pushed the door open a young officer emerged with a stack of files in his arms. Behind him, the director appeared.

"Manfred, come in."

He entered the expansive office and stood in front of the desk as Director Atzmoni took his seat.

"Please, sit."

Lisker made himself comfortable in one of the chairs. "How's the family, Caleb?"

"Good, Manfred. Are you going to make Benjamin's *Bar Mitzvah* this Sunday?"

"I wouldn't miss it for the world. They grow up so fast."

"That they do. Sorry to cut straight to business, but I've got a very full day. As you know, there have been significant funding cuts as a result of changes to the counterterrorism budget. I've had to make some hard decisions on what I can and cannot afford to fund. Unfortunately, your Proteus project has not made the cut."

Lisker exhaled. "The Proteus project is the future of our agent recruitment."

"There is no doubt that the project has shown promise. However, it is decades, maybe more, from showing any payoff and I have more pressing matters that require attention."

Lisker knew better than to attempt to argue the point. The Director was a man of absolutes and once he'd made a decision very little could change his mind. However, he was a reasonable man, and Lisker knew that the closing of one door might provide the goodwill to open another.

"Disappointing but understandable. As you are aware, I am all about delivering capability now as well as in the future. Our recent success employing proxy forces through Tariq Ahmed and his company, Lascar Logistics, is evidence of that. My team has been able to leverage external assets at minimal cost and risk to the agency."

"Yes, both you and agent Bachman have had an element of success in running Lascar assets."

Lisker snorted. "Sir, Bachman is interacting with a foot soldier. I have leverage and access to Tariq Ahmed, CEO of the largest logistics company in the Middle East and the Arab world."

"Bachman seems to have developed a level of rapport with her foot soldier."

"You know as well as I do, Caleb, rapport is limited. Real influence is achieved through leverage."

The director pondered the comment. "Not a believer in the old adage, you catch more flies with honey?"

"I speak from twenty-five years of experience. I've seen agents with so-called loyalty and rapport betray their handlers at the drop of a hat. Real power is holding the leash, not coaxing the hound."

Atzmoni nodded. "You're right."

"Agent Bachman is to be commended for her endeavor. However, a source as influential as Tariq Ahmed needs to be run with an element of finesse. I think it is best that I personally handle all engagement with him and his associates, with oversight by yourself of course."

"You want exclusivity?"

"Yes. Ahmed is a fox and he will slip out from under our thumb if he isn't handled delicately."

"His value is undeniable. I want weekly updates on your activities."

"Of course. I'll have the necessary changes made to the compartment and associated intelligence."

"I'll inform Agent Bachman and her team."

"Appreciated, Caleb. Is there anything else you needed?"

"That is all. Future funding for Proteus has already been redirected, I'm sure you will manage its closure discreetly. Now, I've got an oversight committee meeting to prepare for." Atzmoni rose and shook his hand. "I'll see you on the weekend."

Once Lisker had left his boss's office, he took a phone

from his jacket and dialed his head of operations. "Set me up a meeting with Daniel Ginsberg."

———

EL LEH, ETHIOPIA

When he returned to the abandoned school Krenich found Dula sitting on his barrel smoking the same brand of cigarette. Three armed Somalis stood guard over the group of twenty girls he'd tested.

"Are the tests in?" Dula asked between puffs.

Krenich nodded. "The results were not as good as I hoped. Only six of the girls passed."

Dula grinned revealing a set of tobacco stained teeth. "Yeah, but you pay three times the price and I can sell the others to Al-Shabaab for wives. They don't care what's wrong with them as long as they have a pussy." Dropping from the barrel Dula swaggered across to where the girls were huddled. "What ones you want?"

Krenich took a slip of paper from his pocket and read out six numbers. Dula gestured to the girls and his men unlatched the collars on their necks and shoved them to one side. He watched, emotionless as one of those selected clung to another girl and screamed. The younger of the two, he guessed her age at around twelve, had not been selected. He didn't know who had the worse deal, the girl being handed over to Doctor Morrison or the one who'd find herself married to a terrorist.

"The diamonds?" Dula asked as he caressed his scraggly beard.

"Of course." He took a radio from his belt and spoke into it. "Mukisa, bring the payment."

His muscle-bound bodyguard appeared at the door a moment later. Lumbering inside he passed a velvet sack to Krenich who'd already laid a square of the material atop a drum. He poured a dozen cut diamonds onto the cloth.

"Triple, as agreed."

Dula inspected the gems as his men roped the six selected girls together. The wailing of the youngest girl echoed off the walls of the old schoolhouse making it difficult to concentrate.

"Shut her up," snapped the Somali.

One of his men stormed across and raised a hand in a fist. One of her friends comforted the girl, silencing her by hugging her close. The guard lowered his arm and Dula looked up from his inspection of the diamond.

"Payment is good. You can take the girls."

"Any more news of the *Ibliiski*?" Krenich asked as his bodyguard oversaw the transfer of the girls into his truck outside.

"No. Once I have gotten rid of the girls I won't have to worry about them." He stuffed the diamonds into the pocket of his camouflage smock and lit another cigarette. "Tomorrow these ones will be brides of Al-Shabaab." Dula offered him a cigarette.

Krenich took it and lit it with a silver lighter. "I'll need more girls in a month. Will you be in business then?"

Dula patted his pocket full of diamonds. "If the price is right."

———

TEL AVIV, ISRAEL

Manfred Lisker left his driver in the basement parking lot of the Royal Beach hotel and rode the freight elevator up into the building above. It stopped on the fifth floor and he made a beeline for suite 506. Rapping his knuckles on the door, he waited for it to open.

The man who opened the door was tall with a mane of blonde hair and narrow features. The CEO of Sakkin Industries, one of Israel's preeminent security corporations, wore a blue polo shirt and tan slacks with a knit sweater tied over his shoulders.

"Daniel, how are you?" asked Lisker as he stepped into the room.

"Good, excellent in fact," said Daniel Ginsberg as he closed the door and directed the Mossad officer to a pair of grey fabric couches in the apartment's living room. "The world is in turmoil, the security market is growing exponentially and Sakkin Industries is leading the charge."

Lisker made himself comfortable on one of the couches, crossing his legs and folding his hands over his knees. "It certainly is a growth industry."

Ginsberg sat on the couch opposite. "Have you reconsidered your position on the job offer?"

Lisker shook his head. "I think it's in both our interests that I remain on my current trajectory."

The CEO flashed a predatory smile. "Straight to the directorship of the world's deadliest intelligence service."

Lisker shrugged. "Perhaps, either way my influence within the organization continues to benefit us both."

"That it does."

"Although unfortunately, the Proteus Project did not make it through the latest round of budget cuts."

It was Ginsberg's turn to shrug. "I anticipated as much and have secured alternative funding for the project. When the time is right, you will be able to ensure that our government contributes again."

"Alternate funding?"

"Corporate investment. Relax, Israel has exclusive rights to the IP and end product. Your Doctor Marnisha Copeland will continue to head all development."

"And the facilities?"

"All offshore."

"Excellent."

"Now, having anticipated your unwillingness to jump ship to the corporate world I wanted to discuss a less obtrusive business partnership."

Lisker tilted his head slightly. "Go on."

"I want to establish a clandestine element outside of Sakkin. Resourced with safe houses, transport and funding." He rose and walked across to a side table where he picked up a leather-bound folder. "These are the details." Ginsberg slid it across the table.

"And you want me to establish it?"

The CEO of Sakkin Industries smirked. "You're the man with the contacts and experience."

He stared at the folder.

"The world is burning, Manfred. We can either sit back and watch, or seize the opportunity and thrive."

"I'm all for thriving Daniel. I just don't believe in serving two masters."

Ginsberg shook his head. "This isn't about buying your service, Manfred. This is about enabling you to further 'our' interests."

"Our interests?"

"Yes OUR interests. Israel has more enemies than its security agencies can handle. New recruits don't have the physical and mental attributes required to protect the nation. Our leaders do not have the will to destroy the wolves baying at the gates. Sakkin is Israel's only hope for survival."

"As long as it is profitable, right?"

Ginsberg ran a hand through his blonde hair. "I'm a businessman."

He took the folder from the table and flipped it open. Inside were several credit cards and banking access details, everything he needed to establish his own covert ops program.

"There's only one caveat," said Ginsberg.

"Go on."

"I need a favor."

"So not really a caveat at all."

Ginsberg laughed. "For a man like you, it's a small problem." He took a flash drive from the pocket of his pants and handed it to the Mossad officer. "Isaac Jarvis is the Managing Director of Intelligent Responsive Systems. They're a Californian company working on autonomous drone software. I want to absorb them into Sakkin."

"They're not selling?"

"No, Jarvis is a real hard-ass."

"And you want me to intimidate him?"

Ginsberg shook his head. "No, I want you to eliminate him. Without him his board will fold."

"Wet work on US soil is off limits."

Ginsberg smiled, revealing a shark-like set of teeth. "Good thing he's going to be in Dubai for GITEX technology week. Or, is the Middle East off limits too these days?"

Lisker pocketed the flash drive and tucked the leather folder under his arm as he rose. "Consider it taken care of."

"Excellent."

The men shook hands and a minute later Lisker was in the back of his vehicle on the way to Mossad headquarters. He gave the contents of the leather folder a second cursory glance then slipped it into a briefcase before taking a phone from his jacket and making a call. "Where are you?" he asked when a tone indicated the line was secure.

"Dubai," answered his head of operations, Avi.

"Good, I've got a mission for Mantis. I'll send you the details in the next few hours."

Chapter Four

DUBAI, UAE

"WHERE DO YOU WANT TO MEET?" asked Saneh as she and Bishop entered the climate-controlled environment of one of the Emirates' mega shopping complexes, Dubai Mall. With over 1300 shops it claimed to be the second-largest retail facility on the planet. Teeming with tourists, it was the closest shopping center to their apartment.

"Caribou Coffee's on level two. It's not too bad."

"See you there in twenty?" She kissed him on the cheek. "Stay out of trouble."

"Come on, how much trouble can I get into here?"

She rolled her eyes before leaving him and heading for one of the many escalators. She made a beeline to the third level, aiming for a row of sports apparel stores. Her mission today, as far as Bishop was concerned, was to purchase new gym leggings. In reality she was here for a more clandestine undertaking.

She spotted her handler long before he saw her. Avi

Lerner was a Mossad operative who'd been in the game for a while, but a while wasn't the lifetime of experience that Saneh had. For a split second she contemplated dispatching the Israeli with the double-edged stiletto blade that she never left the house without. She dismissed the idea. If she killed Avi then Mossad would come after Bishop and everyone else she loved.

Avi made her as she approached him in a Nike store. She stopped at a rack of leggings a short distance from where he was inspecting sneakers. He glanced sideways at her and nodded, before moving closer and picking up a basketball boot.

"You have a task." He spoke without looking at her.

"Who?"

"His name is Isaac Jarvis. He's attending GITEX," he said, referring to the Gulf Information Technology Exhibition.

"Mission?"

"Eliminate."

Saneh shook her head as she pulled a pair of Nike leggings from a rack and inspected them. "You want me to assassinate some tech nerd. That's a little below my level sweetheart."

"You'll do it, or you'll pay the consequences."

She clenched her teeth as she selected another size.

Avi moved past her holding the basketball boot. "The details are on the bench. Make it happen."

She watched him leave the store from the corner of her eye before making her way across to the padded bench used by clients trying on sneakers. The basketball boot that Avi had been holding was sitting on it. She picked the shoe up and turned it over. A micro SD card dropped into her hand.

Returning the shoe to the bench she took the pair of tights she had selected and paid for them.

Her blood boiled as she made her way through the shopping center, past the massive five-story indoor aquarium toward the coffee shop Aden had selected. Manfred Lisker had her in the palm of his hand and she felt utterly helpless. Her choices were to continue killing at their command or refuse. The latter came with dire consequences that she was unwilling to accept. She'd almost lost Bishop on several occasions and she wasn't going to let it happen again.

She spotted her lover already seated in the cafe with his trademark New York Yankees cap perched on his head and a coffee in hand. Her mood improved a little when he saw her and a smile lit up his face. For all his flaws, and the man had many, Aden Bishop had the biggest heart of anyone she knew. Nothing he ever did was by halves; he committed his entire being to everything, including their relationship. It tore Saneh up to keep anything from him, let alone her status as a Mossad assassin, but she knew there was nothing he or anyone else could do to throw off the shackles.

He rose and kissed her as she arrived, pulling out a chair for her. "Babe, I ordered you a caramel latte."

"You're the best."

"Did you get what you wanted?" he asked.

"Not really, but I'll deal with it."

Their conversation paused as a waiter delivered her coffee. When he'd left Bishop reached under the table and pulled out a paper bag.

"What's this?" she asked.

"Something special."

She opened the bag, reached inside and pulled out a

naval cap complete with gold braid around the brim. A single brow arched. "For me?"

"Yeah, I mean you can't Skipper a ketch without a hat."

Her brow dropped, replaced with a beaming smile. "She's ready?"

"Sure is. We can head over to Greece and inspect her this weekend."

Bishop's phone buzzed and he glanced at the screen. Saneh registered the look on his face.

"Who is it?"

"Keila, she wants to meet somewhere neutral."

"And you think that's a good idea?"

"We need to discuss it with Vance and Chua."

"But, you think it's a good idea?"

Bishop shrugged. "I don't think it's a bad idea. She's proven that she can be trusted. I think it's in PRIMAL's interest to maintain a relationship with her."

Saneh lowered her drink. "You think it's a good idea to cozy up with the most lethal and untrustworthy intelligence service on earth?"

"I think that's a little harsh—"

"You don't know them like I do." She sipped from her latte.

"Yeah, I know, as an Iranian they're your sworn enemy, I get it. But, as far as PRIMAL goes Keila is an asset." He paused and shot her a smirk. "Or is this less about Mossad and more about my undeniable charm?"

Saneh snorted into her drink. "Aden Bishop, you're about as charming as a warthog's backside."

He laughed. "I happen to think that warthogs are very charming. Now, we should get going if we're going to make the team meeting."

As the pair left the cafe and made their way to the exit, neither of them noticed Avi Lerner watching them from the level above. He waited until they had departed before taking out his phone and texting Lisker.

The Mantis is on the hunt.

———

THE SANDPIT, ABU DHABI

It was the first time that the remaining members of PRIMAL had been brought together in months. Mirza and Mitch were connected via the iPRIMAL network, but Vance, Ice, Chua, Tariq and Saneh were all present at the Sandpit.

They sat in the open plan dining area drinking coffee that Chen Chua had made. A laptop on the breakfast bar displayed a secure video feed. Once Ice had confirmed that Mirza and Mitch were connected Tariq Ahmed, the organization's benefactor, took center stage. The handsome Arab tycoon stood wearing an immaculately tailored three-piece suit that, despite the intensity of the Emirates heat, was not even slightly rumpled or sweat-stained.

"Team, eight years ago when Vance, James and I started this organization I gave it a broad mission, to seek out injustice and set it right. I could have never anticipated the level of success that you as a team would achieve. You've taken on many of the world's worst and, as Bishop would say, you've handed them their asses."

Laughter filled the room.

"However, it's with a heavy heart that I've decided that

it's time for PRIMAL to stand alone. Given the current situation, I firmly believe that you no longer need my support to continue your work. You now have the Nemesis fund to go this alone. I have to consider the well being of the eight and a half thousand people who are employed by Lascar Logistics and its affiliates."

Vance rose from where he was sitting at the breakfast bar and extended a hand to the Arab. "Tariq, it has been a pleasure to work with you on this venture. You will always be the essence of PRIMAL even if you're not directly involved." Grasping Tariq's hand, he pulled him in for a bear hug.

The rest of the team was quick to extend their own thanks. As Chua shook his hand Tariq handed over his iPRIMAL, the custom smartphone given to every operative. Bishop was the last in the line as the Arab made for the door. "Does this mean I'm out of a job?" he asked with a smile.

"Not at all. It would be suspicious if you and Saneh simply left the company. In fact, I've got a special task for you in the next few days."

"Aid delivery to a war-torn region?"

Tariq laughed. "Always on the hunt for action aren't you? No, a protective security detail here in the Emirates."

Bishop feigned disappointment. "OK, well I guess we'll see you then."

"Yes, you will." With that Tariq Ahmed, CEO of Lascar Logistics and the former benefactor of PRIMAL, departed the Sandpit.

"This all seems a little final," said Ice, breaking the silence that had descended on the room.

"It's the end of an era," added Chua.

"So what happens now?" asked Mirza through the video feed from London. "Is PRIMAL going to continue?

Vance faced the laptop. "That's still up in the air. The reality is we need to continue our low profile while at the same time build on the links we have into intelligence agencies and services."

Bishop shot Saneh an 'I told you so' look. She rolled her eyes in response.

"We've got limited resources now," added Chua. "Our access into the world's intelligence networks is going to be our eyes and ears."

"What about the operation in Africa?" asked Ice.

"Kruger and Kurtz are pretty much running their own show," replied Vance. "We've been providing limited assistance. Once that mission is complete we'll be closing down the Sandpit. We intend to move to a cell-based model."

"Like Al-Qaeda," said Mitch through the laptop.

"Why does everyone use that example?" asked Chua.

"Because they employed the technique so successfully," said Saneh.

"Fine, yes just like Al-Qaeda," said Chua.

"Are we going to run any operations?" asked Bishop. "Or is this just posturing?"

"I'm not going to lie to you, Bish. The Africa job is probably going to be the last for a while," replied Vance. "We need to keep things low key till we're reestablished."

"What about the Sandpit?" asked Mirza from the computer.

"Chua, Ice and I will close things down over the next two months. Mitch is getting a new location set up in a slightly cooler part of the world."

"You going to be alright without your Hawaiian shirts?" asked Saneh.

"Without?" said Ice. "I've seen Vance wear a Hawaiian shirt in a snowstorm. He'd wear one in the Arctic Circle,"

Everyone laughed again.

"Like Chua said, this is the end of an era people," said Vance when they'd fallen silent. "PRIMAL has been everything to us. Now we've got the opportunity to pursue other interests alongside our philanthropic pursuits."

"I feel like a toast is in order." Bishop walked into the kitchen and opened the fridge. As usual, the shelves were stocked with international beers. He tossed a Coors to Vance, Chua and Ice and handed a Coopers Pale to Saneh.

"Oh, so I drink your beer now?"

He grinned. "Don't you? Sorry Mitch and Mirza, you'll have to find your own." He hefted his bottle into the air. "To Tariq and PRIMAL, the end of an era."

The others echoed the toast and they drank together. Then the team broke off into separate conversations with Ice chatting to Mirza and Mitch on the laptop while Saneh, Vance, Chua and Bishop gathered around the coffee machine.

"You guys OK with working for Tariq for a while longer?" asked Vance.

"How long is that exactly?" asked Saneh.

"A few months. We need to maintain the status quo as far as Mossad is concerned. Keila and her people need to believe that Bishop works for Priority Movements Airlift. It goes a long way to explaining how he put together a team to get them out of Iraq."

Bishop nodded. "Keila reached out today. Wants to meet somewhere neutral. Saneh and I are planning to head over to Greece to inspect our boat. I figured we could tie in a meeting."

"Unless you don't think it's a good idea," added Saneh.

"No, it's all good," said Chua. "Keila is a link into the most capable intelligence agency in the Middle East. She's going to be a formidable ally in the future."

Bishop spotted the look that passed over Saneh's features. He'd seen the eyebrow twitch before, and knew what it meant. She wasn't happy with the situation, which was understandable. When she was a MOIS operative the Israelis had been her sworn enemy and she'd personally dispatched a number of their agents. Still, that was a lifetime ago. She was PRIMAL now and their views on justice were not aligned to a single nationality or entity.

"So, tell us more about New Zealand," Saneh asked diverting the conversation.

"Who said anything about New Zealand?" said Vance, feigning surprise. "Let me guess, Mitch?"

"He said he was working on something special for you guys."

"All will be revealed in good time," said Vance. "Now, what about this boat of yours?"

―――――

NYAGATARE, RWANDA

Bianca had tracked down the girl through her new fixer, the cab driver who'd abandoned her to the security thugs. She'd guilted him into running some errands, and the promise of cash had incentivized him to find someone who worked at the medical facility she was investigating.

Their meeting place was a teahouse on the outskirts of

Nyagatare. Bianca arrived late in the afternoon and took a seat in the corner of the empty room. Unwinding the bulky headscarf she'd used to cover her blonde hair she gave the establishment a once over. It was spartan to say the least. What served as the kitchen was a low counter at the back with a sink, two kettles and a pile of plastic mugs not unlike the ones she remembered from summer camp. A scrawny teenage boy had taken her order with eyes wide as saucers. Bianca doubted that a westerner had ever visited before much less a blonde woman.

As she waited for her contact she sipped sickly sweet tea and recapped the events that had brought her to this meeting. She'd first learned of the rumors surrounding the medical facility when she was working for a non-profit organization teaching English. The former Canadian Special Operations Regiment non-commissioned officer had left the service eighteen months earlier. It had only taken her a few months to realize that while she'd needed to go her separate way from the military, she still needed purpose and excitement in her life.

Unfortunately, her role at the English school had been short, ending when her agency had been investigated back in Canada for fraud. With funding dried up, she'd been ready to head home when one of her students had told her of the medical facility. Google had proven its existence, and a few queries around town had raised her suspicions.

The laboratory, as it was described online, was a research facility that employed fifty locals in a variety of roles. The company behind it, Lifebright Foundation, also claimed to run several medical aid stations around Rwanda, although she had been unable to find any evidence that the clinics had ever operated.

Prior to the incident with Lifebright's security guards,

she'd had little evidence linking them to nefarious activity. The threat they'd issued had reinforced her suspicions.

A bell attached to the teahouse door jingled and Bianca spotted a middle-aged Rwandan woman with a red scarf tied around her head entering. She half rose as the woman walked directly to her. "Hello, my name is—"

The woman cut her off with a raised hand. "No names."

"OK."

She sat opposite Bianca, waved the teenager over and ordered sweet tea.

"So, how long did you work at Lifebright?" Bianca asked when he'd moved back to the kitchenette.

"Eight months."

"What was your role?"

"I worked in the kitchen. Making meals for the girls."

"Tell me about the girls."

"I only saw them twice. One of the workers did not come to work and I had to stay late to clean the kitchen. When I left, I saw a truck arrive full of girls."

The teen delivered a cup of tea.

"You're sure?"

She nodded. "The second time I saw the same truck from a distance. More girls unloaded."

"Do you know what happens to them?"

She shook her head. "No, I never see them again."

"But you make meals for them?"

"I think so. We make lots of food. More than is needed for the staff."

"But you don't know what they're doing to the girls."

"No." She glanced over her shoulder at the door. "But I think it is very bad."

"What makes you say that?"

"Why do they hide it from us?"

"Good point."

The woman took a sip from her cup then rose. "I have to go now."

Bianca stood. "Please wait. I've got some more questions."

"These are bad people. They need to be stopped. I must go."

She made to follow her but thought better of it. The woman was terrified. Plus, she didn't think she was going to get any more information out of her.

Bianca finished her drink, rewrapped her head scarf and paid the teen along with a healthy tip. Light was fading as she left the teahouse and began walking to the next block where her cab driver waited. Turning the corner she heard a commotion further along the dimly lit street. A small crowd had gathered by the side of the road. As she got closer she saw that someone was lying in a crumpled heap. Her training kicked in and she pushed her way through the group. On the ground was the woman she'd just met.

Her pulse quickened as she saw the woman's head was at an award angle, eyes wide and staring. She didn't need to check her vitals to see she was dead.

"A car hit her and didn't stop!" exclaimed a bystander.

Bianca backed out of the crowd, disappearing into the darkness. For all she knew the Lifebright guards who'd assassinated her contact were still close by. There was no doubt in her mind now, she was up against an evil entity and they'd upped the ante.

LASCAR TOWER, ABU DUBAI

Avi Lerner strolled into the foyer of Lascar Tower and collected a pass from the security desk. Entering an elevator he pressed the button for the top floor.

As it rose at high speed he felt a strange prickling sensation and the hairs on his arms stood on end. No doubt some kind of advanced scanner had confirmed that he wasn't carrying a weapon. Not that the square-jawed Mossad operative needed one. If he wanted to kill Tariq Ahmed he could do it with his bare hands.

The elevator slowed as it approached the top level. The indicator displayed the highest floor, but the doors didn't open, it merely blinked twice and rose another dozen feet.

"Sneaky," Avi murmured as the doors finally opened.

He recognized the attractive brunette behind the sleek white desk in the foyer. "Hello, Emily."

"Mr. Lerner, you are expected."

Avi had no way of knowing that the bookish secretary had a Kriss .45 submachine gun aimed at his torso. A weapon that, thanks to tutelage by Saneh, she was highly proficient with.

Thick opaque glass doors slid open and Avi gave her a wink as he strolled through them.

Tariq was sitting at his desk when the Mossad operative entered. The CEO and owner of Lascar Logistics' attention was fixed on the tablet in front of him.

Avi coughed.

"I'll be with you in a moment."

The Mossad operative made himself comfortable on a white settee.

Finally Tariq looked up and locked eyes with him. "I take it this is not a social visit?"

"Not at all," Avi replied. "I'm here to discuss our business arrangements."

"I'm sure that could have been achieved over the phone."

"Director Lisker wanted me to add a personal touch."

Tariq folded his hands in front of him. "I'm truly blessed. Now if you don't mind, I have business to conduct. So, if we could keep this quick."

"Of course. A company called Dynamic Procurement Holdings will place orders for equipment we need moved. The shipments will primarily be of a humanitarian nature and as such will be shipped into high-risk areas."

Tariq's eyes narrowed. "Humanitarian Aid."

"Yes, I believe you have an outfit called Priority Movements Airlift that is adept at conducting such activities."

"That business unit is closing down."

"Unfortunate. But, with your fleet of aircraft, I'm sure you'll find something to meet the requirement."

"And you expect Lascar Logistics to be at your beck and call."

"Of course not. We'll have an account like anyone else and we'll submit shipment orders just like anyone else. In fact, we'll pay a premium to ensure expedited delivery."

"I don't need your money."

"So you'd provide your services out of the goodness of your heart. Knowing that your actions will further Israel's interests over that of your countrymen."

Tariq exhaled, fighting the urge to draw the pistol he kept in his drawer and shoot the smug Mossad agent in the face. "You've made your point."

"Excellent." Avi rose. "I'll see myself out."

"Please do."

Tariq waited for Avi to leave then rose from his desk. He

walked across to a glass cabinet and studied his reflection. The face that looked back was a face that repulsed him. It was the face of a man who'd betrayed a friend, a man who had sold out everything he stood for.

He lashed out at the glass, cracking it with his fist. His only consolation was that his actions were keeping Lascar employees safe.

Chapter Five

LAVRIO, GREECE

"KEEP THEM CLOSED, BABE." Bishop gripped Saneh's hand as he led her along a floating concrete pier at the Olympic marina in the Greek township of Lavrio. The pair had flown in to Athens that morning and caught a bus to the center of the coastal town. Breakfast at a café was followed by a stroll through streets lined with vibrant white buildings capped with red terracotta tiles. Bishop's research had revealed that the small town had grown around ancient silver mines. The port and subsequent marina had been constructed to manage a growing fishing fleet and shipments of ore.

He stopped her at the end of the pier. "OK, open them."

Saneh let out a sigh as she took in the sleek lines of the yacht that Bishop had purchased. The vessel sported a deep blue hull with polished teak decks and superstructure. "She's gorgeous."

Bishop unhooked a lanyard on the railing of the boat and gestured for Saneh to board the 115-foot vessel.

"So, what makes it a ketch?" she asked as they walked along the deck.

Bishop gestured to the twin masts. "A ketch always has a mainmast taller than the second mizzenmast."

"And the mizzenmast is the one at the rear?"

"Correct."

"Does she have a name?"

"She did, but I didn't like it." Bishop led her to the wheelhouse.

"What was it?"

"The Isabella."

Saneh scrunched her nose, confirming his assessment that she wouldn't like the name either.

"I was thinking *Susurro*," he said.

"*Susurro?*"

"It means whisper."

"I like it." She followed him into the wheelhouse.

The elegant vessel's cockpit reminded Bishop of the control surfaces in a modern aircraft. Sleek black touch panels surrounded the ship's wheel, and a row of waterproof headsets sat on a charging dock. Mitch had organized the refit of the forty-year-old yacht, and Bishop could see that the systems were state-of-the-art. The scent of marine varnish hung heavy as they descended a staircase into the hull. LED panels recessed into the rich honey-colored wood lit the interior.

"Wow, there's a lot more room down here than I expected," exclaimed Saneh as they entered the living area. The open space doubled as a dining room with a well-equipped galley running along one side.

"There're two bedrooms forward and a bunk room, store room and gym aft."

Her eyes shone as she turned and wrapped her arms around him. "She's perfect," she whispered as their lips touched.

"Wait till you see the master bedroom." Bishop slipped his arms around her waist as they kissed passionately.

"Show me," she said huskily when they broke.

He maneuvered her through a narrow doorway into the vessel's master suite, lifted her from her feet and lowered her onto the king-size bed. "Damn I love you," he said as he eased himself onto her.

"Me too," she murmured as he slid his hands under her T-shirt. "And I love this boat."

Bishop pulled her T-shirt off, revealing a lacy bra that he removed with a flick of his wrist.

Her long brown hair spilled out over the bed as she arched her back and let out a soft moan. Bishop kissed his way down her lean body to the top of her jeans.

An hour later Bishop strolled alone through the streets of Lavrio. He wore a bright smile and walked with a skip in his step. Finally he felt like things were back on track with Saneh. They'd had a tough last few years but their relationship was heading in a positive direction. He could tell that she was as excited about the boat as he was.

He found the restaurant he was looking for one street back from the waterfront. The cheerful seafood establishment boasted an outdoor dining area surrounded by white pillars and a seaside view. Taking a seat he ordered a beer and a plate of dolmades. It was a pity that Saneh had stayed onboard the boat, she loved Greek food.

"Hello, Aden."

He turned and locked eyes with Keila Bachman, the

Mossad operative whose team he'd saved during a mission in Iraq. "Keila, you're looking well." She wore her usual sports attire with her hair in a ponytail.

"You too. Do you mind if I take a seat?"

"Of course, I'll get you a beer." He signaled to a waiter.

She sat opposite him. "After everything that's happened, I think I owe you a beer, or ten."

Bishop shrugged. "I'm not about to argue that. So, what's this meeting about? I'm guessing you didn't agree to meet in Greece because you wanted to buy me a beer."

"Correct. I wanted to discuss the future of our relationship and I thought it best to do that in person."

He raised an eyebrow. "You do know I'm already in a relationship."

"Yes, with a gorgeous Persian woman who's deadlier than anthrax. I'm here to talk to you about our professional relationship. What you did for us in Iraq was nothing short of amazing. We'd like—"

"For you," Bishop interrupted.

"I'm sorry."

"We did it for you and your team. Not Israel and certainly not Mossad. I took my people in to Iraq to rescue your people because it was the right thing to do."

"What about Salim?" She referred to the ISIS arms dealer that Bishop and his team had captured and delivered to Keila.

"The guy was an asshole."

Keila laughed. "So, what if I was to point you in the direction of other assholes."

"Enemies of Israel?"

"No doubt. But assholes none the less."

"So, you're talking about a mutually beneficial relationship?"

"Exactly."

Their beers and the dolmades arrived and Bishop gestured to the plate. "Help yourself."

"Thanks." Keila slipped one of the vine leaf-covered morsels into her mouth and chewed it. "Damn, that's good." She wiped her fingers with a paper towel. "So, I've looked into your boss."

"Oh yeah?"

"He seems to be a good guy. Did you know he sponsors a dozen orphanages in Turkey?"

Bishop cocked his head. "That I did not know, but then I've never met the guy."

"You've never met Tariq Ahmed, the CEO of Lascar Logistics?"

"Not personally. He's visited the hangar a few times. I'm not one for hobnobbing with big shots."

"OK, well take it from me, he's a good guy."

Bishop could tell by the tone of her voice that she wasn't buying his story. "What about your boss? He a good guy?"

"Yeah, he's decent."

Bishop finished his beer. "Then I guess this could work then." He waved the waiter over and ordered another beer. When the man had departed, he took a dolmades from the plate. "OK, so let's talk communications protocols."

———

OMORATE, ETHIOPIA

A rooster crowed as Booyah approached a ramshackle cluster of tin huts on the outskirts of a village. As he got closer he spotted a woman crouched over a pot, cooking breakfast. A dog barked as he made toward her and she glanced up with a concerned expression.

"Good morning," he chirped in her native tongue.

She gave him the once over and decided that despite his disheveled appearance, he was probably harmless. "Good morning." She went back to stirring the contents of the earthen pot.

A quick glance around confirmed that the woman and her family were dirt poor. Their hut leaned sideways and was held together by rusted wire and lengths of twine.

"I've been traveling all night. Any chance I could sit and rest my feet. Perhaps warm my hands by your fire?"

She nodded.

Booyah unslung his backpack and took a seat on a worn truck tire. From inside the pack he removed a bag of maize, a bottle of water and some fruit.

The woman eyed the food as she stirred the meager portion in her pot. "Where are you from?"

"Luuq," said Booyah. "I'm looking for my cousin. He's been fighting with the ONLF."

The woman nodded slowly. War was a constant in her part of the world, and everyone had family who'd been killed or was fighting.

Booyah offered her the maize. "Perhaps if you add this to your *misharri* we could share." He reached back into the bag and took out a plastic container. "I've got some sugar."

She nodded, eyes wide. "We haven't had sugar in so long."

Booyah smiled. "Then it was certainly Allah's will that I stop here this morning."

He watched as she stirred in more maize then added a spoonful of sugar and made to hand the container back. "You can keep it."

"Thank you."

"Do you have any family?" asked Booyah as he warmed his hands by the fire.

"Three children."

"A husband?" he asked, softly.

"He was killed in the war."

Booyah didn't bother to ask which one. Wars were so numerous in this region that, for the locals, they had merged into one continuous blur of conflict.

"I'm sorry to hear that. Was he in the ONLF?"

She shook his head. "He was not a soldier."

"Neither is my nephew. That is why I must find him. Do you know if there are any camps nearby?"

"There is one north of the village. It's hidden deep in the thickest part of the bush." She never looked up from the pot as she spoke.

There was a noise from the shack and the door opened. The woman's children appeared; a boy and a girl, early teens, by his guess. Dressed in threadbare school uniforms they watched him cautiously. The girl, the eldest, had a toddler on her hip.

"Come and say hello to our guest." The woman turned to him. "I'm sorry I should have asked your name."

"Booyah. Hello children, my name is Booyah."

The children introduced themselves as their mother spooned maize porridge into empty tins. He felt for the family. His own wife and children had known hunger before he'd started working for the Somali pirates. If he hadn't made that decision they would have surely starved or worse, been sold into slavery.

Booyah sat quietly and ate breakfast with the family. He made a mental note to return and help them once his mission was complete. He'd asked Kurtz and Kruger for a small amount of money for charity previously and he'd been pleasantly surprised by their generosity. Both men had big hearts, which explained why they were so heavily invested in recovering the missing girls.

After the breakfast he thanked the woman and her children before continuing his journey. Once he was gone the woman turned to her eldest daughter. "Go and tell Kofi at the store that the man is looking for the ONLF camp. Make sure he gives you some rice as payment before you describe the man."

The girl nodded, handing her baby sister to her sibling. Then she took off along a different track to their guest. The woman watched as her child disappeared into the thick scrub. She felt a flicker of remorse for the man. However, since the death of her husband, her only concern in the world was feeding her children and giving them a better life.

————

TEL AVIV, ISRAEL

"What the hell?" bellowed Keila from her workstation. "I'm locked out of the Lascar files." She popped up from behind the divider that separated the team's desks in their Secure Compartmented Intelligence Facility or SCIF. "Does anyone else have access?"

"I'm locked out too," answered Abel.

"Same here," added Fahim.

"Just a second," said Jacinta. "Nope, I'm locked out."

"You're kidding me. Someone has locked us out of our own project. I spoke to the Director four days ago about this and secured funding. Who the hell could have trumped us?"

"I think you know the answer to that," said Abel.

"There's only one way to find out." She lifted her desk phone and punched a speed dial button. "Keila Bachman for Director Atzmoni," she said to the man that answered the call.

"One moment."

"Keila, I meant to call you." The Director's voice caught her off guard. She'd expected to be put on hold. "There's been some progress with the Lascar case."

"Yes, sir, that's why I called. My team has been locked out of all the working files."

"Ah yes. The project is being handled by another team. Unfortunately, it now falls under a different compartment."

"That I don't have access to."

"Correct. However, I'm sure that won't hinder an officer of your caliber."

"What about the funding?"

"I allocated that to your team, not the project. I'm sure you'll put it to good use. However, you are to terminate all engagement with any Lascar Logistics personnel."

"Sir, can you at least tell me who is handling the project?"

"Unfortunately not." He paused. "Keila, as much as it pains me to say it, this is outside of my control. Now, I'm already late for a meeting with the Director of Special Operations, I must go."

"Thank you for your time, sir."

Keila returned her phone to the cradle. "Lisker," she hissed between her teeth.

"What's that?" asked Abel.

"Lisker's snatched Lascar out from under us."

"Why would he do that?"

She shrugged. "I'm not sure. But we're going to find out."

"You think he's up to no good?" asked Fahim.

"Who knows?"

"We've still got all the stuff we've been working on in Africa," said Jacinta. "And you've got the new communications protocols that you set up with Bishop."

"Correct, we're just going to have to be very careful with what we report."

Abel cracked his knuckles. "How black are our black ops going to get?"

Keila managed a laugh as she spun a pen in the palm of her hand. "Low key is the term I'm running with."

"You want me to look into Lisker's involvement?" asked Abel.

"Not directly."

Abel winked. "Got it."

"Do we know if 8200 have been able to crack the PRIMAL communications network?" she asked.

Abel shook his head. "Can't check. We're locked out."

"What about the African connections?"

Able returned to his terminal and his fingers raced across the keyboard. "We've still got access to them. Nope, they haven't broken into the network. However, they have identified several non-secure entities nearby. I can use our toolset to break them out and see what I can find."

"Do it. We're now focused on the African networks."

As Jacinta and Fahim moved across to Abel to coordinate their efforts, Keila pondered the conversation with the director. There was no doubt in her mind that Lascar and Priority Movements Airlift were gone. However, she got the distinct impression that Caleb Atzmoni had been forced to shut her down. If that was the case, then Manfred Lisker had a serious amount of influence. That was something she was going to have to skirt around if she was going to continue working with Bishop. Additionally, she would have to explore other options for keeping tabs on 8200's access to PRIMAL. If that meant entertaining the romantic approaches of a handsome signals officer, then so be it.

CHUHUIV, UKRAINE

Rain lashed the cockpit windows of the Lascar Logistics Ilyushin-76 transporter as it made its runway approach at night. The pilot, Mike Summer, made a subtle adjustment to the jet's trim as he lined it up with the barely visible runway lights. A veteran of both Lascar Logistics and Priority Movements Airlift, Mike was comfortable in the adverse conditions. He and his co-pilot, Elaine, calmly set the two-hundred-thousand pound behemoth down on the wet tarmac and brought it to a roaring halt in front of a row of rusted aircraft hangars.

He turned the jet in a tight circle before throttling back the turbofans to idle. Then he unbuckled his seat harness and rose. "I'll drop the ramp."

As he left the cockpit he contemplated the instructions Tariq had given him regarding the mission. Mike was permitted to leave the cockpit to lower the ramp and then check the incoming load was secure before takeoff. Other than that he was not to have any interaction with the ground crew or the cargo.

Wind and rain whipped into the empty cargo hold as the clamshell doors opened and the ramp dropped. Mike glanced out into the darkness but saw no sign of activity before he turned and made his way back to the cockpit.

"All good?" asked Elaine as he dropped into his seat.

"Shady as…" he murmured.

"Have you done many gigs like this?"

"You could say that." Mike couldn't help but smile as he recollected the dozens of covert flights he'd conducted for Bishop, Saneh, Mitch and the rest of the PRIMAL team. He had penetrated hostile airspace, conducted hot extracts and delivered resources in some of the most hostile conflict zones on the globe.

"So this is normal?"

The aircraft shuddered. Mike glanced at the camera feed from the cargo hold. On screen two men dressed in black with their faces covered by balaclavas guided two pallets of crates off a low loader into the jet.

"No, not really," he replied, wondering why Bishop wasn't on the flight. None of team PRIMAL had been tasked since the Syria job. Instead, Tariq was micro-managing the delivery.

"What do you think is on the pallet?"

Mike shrugged. "The manifest says medical supplies."

One of the men gave a thumbs-up to the camera then they left the jet, backing the cargo carrier away into the darkness.

"I think we both know it's not medical supplies," said Mike as he climbed out of his chair. "Let's prep for takeoff."

After Mike raised the ramp and closed the doors he inspected the two pallets of alleged medical supplies that now occupied the hold. He shook his head as he lifted the cargo netting to check one of the large wooden crates. The white paint looked fresh and there was an obvious spelling error among the words stenciled haphazardly on its side.

FIRST ADE BANDAGES

Mike had seen enough military hardware to recognize the crate as the type used to transport munitions such as rockets and missiles. "Medical supplies my ass."

Back in the cockpit he strapped in and turned to Elaine. "OK, let's get this hog airborne. You have the stick."

Elaine deftly maneuvered the hulking aircraft onto the main runway and sent it rocketing down the tarmac. As soon as they were airborne and climbing toward cruising altitude Mike excused himself and made for the communications room. The cramped space behind the cockpit, formerly occupied by the aircraft's radioman, now served as a galley. Mike turned on the coffee machine before taking a satellite phone from a shelf. Dialing a number he raised it to his ear and waited.

"Mike, go ahead," said Tariq Ahmed.

"We made the pickup. You were right, it's not what's on the manifest."

"As expected. Can you determine the contents without disturbing the load?"

"Already have. We're definitely shipping ordnance. Two pallets of bandages don't weigh eight ton."

"That is suspicious. OK, can you document everything and forward it to me once you have made the drop."

"Will do."

"Thank you, Mike. I appreciate your discretion with this."

"Always, and if you need any additional help…"

There was a pause as CEO of Lascar Logistics considered the offer. "I think it's better if I deal with this personally."

"Roger."

"Safe travels."

Mike returned the phone to its place and contemplated

the situation as he made coffee. The manifest for this shipment had cited a company that Mike wasn't familiar with. A quick Google search had revealed a basic website but very limited information, a reasonable indicator that it was probably a shell. That meant that someone was using Lascar Logistics to ship contraband from the Ukraine into the Central African Republic. It certainly wasn't the first time that he'd been involved in 'grey' activities, but it was the first time it hadn't involved a PRIMAL operative. As he added milk to a coffee he pondered why Tariq was managing this personally. At least his boss seemed to have it well in hand and there weren't many who played the subversion game as well as the former head of the UAE's Special Tasks Branch.

Back in the cockpit he handed a mug to Elaine. "Good take off."

"Thanks, skip. So what are we actually hauling to Africa?"

Mike shrugged. "Your guess is as good as mine."

Elaine took the hint and settled back in her seat, autopilot activated and coffee cupped in both hands.

"So, what made you leave Virgin?" asked Mike.

"Got tired of trucking planeloads of assholes around the globe."

Mike laughed. "Yeah, I can relate to that. No day's the same flying for Lascar Logistics, that's for sure."

She raised her coffee in a mock toast. "And we wouldn't have it any other way."

Chapter Six

ABU DHABI, UAE

DAISY, the Border Collie, snarled aggressively as Bishop tried to shake a rubber chew toy from her jaws.

"Let it go you demon," Bishop said as he lifted her from the floor by the toy.

"You're going to pull her teeth out," said Saneh from the kitchen where she was preparing breakfast.

"Are you kidding? She's got a bite worse than yours." He shot his partner a cheeky grin and was rewarded with a dark look.

"You can't still be angry with me."

Her almond-shaped eyes narrowed further.

"Okayeee." Bishop turned his attention back to the dog. "Well, at least Daisy still appreciates me."

"I'm sure she wouldn't if you decided to buy a cat."

"Oh, I see what you did there." Bishop laughed and from the corner of his eye he spotted an ever so slight smile on Saneh's face. Dragging Daisy across the polished floorboards he maneuvered her into the kitchen. Finally releasing the toy, he laughed as Daisy escaped with it and bolted for the apartment's spare room. Turning he wrapped his arms around Saneh's slender waist and kissed her ear gently. "You know you're the only woman for me."

"I know, I'm the only woman who'll handle your stupidity."

Bishop slid his hands to her hips and kissed his way down her neck, nuzzling into her silky dark hair.

She let out a soft moan as he slipped a hand under her loose fitting T-shirt and caressed her breast through the sheer Lycra of her sports bra. She turned and their lips touched in a passionate kiss that sent electricity shooting through Bishop's body.

Saneh braced her hands against his chest as he cupped her buttocks in his hands, and hefted her onto the countertop.

"This doesn't mean you're forgiven." She panted between kisses.

"Of course not."

At that moment Bishop's phone vibrated on the counter next to them.

They both ignored it as he pulled her T-shirt and bra over her head and lowered his lips to her breasts.

"OK, maybe a little bit forgiven." She arched her back and gripped his hair with both hands.

Bishop's phone stopped vibrating. A moment later Saneh's rang.

She glanced sideways. "It's Tariq," she exclaimed as Bishop slid his fingers into the waistband of her tights. "He's got a job for us."

"Really, because I've already got a job and it's pleasuring you."

"Aden, this might be important."

"Fine." He extracted himself from her clothing, reached for his phone and dialed.

"Aden, I trust you and Saneh are well," said the CEO of Lascar Logistics as soon as the call had connected.

Bishop made a face at Saneh as she slipped her bra back on. "We're good, what's up?"

"I have a task for you both."

"Roger, where are we flying?"

"No, nothing high speed, a simple close protection mission in Dubai."

He frowned. "OK, shouldn't be a problem."

"Excellent, I'll send through the client details and his itinerary."

"Is there a real threat to his life or is this more of a VIP type treatment?"

"A little of both. Isaac Jarvis is the CEO and lead engineer of a technology firm working on artificial intelligence algorithms, primarily for autonomous security systems. His company has been the target of several failed hostile takeovers."

"Corporate brigands don't really demand our particular skill set."

"I agree. However, he's concerned that competitors will stop at nothing to acquire his firm, including kidnapping the CEO."

"Pretty unlikely scenario, but work is work, and we're keen to help out."

"Appreciated, I'll send that info through. He arrives on Tuesday, I'll check in with you before then."

"No problems." Bishop ended the call, tossed the phone on the counter and placed his hands back on Saneh's waist. "Now, where were we?"

She planted a kiss on his lips. "What's the job?"

"Protection detail for a VIP."

She feigned a yawn. "Boring, who's the client?"

"Some engineer CEO called Isaac Jarvis."

Saneh leaned closer and rested her head on his shoulder.

"What's up?"

"Nothing," she replied as he wrapped his arms around her. "I was just hoping we could bring the boat over soon."

"This job won't take long. Then we'll head over and spend two weeks sailing her back."

"Or we could just sail into the sunset," she murmured.

"Now that's an idea."

———

TEL AVIV, ISRAEL

Keila spotted Asher sitting in a booth at the rear of the burger bar in Tel Aviv's upmarket district of Rothschild. She had to admit, the 8200 SIGINT specialist was good looking. He had a lean build, black hair, grey eyes and an easy going smile. In fact, he kind of reminded her of Aden Bishop, although slightly less masculine.

He stood as she approached, and flashed one of his trademark smiles. "Hi."

"Hey." She sat opposite and reached for the menu that was sandwiched between a bottle of ketchup and a jar of American mustard. "You eat here often?"

Asher nodded. "Yeah. It's a bit of a fave with the team. The Hawaiian burger is awesome."

She pursed her lips. "So you're a pineapple on pizza person?"

"You know what they say. There're two types of people in the world, people who have pineapple on their pizza and people who are wrong." He paused, expecting her to laugh.

She didn't. "Well I guess I'm wrong then."

"Oh."

Keila winked. "I'm just messing with you. I love pineapple."

Asher shook his head. "You got me good."

They made small talk until a waiter appeared and then ordered two Hawaiian burgers.

"So, why did you finally agree to grab a bite to eat with me?" asked Asher as their food arrived.

"I was impressed by your persistence." She smiled. "And you're pretty cute."

"You too."

"I was disappointed to find out we won't be working together as much anymore."

"How do you mean?"

She took a bite of her burger, chewed and wiped her chin with a napkin. "The Lascar network. It's been handed off to another team."

"Oh yeah. I saw that."

"It's the Mossad way. You do all the hard work and then some prick slides in and snatches it out from under you."

"And he is a prick," murmured Asher before he tucked into his burger.

"Everyone knows it. Seriously, my people put so much work into this asset."

"Yeah, I'm sorry for the way it panned out. The work you did in Syria was impressive. We'd been trying to pinpoint Salim for months. Then you slide in and take him down."

Keila shrugged. "Damn this is a good burger."

"Told you."

They ate in silence until she had devoured her meal. "Hey," she asked as she wiped her fingers with a serviette from a basket on the table. "Is there any chance you could keep me in the loop on your project, informally of course."

Asher placed what remained of his burger down and stared at her intently. "Is that what this is about?"

She shook her head. "No, this is about me getting to know you."

He took a sip from his cola. "I'm going to need a dinner date."

The corner of her mouth lifted slightly. "What's the current status of your project?"

"We're close."

"Hmmm, any chance you could give me a little head start on our friend the prick?"

It was his turn to smile. "Depends how well the date goes."

Keila took a knife from the cutlery container, spun it in her palm and then around her hand as she contemplated the offer. Asher watched intently. "OK, but I choose the restaurant." She tossed the knife back into the basket.

"Deal. So, how exactly did the prick snake you?"

"Is that the call sign we're running with?"

"Yep, totally."

"Well, I'm not exactly sure how he managed it."

"Guy's got more reach than an octopus and he's twice as slimy."

Keila laughed as she waved over a waiter and ordered a milkshake. "Do you have much to do with the prick?"

"I try to avoid it. He threatened to have me sacked after one of his teams screwed an exploitation job. They botched the physical tap and we couldn't remote in."

"So clearly not your fault."

"We eventually found a workaround."

"You're pretty sharp on the tools."

"So are you." He gestured to the cutlery basket.

"You intimidated?"

"A little. But, it's also kinda hot."

Her milkshake arrived and she took the straw in her mouth as they locked eyes. Asher's gaze narrowed and he smiled suggestively. Keila smirked as she slurped the milkshake with a horrendous sound.

Asher threw his head back and laughed. "You're out of control."

"Oh, you haven't seen anything yet."

OMORATE, ETHIOPIA

Booyah found the camp exactly where the woman had told him it would be. He'd followed a well-worn path into a dense forest of elephant thorns. It was an excellent choice for a base. The thorny bushes were impenetrable to people and vehicles, keeping them to tracks that could easily be monitored and ambushed. The dense vegetation offered excellent concealment from the sky rendering a drone mission useless.

As he made his way along a pathway he noted an increase of trash in the bushes on either side. Noodle wrappers, drink containers and cigarette packets indicated that the rebels had been using the location for some time. That meant they were probably comfortable in their routine.

He smelt rather than saw the first traces of the camp. The earthy stench of a dung fire wafted past his nose, reminding him of his childhood. He and his siblings had scrounged manure so their mother could cook what little food they'd had. It had been a hard life, but his parents had filled their house with love and laughter, until a marauding militia had murdered all of them while he and his sister had been at school.

Booyah clenched his fists as he crouched low and worked his way around a particularly dense wall of thorns. As he reached its limits he glimpsed ramshackle huts. He shuffled a little further and counted a dozen men milling around a central fire pit. They were dressed in the usual mix of military and civilian clothes and had weapons at arm's reach.

Behind them, through the bushes, he spotted more huts and what looked like a large wooden cage. The thick vegetation blocked his line of sight and he couldn't see if there was anyone in the makeshift prison. He considered moving around for a better look, but quickly discarded the idea. He'd located the camp. The rest was up to the crazy K, as he'd taken to calling Kruger and Kurtz. He made to turn and make his way out of the thicket when he heard the crack of a dry branch.

"I've found the spy," said a voice.

He spun and found himself staring into the wide eyes of a teenage soldier aiming an AK-47 directly at him.

"Spy?" said Booyah. "No, I'm just looking for my nephew. His name is Yonas. Here, I have a picture." He reached into his pocket and removed his phone.

Other men joined the boy and enemy fighters soon surrounded Booyah.

"I am looking for my nephew." He unlocked the phone and held it up to show the men the picture of a teenage boy in school uniform that was on the screen.

One of the men snatched the phone from his hand. "You are a liar. You are a spy."

They shoved him out of the bushes and along the path to the center of the camp. As they emerged into a clearing he caught a glimpse of small figures huddled in the corner of the makeshift prison. Scared, haunted eyes watched as the men pushed him toward the dung fire and others who were gathered around it.

"I found this guy," announced the teen. "He was hiding in the bushes."

"I'm looking for my nephew." Booyah didn't need to feign fear. He knew there was a good chance that the men would kill him. Life was cheap for these people.

One of the men, narrow-faced with a scraggly beard, rose from the ammunition box he was using as a seat. "Are you here for the girls?" he asked with a hiss.

"What girls?" Booyah shook his head vigorously. "No, I'm trying to find my nephew. He joined a militia a year ago. I've been searching everywhere. My phone has a photo."

The man stared at him with cold dead eyes. "You're working for the *Ibliisku*, aren't you?"

Booyah knew the term, it meant devil.

"The ones who are hunting for the girls."

Ibliisku, that made sense, he thought. Word of crazy K's success in killing militants had spread and they'd named them *Ibliisku*. He fought the urge to smile. These men were terrified.

"Please General, I know nothing of any devils. I just want to find my nephew." Booyah shivered involuntarily as the militia commander stared at him with cold eyes.

"I think you're lying to me. Do you know what we do to liars?"

He shook his head. "I'm not lying. I'm telling the truth. I swear to you in the name of Allah the merciful."

The man spat into the dust. "Bring the block."

Hands grabbed Booyah's shoulders and arms while the teen who'd captured him moved to one of the huts and hefted a log-round into his arms.

He struggled as a belt was dropped over his head and tightened against his neck. The teen positioned the blood-stained log in front of him and Booyah realized he was in real trouble.

A piece of rope was looped over his hand, pulled tight, and a machete appeared in the leader's hand. The men forced him to his knees and stretched his arm across the log.

Adrenaline surged through Booyah's body as the militia commander waved the rusted and burred blade in front of his face.

"Who do you work for?"

"No one," blubbered Booyah. "I'm here for my nephew."

"You are a liar and no one lies to Dula." He raised the blade high.

Booyah swallowed against the belt and let all sign of fear drop from his face. "Dula, know that even if you take my arm, even if you chop me into tiny pieces and bury me deep. They will come and when they do you will tell them everything you know before you die."

Dula paused and seemed to consider the threat. Then a weak smile spread across his face. "They'll never find you or me."

At that moment a 300 Blackout 190-grain projectile tore through Dula's shoulder with a wet slap. He managed a blood-curdling scream as it knocked him sideways.

Bullets thudded into bodies as Booyah snatched his arm

free and dove to the ground. Terrified screams filled the air. He knew better than to move and hunkered low as an automatic burst lashed the camp with high-velocity rounds.

Finally, after what seemed like minutes, but was literally seconds the carnage ceased.

"Hey Booyah, you drop a dollar?" Kruger's voice bellowed.

The scout tore the belt from his throat as he scrambled to his feet and surveyed the damage. Bodies littered the ground around him. "You guys couldn't cut it any finer?"

"Sorry, the brush was a little thick," replied Kruger as he and Kurtz materialized from the bushes clad in their signature camouflage and body armor.

"There are girls here," said Booyah, gesturing toward the makeshift cage. Then he recovered Dula's machete from the ground and stood over the whimpering Islamist who was clutching his shattered shoulder with his other arm. "And this guy knows where the rest of them are." He bent down low till he was face to face with the terrified human trafficker. "I told you they would come."

"I'll tell you everything. Just, just don't kill me," stammered Dula.

"Where are the rest of the girls?" asked Kruger.

"Another man took them. A white man called Krenich."

Kurtz took a seat on the bloodstained log. "Booyah, check on the girls with Kruger and see what they know. I'll finish up here." The tall German balanced his assault rifle across his knees. Dressed from head to toe in camouflage with a wrap across his mouth he personified the *Ibliisku*. "So, how do you get in touch with Krenich and where can I find him?"

"I have a satellite number. He's based in Uganda."

Kurtz took a notebook from his chest rig. "What's the number?"

Dula gave it to him between shallow gasps.

"What does he do with the girls?"

"I don't know."

He flicked the safety off his rifle and aimed it at the man's face. "You're not much use to me then are you?"

Dula released his shattered shoulder and raised a palm. "Wait, wait. I know more and I have diamonds." He fished in his jacket with a bloodied hand and removed a black velvet sack. "You can have it if you let me live."

Kurtz chuckled as he snatched it from the injured man. "You're not really in a position to negotiate, my friend. What is Krenich doing with the girls?"

"He tested their blood. That's all I know. He only wanted the ones who passed the test."

That piece of information was a revelation to Kurtz. This was the first time they'd heard of the girls being used for anything other than sex slaves or wives. It suggested that someone was using them for medical testing. It possibly meant it would be easier to find them and, if they moved fast enough, they might even still be alive.

He rose from the log and made his way across to where Booyah and Kruger were helping a dozen girls from the cage. As he got closer he locked eyes with the Somali scout and handed him the velvet bag of diamonds. "Make sure the girl's families get these."

"You're going to let that piece of shit live?" asked Kruger as Kurtz surveyed the small group of dirty, terrified teenagers.

He shrugged. "He's in shock with significant blood loss. If he survives till dark the baboons will kill him. Right, let's call up Toppie and get these girls home. We've got a new lead to chase."

Chapter Seven

LIFEBRIGHT FOUNDATION FACILITY, RWANDA

JAMILAH and her sister were laughing and skipping as they made their way across a field heading home from school. They stopped to pat the cow tethered under the sweeping branches of an oromo tree.

She climbed into the tree and snapped off a branch, dropping it to her sister who offered it to the doe-eyed animal. The younger sister's giggles made her smile as she climbed down from the tree.

"Her tongue is so funny," said her sister. "It's like a snake."

Jamilah joined her, and the two of them watched the cow use her long brown tongue to strip the lush green leaves from the branch.

Her sister wrapped her arms around Jamilah and hugged her tightly. "I love you so much."

"I love you too."

"Don't let them take me away."

Jamilah looked into her sister's tear-filled eyes. "Who's going to take you away?"

"Don't let them take me away!"

"No one's going to take you from me."

"JAMILAH!"

In a flash the blue sky had disappeared, replaced by the flat white paint on the ceiling of her prison cell.

"NOOOO!" her cell mate screamed. Jamilah jolted off her bed and saw two white-jacketed orderlies dragging her friend from the room.

"Leave her!" she yelled, leaping at the men. Scratching and biting she forced one of them to release the girl's arm.

"You little bitch." He slapped her with an open hand, sending her reeling.

Collapsing to the floor, she took a second to gather herself. By that time the men had dragged her screaming roommate outside and slammed the door. Jamilah threw herself against it, hammering her fists against the bars.

She managed to keep up the furious assault for a minute before slumping to the ground and sobbing. "I'm sorry," she repeated over and over until she was overcome with exhaustion.

DUBAI, UAE

Isaac Jarvis paced the living area of his hotel suite as Bishop and Saneh sat drinking coffee on a leather couch. The CEO of Intelligent Responsive Systems was dressed in brown pleated slacks and a blue polo shirt with his company logo emblazoned on it. His shock of grey hair was parted to one side and his brow furrowed above close-set brown eyes.

Bishop thought that he looked like a tractor salesman rather than the genius head of a cutting edge technology firm responsible for developing the world's leading security software systems.

"So, have there been any direct threats to you or your company?" asked Bishop.

Jarvis stopped and turned to the pair. "Not directly. However, we've been the target of several hostile takeover attempts and I believe the firm behind them will stop at nothing to acquire my patented technologies."

"What exactly does this technology do?" asked Saneh.

"It's an integrated security system with algorithms capable of independently identifying and tracking threats."

"That sounds like artificial intelligence," she said.

"That sounds like *Skynet*," added Bishop. "Does this system of yours decide who to kill?"

"No. I have built-in measures to ensure it is not used for direct targeting."

"Measures that someone else could remove if they took over your company."

Jarvis nodded. "Exactly. If Sakkin Industries gets its hands on the system things will move in a sinister direction. Before we know it armed drones will be engaging targets with no human oversight."

"So Sakkin industries is the firm you're concerned with?" said Bishop.

"Yes, have you heard of them?"

Bishop shook his head. "No. Are they American?"

"Israeli."

Bishop shot Saneh a sideways glance and noticed that she seemed a little unsettled.

"They're rapidly evolving into the most significant

player in the security sector in the Middle East and Africa. They're utterly ruthless."

"And you think they might make an attempt on your life?" asked Bishop.

"It's the only way they're going to get their hands on the software. I've already turned down a half-billion dollar offer."

"Well, we've been over the hotel's security. It's pretty tight. You've got a duress alarm and we'll be right next door. What we need to cover now is your movement plan. You're most at risk outside of the hotel."

Forty minutes later Bishop and Saneh had finished with Jarvis and returned to their suite. Bishop sat at a desk in the corner of the room as his partner lay on the bed and stared at the ceiling.

"You OK?" he asked after he'd updated his notes on a tablet computer.

"Yeah, why?"

"You didn't say much through that entire meeting. That's not like you." He left the desk, sat next to Saneh and touched her hand. "You feeling OK?"

"I'm a little under the weather."

"Hopefully you're not coming down with something."

She shook her head. "I don't think so." Rising from the bed, she grabbed her bag. "A workout and a sauna will clear my head. What time is our first movement with Jarvis?"

Bishop checked his watch. "Nineteen hundred. You've got a couple of hours."

"Great."

Bishop went back to his tablet as Saneh dressed for the gym and left without saying goodbye. As she rode the elevator down to the basement and fitness center she almost broke into tears. Lisker had ordered her to kill a man who by all accounts was completely innocent of wrongdoing. What made it worse was the fact that Tariq had tasked her and Bishop to protect the very same man. She was at a crossroads. Failing to complete her mission could result in the death of people she cared deeply about. Successfully completing it would mean betraying the man she loved and killing Isaac Jarvis.

———

LASCAR TOWER, ABU DHABI

The mellow crooning of Buffalo Springfield's *Stop Children What's That Sound* filled Tariq Ahmed's opulent office as he scrolled through the Wikipedia page for the Central African Republic. Despite being rich in resources the country was the tenth poorest in the world. It had also been wracked by civil war for as long as it existed. Originally a French colony the region was dominantly Christian with a small population of Muslims. There was also currently a Peacekeeping contingent deployed to monitor a cease-fire between the government and rebel forces.

Tariq turned his chair and gazed out over the Arabian Gulf as he contemplated these facts. Why would Lisker be covertly shipping arms to a former French colony two and a half thousand miles from Tel Aviv? Was Israel trying to secure a foothold in the area? From what he understood of their international engagement they were focused on East Africa, in particular, Uganda, Sudan and Ethiopia. Then again, what did it matter? Lisker and Israel's motivations were not his concern. He needed to focus on gaining leverage that would, in turn, allow him to negate Mossad's influence over him. He needed to find dirt on Lisker and he needed to find it fast.

For a moment he contemplated contacting Chua. PRIMAL's Chief of Intelligence seemed to have connections into almost every intelligence agency. Then, as quickly as he considered the idea, he discarded it. Exposing Chua and the team to Lisker would only make the situation worse. It was bad enough that Saneh and Bishop were exposed; he couldn't risk the rest of the team.

He'd been forced to sell out Saneh to protect the PRIMAL team, his family and the eight thousand Lascar Logistics employees that relied on him for their wellbeing. However, despite knowing that Saneh was the former Iranian assassin known as the Mantis, Mossad had yet to make a move against her. That meant that Tariq still had a chance for redemption.

He turned his attention back to his computer. He needed to know more about the arms shipments.

The sharp trill of his desk phone interrupted his thoughts and he answered.

"Sir, Mr. Bishop confirms that they have met with the client and established security protocols. He will be attending the conference tomorrow."

"Very good."

"Did you have anything you wanted to pass to them?"

"No. Everything seems in order. Can you have my driver ready, I'll be leaving in the next ten minutes."

"Yes, sir."

Tariq returned to his screen. The protection mission was a favor to an old friend who'd provided most of the seed capital for Intelligent Responsive Systems. Additionally, it gave legitimacy as to why he would have the likes of former Australian and Iranian intelligence operatives on his payroll. He also figured if he kept Saneh and Bishop within the UAE, then Mossad was less likely to go after them.

He closed his laptop with a sigh, rose and donned his jacket. Investigations into Lisker would have to wait. His wife had scheduled a family dinner and Famika Ahmed was one person you didn't keep waiting.

―――――

LIFEBRIGHT FOUNDATION FACILITY, RWANDA

As Tariq Ahmed was being chauffeured across Abu Dhabi in the comfort of his long-wheelbase Range Rover, several thousand miles away Bianca Paquet lay in the darkness below a bush that smelt like it had been used as a urinal by a football team. The heavy stench of musk clung to the hessian sacking that she'd shredded to form her makeshift sniper suit.

After the Lifebright Foundation's security had killed the woman in Nyagatare she'd ordered some equipment online. The Chinese night vision scope she'd purchased was nowhere near as good as the thermal one that had graced her HK417 when she was on team, but it got the job done. Instead of the rifle, the scope sat on a tripod beside her long lens camera.

The position she'd selected was a little over three hundred meters from the Lifebright Foundation's facility. She'd trimmed vegetation and constructed a hide giving her line of sight into the facility's loading dock and rear access point. From here she hoped to take images that she could use to expose the foundation and shut it down. So far she'd observed trucks making deliveries of boxes and crates, but nothing untoward and nothing relating to the abduction of children.

Bianca yawned, fighting the urge to nap as she took a pinch of roasted coffee beans from a bag that lay next to her and slipped them into her mouth. It was a technique she'd first used during basic training. As she crunched the beans she heard the rumble of an engine.

A moment later a truck emerged from the bush and stopped at the facility's security gate.

She'd already scouted the perimeter and spotted the extensive security measures protecting the facility. No, protecting wasn't accurate. Yes, the cameras, tremble sensors and electrified razor wire fence were designed to keep people out, but they were also there to keep people in. Innocent girls being pumped full of god knows what.

Through the night vision scope she watched as the truck passed through the gates and turned into the parking area in front of the loading docks. As it came to a halt a figure exited the building. She instantly recognized the stocky head of security as he greeted a man who stepped from the truck's cabin. She grabbed her camera and aimed it through the scope as the men talked, snapping a dozen shots as guards surrounded the truck.

She gasped as the tailgate was dropped and a line of manacled figures appeared from inside the truck. She adjusted her focus and captured more images. Then she lowered the camera and placed the night vision scope against her eye.

Even though the image was grainy she could tell that the figures were children. Fury boiled inside her as she clutched the tripod. If only it were her rifle. She fantasized about sending a 7.62mm bullet slicing through the head of security's skull. With her 417 she was confident she could clean up the majority of the guards, but that was never going to happen. She was on her own now with a cheap night scope instead of a rifle, and a greasy cab driver as backup instead of a platoon of gunned-up operators.

The children were marched inside and the guards disappeared. A moment later the truck passed out through the security gates.

Bianca shrugged off her camouflage suit as she climbed to her feet. Leaving her equipment she crashed through the bushes toward the road as the truck's headlights grew in size. She crouched by the side of the road, waiting for the vehicle to pass so she could see its license plate.

As it flashed past she caught a glimpse of where the plate should have been, it was missing. The truck continued on its way, taillights fading into the darkness. She felt a moment of frustration before remembering the photos she'd captured and managed a smile. Finally, she might have the evidence to shut down the Lifebright Foundation.

Chapter Eight

DUBAI, UAE

SANEH STOOD a dozen feet from Isaac Jarvis as the engineer discussed something of incredible complexity with another attendee of GITEX, held in the Dubai World Trade Centre.

The CEO of Intelligent Responsive Systems was in his element surrounded by the fellow engineers, technicians, enthusiasts and geeks who were attending the Middle East's largest computer and electronics fair.

Bishop, a notorious gear fiend, had initially been excited to attend the event. However, after four hours of motherboards and logic algorithms even he was bored.

Saneh had purposefully distanced herself from Jarvis, or the objective, as she had mentally named him. The last thing she needed was to develop a relationship with a man she had been ordered to kill.

"You doing OK?"

She turned to Bishop and managed a half-smile. "Yeah,

just a little tired. I'm going to do a room sweep." Saneh left Bishop and made her way around the perimeter of the tennis court-sized exhibition room.

The space was jammed full of stalls and salespersons pitching their electronic wares. Saneh avoided eye contact as she scanned the room. Being a woman at a male-dominated forum was proving to be more of a hindrance than she'd anticipated. If it wasn't a salesman trying to grab her attention it was another guy making a pass.

She was making her way along the rear of the hall when she spotted a familiar face. Avi, her Mossad handler, was standing at an information booth that looked to be promoting a brand of thermal camera.

A glance toward Bishop's position confirmed that she wasn't going to be seen by him or the objective. Casually she moved across and took a pamphlet from the stand next to Avi.

"Now you can see the dilemma," she said, softly. "I can't kill a man I've been hired to protect."

"Can't or won't?"

"If I do, I've blown my cover and my use to you ends." She turned and met his stern look with a glare. "And I don't know what happens after that."

He considered her point. "Give me your hotel pass."

Her eyes narrowed. "I need it."

"You can have it back."

Reluctantly she took the pass from the pocket of her suit jacket, slipped it into a pamphlet and passed it to him. The card disappeared into his coat and a few seconds later he handed it back.

"What now?" she asked, imagining jamming her stiletto blade into his chest.

"I'll be in touch."

Avi turned away and disappeared into the crowd. Her mind raced as she pretended to read the information board in front of her. Was she off the hook regarding Jarvis? Was Avi going to reallocate the job to another operative?

Stepping away from the booth she made her way back to where she'd left Bishop and the objective. As she approached, Aden turned and flashed her the roguish smile that seemed to always adorn his rugged features. The look hit her like a sledgehammer to the heart. If Jarvis was killed on Bishop's watch, he was going to be devastated. What's more, if he ever found out she was linked to the death he'd probably never forgive her. She forced a smile in return, and went back to scanning the room.

———

MADIINO, SOMALIA

Kurtz's boot connected with a rusty tin and the container sailed through the air with a loud clang. It landed in the scrub that surrounded the team's makeshift camp.

The sense of satisfaction from returning the girls they had found in Ethiopia had long since been replaced by frustration. It was another seemingly hopeless dead end. Booyah and Toppie had been unable to find any additional information on Krenich, the name the militia leader had given them. They had a satellite phone number, but without the assistance of Chua and his team, there wasn't much they could do other than ring it. Kurtz had considered doing precisely that. However, all that would achieve was alerting Krenich to the fact he was being hunted.

"You want a beer, bro?"

The lanky German turned to find his South African

teammate with a bottle in each hand. Behind him, Toppie sat on a fuel drum smoking as he conversed with Booyah.

"*Ja*, that would be good."

Kruger twisted the cap off an ice-cold Heineken and handed him the beer.

"Maybe we should ask Chua to run the number?"

"Maybe," replied Kurtz.

The two men strolled across the clearing to where Toppie's Mi-17 helicopter was parked with the rear doors open. They sat in the tail of the chopper and gazed out across the scrubby landscape as they drank their beer.

"We're going to find the rest of them," said Kruger between sips. "We won't stop till we do."

"Won't matter if they're all dead."

Kruger went silent as he contemplated the grim prediction. Like Kurtz, this mission had become intensely personal for him. While he didn't have children of his own, he'd chosen the life of a warrior, he did have two nieces who were a similar age to the kidnapped girls. "Isn't there someone else who can run the number?"

Kurtz frowned. He could possibly ask Saneh or Bishop, but inevitably they'd go straight back to Chua. He had some contacts from his former life as a police officer in Germany's elite counter-terrorism organization, GSG-9. However, none of them knew where he was or what type of work he was doing.

"The Sandpit is probably the best option." Kurtz referred to PRIMAL's safe house in Abu Dhabi.

"Pretty much our only option."

"What are you reprobates up to, eh?" asked Toppie as he and Booyah joined them at the rear of the chopper. "You found this Krenich guy yet?"

"*Nein.*"

"Comes after eight. Look, the trail is going cold and we need to get after this guy," snapped the portly pilot.

Kurtz glanced at his watch. It was late in Abu Dhabi. "I'll make the call first thing in the morning."

KIGALI, RWANDA

"The Human Rights Advisor will see you now," said the assistant, a twenty-something from Boston who thought her service with the UN was making a difference.

Bianca checked the clock on the wall of the UN Human Rights office in Kigali as she rose. It was 1115. Her appointment had initially been scheduled for 0900. She had been waiting over two hours despite making it perfectly clear she was here to report a violation of human rights.

The UN website hadn't included a picture of Doctor Jay Philips but had summarized an impressive academic background in the study of human rights. She'd assumed the regional human rights advisor was a man. Bianca was pleasantly surprised to find that the doctor was a middle-aged woman.

Philips was reading a document at her desk when Bianca entered. She glanced up and gestured to a low table with a sofa on either side. "Please, take a seat."

Bianca sat, placing a brown envelope on the table.

"Elaine, be a dear and bring us some tea," Philips said as she left her desk and sat opposite Bianca. "So, Miss Paquet, what compelling evidence have you brought me that couldn't be discussed over the phone?"

"Ma'am, for the last two months I've been investigating

the Lifebright Foundation under suspicion that they've been testing drugs on kidnapped children."

Philips raised her eyebrows. "Investigating? Are you a journalist?"

"No."

"Interpol?"

"No."

"Sorry, I'm confused. Who exactly are you?"

"A concerned international citizen. Look, I first heard rumors regarding the foundation when I was teaching English in Nyagatare."

"So you're a teacher not an investigator."

The woman's tone told Bianca that she needed to cut to the chase. "I met with a former employer of Lifebright who reported the presence of children at their facility. After meeting me she was killed by their security people."

"I heard about that. She was hit by a car at night, all too common in a town with no street lighting."

"She was murdered. I was also threatened by Lifebright security guards."

At that moment Elaine returned with cups and a pot of tea. She poured two servings as Bianca continued.

"For a research foundation, Lifebright's security is unparalleled."

"Not surprising considering the importance of their work. You do realize they're developing technologies that may cure diabetes?"

Bianca opened the envelope and removed copies of the photos she'd taken. "This is actual evidence that they're shipping children into their facility."

Philips took reading glasses from her jacket pocket and inspected the images one by one. "You say these are from the Lifebright building?"

"Yes, by the border. You can see that's a military truck."

"If you say so." She put down one photo and picked up another. "How did you get these?"

"I spent a night watching the facility."

Philips eyeballed her over her glasses. "You spied on them."

"It's called surveillance, and it's an investigative technique."

The Human Rights Advisor placed the photos on the table and leaned back into the sofa as she removed her glasses. "Miss Paquet, what you have here is not an investigation. It's an accusation based on rumors and barely interpretable grainy photos. The Lifebright Foundation funds more than a dozen medical clinics across Rwanda and provides financing to a range of other projects. The idea that they would test on kidnapped children is utterly ridiculous."

Bianca was lost for words.

"What's more your investigation is borderline criminal and I have half a mind to refer you to the police."

"That won't be necessary," she managed through gritted teeth as she gathered up her photos.

"I suggest that in the future you email your concerns and refrain from wasting my time."

Bianca's frustration had peaked by the time she reached the street and flagged a cab. There was no doubt in her mind that the Lifebright Foundation was involved in child trafficking and most likely testing. What she needed now was a plan to shut them down.

THE SANDPIT, ABU DHABI

Chen Chua's iPRIMAL rang as he was halfway through a set of twenty-five chin-ups. The ringtone was barely audible over the heavy metal music blaring from the gym speakers. He touched his chest to the bar attached to the wall of the Sandpit's garage before dropping nimbly to the ground.

"Hang on!" he yelled as he answered the phone, fumbling with the stereo remote and killing the music. "OK, go."

"Chua, it's Kurtz."

"Hey, how's the mission going?"

"We've hit a dead end."

"Sorry to hear that. Anything I can do to help out?"

"That's the reason I called. The only lead we've got is a satellite phone number for a human trafficker called Krenich. According to a local source he has some of the girls."

"How many of the girls have you recovered?" Chua left the garage and climbed the stairs to the kitchen.

"Fifty-five of the original seventy."

"That's pretty good."

"Not good enough. Can you track the number?"

Chua took a protein shake from the fridge. "We've shut down all SIGINT operations now that Flash is working for Lascar Logistics." Flash was previously PRIMAL's technical analyst, a genius when it came to all forms of electronic warfare and signals intelligence. "However, I do have a few other options to explore. Leave it with me for a few hours and I'll get back to you."

"*Danke.*"

"You guys are doing great work out there. Those girls wouldn't stand a chance without you."

"So Vance isn't angry?"

"Not at all. You're keeping it real discreet and professional. This is exactly the type of operation we'll be doing going forward. Now, let me chase up that number."

Chua pocketed his phone, shook the protein shake and wandered out through the building's open glass doors into the intense Middle Eastern sun. He spotted Vance and Ice at the far end of the swimming pool. The two men wore only shorts and were finishing a heavy deadlift session followed by a plunge into the icy water. Both were in impressive condition for their age. With extensive scarring across his lean torso and face, plus a prosthetic hand, Ice resembled a muscle-bound cyborg. Vance was even more heavy-set, the culmination of decades of powerlifting.

"You finished your circuit already?" jibed Vance as Chua approached.

"We're not all gorillas like you two. I got a call from Kurtz."

"They need backup?" Ice asked, eagerly.

"No. They need some intel assistance. They've got a satellite number that they want traced."

"You tell them we've shut all our tech down?" asked Vance.

"Yeah, but what if we get Bishop to hit Keila up for support? She'd have the basic tools at her fingertips."

Vance grabbed a towel from the back of a sun chair and used it to wipe the sweat from his forehead. "Does that compromise our operation?"

"No. The number isn't linked to the boys and if they run some tight counter-intel drills, it'll let us know if we can trust Keila."

"Well, she does owe Bish one after Iraq."

"And the rest," added Ice. "I'm happy to help the team out if they need it."

"Workout's too tough for you, brother?" asked Vance.

"Please, I warm up with what you max."

Chua rolled his eyes. "So I'm good to pass the number to Bishop?"

"Yeah, make it happen."

———

CAPE TOWN, SOUTH AFRICA

As the Sikorsky S-76C business helicopter descended Manfred Lisker adjusted his glasses and peered out the side window at the structure that blocked his view of Cape Town. The skeleton of a modern skyscraper glistened in the setting sun as the light reflected off steel girders and sleek glass panels. Clearly Sakkin Industries wasn't short on cash, he thought as the chopper touched down.

Lisker had been attending a conference at the Israeli embassy in Pretoria when the CEO of Sakkin Industries had extended him an invitation to the new facility. He'd expected a low-key complex on the outskirts of the city, not the monolith that towered above him.

Daniel Ginsberg greeted him as he stepped down the helicopter's stairs. As usual, the CEO looked as if he'd stepped straight from the pages of a Ralph Lauren catalog. The man never bothered with business attire.

"Very impressive, Daniel." He nodded toward the tower. "I didn't realize you were so heavily invested in Africa."

"Africa is the future," Ginsberg replied. "A continent of boundless opportunities. Let me show you around."

He led Lisker across the helipad, down some stairs and into a series of transportable buildings. The first room they entered was brimming with engineers, computer screens and had blueprints, images and diagrams attached to the walls.

Ginsberg paused in front of an artist's impression of the completed structure. "The building will house offices, a command center and a technology and research complex. From here we're going to be able to run our activities across the continent."

"Activities?"

"Sounds less hostile than security operations."

Ginsberg tipped his head toward a door at the side of the building. "Through here." He punched a number into a keypad on the door and led Lisker into his office.

"How are you tracking with Jarvis?" he said once the door closed.

"That will be dealt with shortly."

"Excellent, in the meantime I've got another small problem that I need you to deal with."

"What type of problem?"

"Someone is getting too close to the Proteus project in Rwanda."

"Rwanda?"

"Yes, we've got a shell company called the Lifebright Medicine Foundation that has a facility on the border. It's where Doctor Copeland's research is being continued. The problem is someone is sniffing around."

"Who?"

Ginsberg took his phone from his pocket and aimed it at one of the screens on the wall. The screen came alive, displaying images of a woman in uniform.

"Her name is Bianca Paquet and from what little information is available online we've been able to deduce that she's former Canadian military."

Lisker adjusted his glasses. "Exactly how much have you been able to find?"

"Just a handful of images."

"No social media?"`

"No, no banking, no social media."

"Then she's either special forces or intelligence."

"Either way, we need her taken care of."

"And your people are not up to the task?"

Ginsberg shook his head. "It would seem not. These situations are the exact reason why I'm funding your capability."

"I'll have it taken care of."

"Excellent. Now, if you don't mind, I'll have the helicopter drop you at the country club. I'll meet you there in an hour. I've got a few things I need to deal with."

"I'm happy to wait. I've got several calls to make."

"You can use my office."

"Appreciated."

Lisker waited till Ginsberg had left before calling Avi from his secure phone. "Re-task Mantis. I'm sending you the target details. Use another asset to deal with Jarvis."

"Got it."

"And Avi."

"Yes, sir."

"Once Mantis is done, terminate her."

"My pleasure."

Chapter Nine

DUBAI, UAE

BISHOP TOOK containers of Thai food from a paper bag and placed them on the hotel room's corner table. "Babe, food's up."

Saneh emerged from the bathroom clad in skin-tight active wear. "I'm going to hit the gym. I'll eat after."

"I thought we could have dinner together?"

She crossed the room and touched his shoulder. "I've been on my feet all day. I need to stretch out."

"The food will get cold."

She made for the door. "I can always order more."

As she reached for the handle Bishop's phone chimed. She paused as he checked it.

"It's from Chua, he wants me to contact Keila."

She turned. "Why?"

"They want a phone number tracked. It's for Kurtz and Kruger in Africa."

"Yeah, well I'm sure you can convince her to do that."

Saneh left the room and walked along the corridor toward the hotel elevators, her fists clenched. Bishop's willingness to work with the Mossad agent infuriated her. Not because she was jealous, but because she knew they couldn't be trusted. Her current predicament was evidence enough of that.

As she strode along the corridor she passed two men dressed in grey coveralls pushing a cleaning cart. Both looked Middle Eastern or at least Mediterranean, not something you usually saw in the Emirates. Pakistani or Bangladeshi migrant workers handled most of the labor.

The elevator doors opened as she stabbed the button. Stepping inside she selected the gym floor and waited for the doors to close. As they slid shut one of the cleaners glanced over his shoulder at her. Their eyes met and she detected a hint of recognition in them.

As the elevator dropped, it clicked. They had to be a Mossad team sent to kill Jarvis. Adrenaline kicked in as she reached for the button to the next floor, but something held her back. If she compromised the team then the next assassins would come for her and Bishop, and they wouldn't stop till everyone they knew was dead. Her hand shook as the floor indicators dropped. Jarvis's face appeared in her mind and guilt assailed her as she realized she held an innocent man's life in her hands.

"Damn it!" She stabbed the button for the floor below. The elevator stopped. Doors opened and she sprinted for the fire stairs. As she climbed her phone let out a high-pitched shriek, Jarvis's duress alarm.

It took her under a minute to reach the floor. Bursting out of the elevator she sprinted toward their client's suite.

The door was open, the cleaning cart down the corridor. She entered and found Bishop kneeling over a convulsing Jarvis, his palms slamming down on the man's chest.

"Med kit."

She raced next door to their suite and grabbed a backpack. Unzipping it on her way back to the room she laid it out alongside Jarvis.

"EpiPen by two." He grunted between compressions.

She took two of the 300-milligram injectors from their sleeves, twisted the caps off and jammed them one after the other into Jarvis's convulsing thigh.

The CEO's back arched and he gasped for air as the chemical coursed through his veins into his heart. But, then he slumped back to the ground as Bishop ripped out the leads for the pack's internal defibrillator.

Saneh knew the move was a last ditch attempt to restart the man's heart. If the adrenaline hadn't worked there was very little that the machine could do.

"Clear," Bishop announced, before punching a yellow button.

It let out a soft whine then sent a charge pulsing through Jarvis's body.

"Fuck!" screamed Bishop as it failed to register a pulse and cycled through again. "More adrenaline."

Saneh prepped another pen and handed it to him. "You know the risk."

He turned to her and she saw the frustration etched into his features. Tears welled in his eyes. "Yeah, I know." He punched the pen into Jarvis's leg.

This time the body barely responded.

"Aden, he's gone."

The defibrillator let out another warning and delivered an additional shock to the body as they heard shouting from the corridor. Paramedics appeared at the doorway with a stretcher. Bishop must have called them as soon as he found Jarvis.

"We think he's been poisoned or had an allergic reaction. He's had three EpiPens and we've attempted resuscitation," declared Bishop as they entered.

"We've got it from here," one of them said.

"OK." Bishop stepped out of the way, grabbed Saneh's arm and dragged her into the corridor. "Did you see anything on your way out? The killers could still be in the building."

"There was a cleaning crew."

"That has to be them. We need to lock down the hotel and check the security footage."

"That is being taken care of." The voice belonged to the hotel's head of security. "My people are liaising with the police as we speak. I suggest that you return to your suite and be prepared to give a statement."

Guilt assailed Saneh as she reached out and took her partner's hand. "Aden, that sounds like a good idea. There's nothing more we can do here."

Bishop glanced back at the door to Jarvis's suite. "I need to call Tariq. Then we're getting out of here."

DUBAI, UAE

"The cleaning crew you saw, what did they look like?" asked Bishop. He and Saneh had provided statements to the Abu Dhabi police and returned to their suite.

"Two men, average height and build, Middle Eastern appearance," replied Saneh.

"And that didn't set any alarm bells ringing?" he snapped. "When have you ever seen an Arab on a cleaning crew?"

Saneh folded her arms. "I'd had a long day and I wasn't paying that much attention."

He shook his head. "We always pay attention."

"I wasn't the one who assessed the hotel as low risk." The look on his face told her the comment hit hard. "Look, we both need to clear our heads. I'm going for a ride."

"Tariq wanted…" Bishop thought better of the comment and stopped. "Good idea. I'll see you when you get back."

Tariq had been beyond furious when Bishop had told him Jarvis had been murdered under their watch. He'd immediately suspended them from all Lascar related activity and advised them to stay in their apartment until he sorted things out. That didn't stop Bishop from wanting to know what had gone wrong.

Fifteen minutes later and Saneh was gunning her Ducati along a desert highway. Clad in armored leathers and helmet other drivers had no way of telling a woman was piloting the superbike. It gave her freedom in a city where, despite progress, females were still treated like second-class citizens.

It took her a matter of minutes to cover the fifteen miles between the city and a small outlying settlement. Swerving onto an off-ramp she downshifted, relishing the snarl of the powerful engine as she slowed the bike to a manageable speed.

She spotted a gas station ahead and turned off the road into the sprawling facility. Cruising past the pumps she pulled in alongside a non-descript SUV and let the bike sit on its stand. Over the ticking of the cooling engine she heard the faint whirr of a power window and turned to face the driver's side of the SUV.

"You've got a new assignment," said Avi from inside the

air-conditioned comfort of the vehicle. He handed Saneh a printed photo. "Her name is Bianca Paquet and she's currently located in Nyagatare, Rwanda."

She took the photo and studied it from behind her visor, jaw clenched. The woman was pretty in a hard no-nonsense kind of way. She had grey eyes with wrinkles around them that suggested she smiled a lot.

"Neutralize her."

"And then what?"

"You come back to Abu Dhabi."

"So you can task me to kill another person like Jarvis? Some innocent pawn caught up in Lisker's bullshit plans?"

"Please, you didn't have it in you to kill him. You're slipping Saneh, and it's going to cost you. Now get this job done, or do you need me to remind you what will happen to your small family if you don't."

Saneh raised her visor so that Avi could look into her eyes. "You go near Aden or his dog and I'll kill every last one of you."

The Mossad operative smirked. "That's the Mantis we know and love."

She scrunched the photo into a tight ball and tossed it through the window of the SUV. Then she dropped her visor and started the bike. Applying the front brake she whipped the rear wheel around in a haze of smoke then roared across the parking lot and back out onto the road. The bike screamed as she sent it blaring back onto the highway.

Weaving the bike through traffic she hammered south away from Abu Dhabi. Fueled by rage she pushed the bike harder than she'd ever raced before. The edges of her vision blurred, the speed pushing everything from her mind as she clung to the bike. Part of her wanted the motorcycle to clip one of the trucks and end her life. But, she knew that Lisker would terminate Bishop anyway. At this point in time her compliance with his tasking was the only thing keeping them both alive.

Slowing she turned off the highway, looped onto an overpass and rejoined the gleaming asphalt road back to Abu Dhabi. Traveling just under the speed limit it took her half an hour to return to their apartment complex. Unable to face Bishop she spent another two hours working on the bike in their garage before she finally returned to the high-rise penthouse.

It didn't surprise her to find that Bishop and Daisy weren't there when she opened the door. He often blew off steam by taking the dog for a run around the Marina.

She found a note on the kitchen counter. It was short and to the point.

Need some time to think. Have taken Daisy home.

There was only one place that Bishop referred to as home; his parent's cottage outside of Requena, Spain. The message hit Saneh like a punch to the gut. She realized she'd been distancing herself from Aden ever since Lisker had blackmailed her into working for Mossad, but she'd never intended to drive him away.

She tossed the note on the bench as she fought back tears. The death of Jarvis, Lisker's new task and now Aden leaving had left her emotionally drained.

Bishop kept an extensive collection of whisky on the bench top. She took a glass from a cupboard, filled it with ice and worked the cork out of a bottle of 21-year-old Hibiki.

Sitting on the couch she sipped while she considered her

options. She could chase Bishop, but that meant failing to achieve Lisker's task. After Jarvis, she doubted he would tolerate further failure. Avi was right, she needed to get back to being the lethal operative of old. Bishop's life was counting on it.

LIFEBRIGHT FOUNDATION FACILITY, RWANDA

Jamilah cowered in the corner of her cell as the door swung open and two masked orderlies burst inside. She screamed and kicked as they grabbed her arms and dragged her along a sterile corridor into a laboratory.

Forcing her into a chair they systematically pinned her limbs and fastened them with straps. Eyes wide she thrashed against the restraints as a thin needle slid into her upper arm. It took less than a minute for the sedative to do its work. Her head lolled to the side and her eyes rolled toward the ceiling as the orderly stuck sensors to her and inserted a line into her arm.

Lifting her shirt they fastened it so her stomach was bare. One of the men rolled across a stand that held a tablet screen and a device that looked like a showerhead.

While the sedative may have rendered Jamilah incapable of motor functions her brain was merely clouded. She was still conscious as the door opened and an elderly white man dressed in blue medical garb entered.

He shot the computer monitor a cursory glance before inspecting a sheaf of papers that lay on a stainless bench. Then he turned to face her.

The man stared at her with an utter lack of emotion in his cold eyes. It was as if she was a side of beef hanging from a butcher's hook. "This one is almost ready," he stated to the masked orderly. "Earmark her for surgery in four days."

"Full procedure?"

The doctor took the device from the stand and ran it back and forth across her stomach and pelvic region as he studied the tablet. "Her womb is in pristine condition," he murmured. "Yes, full procedure."

Jamilah caught the sad look that the orderly shot her as he made a note on the sheaf of papers. She had no idea what a 'full procedure' was, but that look all but confirmed it was a death sentence.

The girl who she shared her cell with, Bilan, had been taken a day earlier and never returned. Jamilah was sure that the doctor had killed her.

Doctor Morrison flicked his rubber gloves into a surgical bin as he left the inspection room and returned to his office. He had a feeling that subject 173X was going to provide the breakthrough he needed to reach the next stage of the project. So far her body hadn't shown any sign of adverse reaction to the concoction of drugs that prepared the womb for removal. Unfortunately the last few subjects had not been as receptive. He'd successfully harvested the required organic components but they had not survived when attached to artificial life support.

He entered his office where Elias was waiting.

"You wanted me?" the head of security asked.

"Yes, Copeland informs me that a specialist is being sent to deal with the Canadian."

Elias crossed his tattooed arms. "We don't need a specialist–"

Morrison interrupted him with a raised hand. "You allowed her to go to the UN. It is too risky to have someone associated with the project deal with her now. You missed your chance. Leave it to the professionals."

"If you say so." Elias stormed out of the office.

"Animal," mumbled the doctor as he sat behind his computer and waited for his daily conference call with Copeland. At least he had the good news of 173X to share with her.

———

TEL AVIV, ISRAEL

Keila glanced at a scrap of paper on her desk and punched the digits scribbled on it into the computer. Drumming her fingers she waited for an analytical program to run the sequence and provide her a return.

The satellite phone number had been supplied by Bishop, a favor that, considering what he'd done for her team, she wouldn't refuse. Additionally, it might provide some further insight into the reach of his capabilities.

A warning appeared on her screen indicating that someone else was already covering the number and the information was restricted. If she were a betting person she'd put money on Lisker being the approving authority however she didn't have the access required to check that. If she wanted to get Bishop the information requested she was going to have to call in another favor with Asher. She caught herself smiling as she contemplated dinner with the handsome Captain. There was something about his relaxed demeanor and dry wit that she found desirable.

"Hey boss," Abel called out from his cubical. "You see the news on that American guy being shwacked in Dubai?"

"Huh. No, what are the details?"

"CEO of a technology firm working on autonomous drone systems. Found dead in his hotel room from a heart attack."

"How old?"

"Mid-forties."

"What makes you think he was killed?"

"Oh come on." Abel raised his hands and used them as exclamation marks. "Heart attack. Please, more like dosed up on beta-adrenoceptor blocking agents."

"Right, and who specializes in that level of deniability?" added Keila as she reached for her phone. "The Saudis or Emiratis?"

"Nah, they just chop people up."

"Exactly, so if anyone assassinated this guy it would have been us. But why would Mossad kill the CEO of a US tech company? It's more likely the guy liked his fries a little too much and keeled over on holidays." She punched in the number for Asher's desk.

"Whatever. Still think he was knocked off," mumbled Abel as he disappeared behind his partition.

"Always a conspiracy with you." She laughed as she waited for the signals intelligence officer to pick up.

The dial tone stopped

"Keila, nice to hear from you," said Asher before she could speak.

"Hey, you free for coffee this afternoon?"

"No, but I can do dinner."

Doesn't miss a beat, she thought. "What makes you think you deserve a dinner date?"

"Because I've got something you want."

She frowned. "And what might that be."

"There was a reason you called, and it wasn't for coffee."

She glanced at her screen and figured out exactly what he was telling her. The number she inputted was flagged and it was part of the target set he was monitoring. Straight away that told her it was likely related to Lisker, but she needed more for Bishop. "OK, dinner. Where are we going to meet?"

"I know a place," he said. "I'll send you the address. You good with eight?"

"It's a date." She cringed as the words left her mouth and slammed the phone down in its cradle. Glancing around the room she saw that all the team members present had popped their heads over the partitions and were staring at her. Abel was smirking, Jacinta was grinning like an idiot and Fahim's eyebrows were raised.

"It's not a date. Get back to work."

The room broke into laughter and Keila shook her head as she turned her attention back to the computer. "I seriously hate you guys."

Chapter Ten

THE SANDPIT, ABU DHABI

"HAVE YOU SPOKEN TO BISHOP?" Vance asked Chua as he entered the Sandpit's operations room.

The intelligence chief sat at the conference table scrolling through his iPRIMAL. "No, he sent me a message saying he was heading to the cottage in Spain."

"Saneh with him?"

"I'd say so."

"You get any additional intel on their client's death?"

Chua shook his head. "According to the media reports, it was a heart attack. No mention of foul play."

"Hmmm." Vance sat at a vacant terminal and stared at the blank screen.

"Maybe you should call Tariq and ask him."

"No. He made it perfectly clear that PRIMAL wasn't to be involved in any of his activities and vice versa. If he thought it was suspicious and wanted our help, he'd reach out." Vance turned his chair to face Chua. "This just doesn't feel right."

"The death?"

"No." He made a sweeping gesture with his hand. "Seems like yesterday we were running operations across the globe. Now we're sitting here waiting to wrap things up and get out of town."

"Yeah, it's a different pace."

"Gonna take some getting used to. Right, so where are we at with Kruger and Kurtz?"

"They're waiting on intel from us before they can continue their operation. Bishop passed the number to Keila and he's waiting for a response."

"Any thoughts on operations once they wrap this up?"

"I was going to recommend that we focus them on network development. Take the downtime to build our capability in case we want to step things up again."

"I think that's a smart move. Africa could become our new stomping ground. When the time is right."

"And when is that likely to be?" asked Ice from the door.

Vance turned and shot the big man a wink. "All in good time, brother. You'll get your chance."

"When are you guys heading down under?"

Vance shot Chua a look. "How the hell does everyone know about that?"

"Because," said Ice, "you guys are crap at keeping secrets."

———

TEL AVIV, ISRAEL

"I want to know all of Tariq Ahmed's secrets," Manfred Lisker announced as he entered one of the secure briefing rooms in his department within Mossad's headquarters.

Avi Lerner, his head of operations, sat at the conference table, only recently returned from Dubai. Beside him sat the department's lead analyst, David Hitzig. The two men glanced at each other.

"Does this mean you've got nothing?"

"Not exactly," said Avi. "But it is proving difficult."

"Difficult?" Lisker looked at David as he sat at the head of the table.

"8200 has identified a secure communications network being used by Tariq's employees within Priority Movements Airlift," said David.

"His militant arm," said Lisker.

"Yes. They're using a highly sophisticated encrypted network to communicate. It's taking a significant amount of analytical and processing power to break it."

"Do we have an estimated timeframe?"

"As yet, no. However, the process would be significantly enhanced if we had access to a physical device."

"Could Mantis provide that?" Lisker asked Avi.

Avi shook his head. "That would burn the network. We can't trust her not to alert the others."

"Her termination may achieve the same effect," added David.

"True. We will delay her retirement until after we have gained access."

The scowl on Avi's face flagged his disappointment. "It may well be that she and Aden Bishop are Tariq's only active operatives."

"Not by my assessment," said David. "8200 have indications that the network is extensive with at least a dozen active members and possibly many more who are dormant."

"What about locations?" asked Lisker. "Do we know where any of these people are? Can we target them?"

"Not until they break the encryption. However, I am looking into Lascar real estate holdings, particularly in the UAE. I think they may have a safe house in the area."

"Anything else?"

"Not at the moment."

"Thank you, David."

The analyst took the cue and left Avi and Lisker alone in the room.

"Well done on the mission in Dubai. Has Mantis left for Africa yet?"

"In the next few hours. I'll also have one of my men on the ground to clean up."

"Off the books?"

Avi nodded. "The best money can buy. How did South Africa go?"

"Ginsberg is building an impressive facility. His ongoing patronage will be paramount to our expansion into Africa."

"A continent of opportunity," agreed Avi. "When you green light Mantis's termination do you want her boyfriend neutralized?"

"Not immediately. I want him to reveal the rest of the network. Keep him under surveillance. Then, when the conditions are right, we clean house. In the meantime I need you to recruit the required field teams. Use the Sakkin funding as you see fit. Additionally, I want an update on the operation in Egypt."

"We're ready for the next phase. All I need is the anti-tank weapons."

Lisker rose from the table. "The shipment's ready. Have Lascar make the delivery."

————

TEL AVIV, ISRAEL

Asher spotted Keila as she entered the upmarket seafood restaurant on the Tel Aviv Promenade. The Mossad operative wore a full-length blue and white polka dot dress with an elegant V neckline. She'd let her brown hair down to her shoulders, framing her green eyes.

He rose from the table and caught her eye with a raised hand. As she crossed the room he noticed a hint of makeup around her eyes and the faintest possibility of lipstick on her full lips. "Keila, you look lovely."

"Thank you." She smiled as she gave his white cotton shirt and linen pants the once over. "You don't look too bad yourself."

They took a seat and Asher offered her the wine menu. She chose a bottle of sauvignon blanc and their waiter soon had both glasses full as they perused the extensive Mediterranean menu.

"How did you find this place?" Keila asked.

"My sister recommended it. She's a real foodie."

At the mention of his sibling she realized that she knew very little about Asher, other than the details of his military career. "Do you have any other siblings?"

"No, just a sister. Chantal works in banking here in Tel Aviv."

The small talk continued and Keila soon found herself

divulging the details of her own family and childhood. There was something about Asher that made her feel comfortable telling him things that even her teammates didn't know. In fact, she couldn't remember the last time she'd had a candid conversation with someone.

The conversation paused as they ordered their meals then Asher went on to tell her a little more about himself. It turned out they shared quite a few common interests, including a love for the outdoors, in particular, hiking.

When their meals arrived the conversation had progressed to their jobs. Keila was pleasantly surprised to find that Asher, like herself, wasn't looking for a career. However, unlike her, he actually had a post-service plan. His dream was to leave the military and run his own business guiding clients on luxury hiking experiences.

"So," said Asher once their plates had been removed. "I guess you want to know about the number."

Distracted by good food, wine and great conversation Keila had forgotten all about the information Bishop had requested.

Asher took a folded piece of paper from his pocket and slid it across the crisp white tablecloth. She placed her hand over it and slipped it into her palm.

"His name is Ross Krenich and he's a people smuggler based in Kampala, Uganda. You've got the address on the paper."

"Who had him on cover?" she asked.

He winked. "Some prick."

"Why the hell would Lisker be interested in a scumbag smuggler in Uganda?"

He shrugged. "I just do as I'm told."

"OK, last question. Any news on the Lascar network?"

"We're close, very close. I'll let you know when we crack it."

She smiled. "OK, but enough about work. How do you feel about coffee and sweets?"

"I feel like that's a great idea. There's a wicked little bar a few blocks from here. They do an amazing caramel torte."

"How did you know I like caramel?"

"Just a guess. Come on, let's get out of here."

Later that evening, once Asher had dropped her home, she dialed Bishop from a burner phone. He'd given her a new number during their meeting in Greece. Despite the late hour he picked up quickly.

"Hello."

"Aden, it's Keila. I've got the information you wanted." She read off the name and address from Asher's note.

"Thanks, greatly appreciated." He sounded tired.

"You OK?"

"I'm fine. Just taking a little time off. How are things with you?"

Keila took a second to reflect on the date with Asher. The evening had been perfect and not surprisingly, she was looking forward to seeing him again. "I'm great. Life is really good."

"Glad to hear it. Thanks again for the info."

"Anytime."

Keila placed the phone on her bedside table. She should have asked what Bishop's intent was regarding Krenich. However, something told her that a little justice was coming to the people smuggler. The bonus was it might throw a spanner into something Lisker was planning, whatever that was.

NYAGATARE, RWANDA

Saneh parked her rented SUV out the front of Nyagatare's Cityblue hotel and walked into the reception area with a barrel bag over her shoulder. Dressed in khaki slacks and grey polo shirt with her hair in a ponytail she looked every part the medical contractor that was her cover.

She'd flown into Kigali on a direct flight from Dubai, hired the car and driven it three hours to reach the town where her target was last reported to have been located. Given that Bianca was a blonde caucasian in a small Rwandan town, it wouldn't take long to find her.

By the time she'd checked in and unpacked it was early evening. She grabbed a bite to eat in the hotel's bistro then made a beeline for the bar. As she pushed through the frosted glass doors she was greeted by the mayhem of happy hour. The place was packed with exactly the crowd she was expecting.

It was wall to wall with UN and NGO workers as well as the usual security types and a smattering of local and international businessmen. She found a space and caught the eye of the bartender. Ordering a gin and tonic she scanned the room for her target. It didn't take her long to see that Bianca wasn't there. For a moment she considered staking out the bar for the evening, but she didn't have the time or the patience. She wanted to get this job done and then head directly to Spain to find Bishop and salvage their relationship, if that was possible.

Waving the bartender over she slid a phone across the table with a picture of Bianca on the screen. "You seen this woman?" she asked in a faux American accent.

He nodded. "Yeah, she came in last week."

"Have you seen her since?"

"Not here. But she's been over at Pepe's Sports Bar on the other side of town."

Saneh shot him a judging look.

"It's my other job."

He scribbled the address on a piece of paper and handed it to her. She downed her drink and made for the door. As she crossed the room she spotted two men watching her from a corner table.

They were both white, well built and wearing clothing that indicated they either had or still served in a government agency. She committed their faces to memory as she left the bar and asked the concierge to bring her SUV around.

Twenty minutes later she'd located Pepe's, a dingy drinking hole that felt way more local. She lodged herself in the corner of the bar with a viewpoint of the entrance and feigned an interest in the football match being played on the 80s-era television perched on a refrigerator. Unlike the hotel the place was relatively empty, obviously more of a late nightspot. She ordered a local beer and prepared herself for a long wait.

KURDISTAN, IRAQ

The Lascar Logistics Iluyshin-76 cargo jet thumped down on a short stretch of tarmac, its engines roaring as the pilot applied reverse thrust. The thirty-five-ton aircraft's nose dropped as it braked, wheels squealing and smoke billowing.

It came to a halt only a few yards from the yellow sand that stretched for hundreds of miles in each direction of the remote airstrip. As the jet backed up and turned to prepare for takeoff a second aircraft appeared in the sky.

The approaching aircraft circled the strip at high speed, a sleek business jet with two massive propellers. As it came closer the props rotated skyward and the aircraft commenced to decelerate as it transformed into a rotary wing aircraft. Like a dragonfly it hovered in front of the Iluyshin then landed. When it touched down the blades flattened, and the side door opened and lowered into a set of stairs.

A suited figure stepped out and strode across the tarmac. His jacket flapped in the wind as he climbed the stairs into the waiting transporter where the pilot met him.

"Tariq, good to see you."

The CEO of Lascar Logistics shook his pilot's hand. "You too, Mike. What have you got for me?"

Mike directed him into the cargo hold and pointed to two large crates marked with red crosses strapped closest to the ramp.

Tariq removed his jacket and tossed it on another crate that looked almost identical to the others.

"The one on the end." Mike passed Tariq a pry bar and used a hook knife to cut the straps holding the crate shut. Tariq pried the lid off with the bar and slid it onto the other crate. Sweeping the packing material aside he exposed green military munitions tubes.

"Why the hell is Mossad shipping rocket launchers to Egypt?" asked Mike. "The last time I checked, a stable Egypt was high on Israel's wishlist. What do they have to gain from rockets going off all over the place?"

Tariq placed the pry bar on top of a crate. "I think it's a safe assessment that the individual who's authorizing this is not doing it in the interests of his government."

"That would explain why we're making the drops. Are we going ahead with the mission?"

"Yes, as briefed."

"Roger."

"And Mike."

"Yeah."

"This stays between you and me."

Tariq Ahmed left the Il-76 and a moment later his private AW609 tiltrotor rose off the tarmac, banked and raced away to the east. As it gained speed Tariq Ahmed stared out of a window at the desert racing past below, his hands clenched on the armrest of his leather chair. It was one thing to be manipulated by a nation-state; it was another for it to be a man driven only by his self-interest.

Chapter Eleven

ABU DHABI, UAE

"ARE WE UP?" the driver of the blue van asked the two men sitting in the rear of the vehicle.

"Two minutes," one of them replied as he inputted commands into a laptop.

"Geeks, always dragging their asses."

The three-man team were security contractors hired to conduct a technical surveillance sweep of an upmarket coastal suburb located a dozen miles south of Abu Dhabi. Former members of intelligence agencies, they'd all made a move into the far more lucrative world of corporate espionage.

"OK, we're on," said the technician.

"A-firm," replied the driver.

The vehicle pulled out of a gas station and cruised along a stretch of highway, before turning on to a land bridge. They passed between rows of palm trees before entering a community of luxury villas built on an artificial island.

"What we looking for?" asked the other passenger.

"Anything out of the norm," replied the tech. "More specifically, increased comms signatures."

"They give us any context or is this just another trawl?" asked the driver as they turned down a street lined with mansions.

"We're trawling. But, my guess is someone's running a high-end hack shop out here. Or at least our client thinks they are."

The driver caught a glimpse of the sea between two houses. "Imagine what one of these places is worth. Not a bad spot to get your geek on."

"Except they're probably in the garage mining bitcoin," said the passenger.

"How on earth do you mine a digital currency?" asked the driver.

"It's easy," said the passenger. "You get kids to play computer games and they find it in the different levels."

The technician raised his eyes from his laptop. "Really? You actually think that's how you mine bitcoin? Seriously, I'm working with idiots." As he glanced back at his screen, he spotted a spike of activity. "Hey slow down."

"You find some bitcoin?"

"No, there's a lot of Wi-Fi traffic in the area. Way more than normal. Turn left up here."

The driver followed his directions and they cruised into an area still under development. The roads were empty and many of the luxury villas that fronted a man-made beach were half constructed. "Do you think people actually live here?"

"Slow down." The tech's fingers raced across his keyboard. "Yeah, definitely something fishy going on."

"Wicked," said the passenger. "How awesome would it be if they let us bang it in? We'd scare the crap out of those bitcoin hackers."

CAMP, SOMALIA

Kurtz was lying on his stretcher staring at the mosquitoes bouncing against the ceiling of his tent when his phone chimed. It was a little after six in the morning but he'd been awake for over an hour, dwelling on their failed mission to find the last of the girls. As he read a message from Chen Chua his frustration evaporated.

"We've got a location!" he yelled as he rolled off the stretcher and stormed out of the tent.

There was a loud groan from the back of the Mi-17 helicopter where Toppie slept and a grunt from Kruger's tent.

"Where is it?" Booyah asked from where he was crouched over a small fire tending a pot of coffee.

"Kampala, Uganda."

"That's not far. We can get there real fast in the helicopter," said the scout as he poured thick black coffee into enamel cups.

"Chua came through?" asked Kruger as he emerged shirtless from his tent. The South African was built like a gorilla with massive arms and a barrel chest covered in hair.

"*Ja*, we have a complete target pack on Krenich and his residence." He took the cup that Booyah offered him. "I'll put it up in the chopper." He climbed into the rear of the

Mi-17 helicopter and was immediately hit by the smell of booze and cigarettes. "Toppie, wake up you stinky *dummkopf.*"

The pilot was asleep on the floor of the aircraft wrapped in a poncho liner.

"I'm awake you Kraut bastard."

Kurtz activated the LED screen they'd bolted to the back of the cockpit wall and transferred the target package from his iPRIMAL. He felt the aircraft lurch and turned to see Booyah and Kruger join him and Toppie inside. The scout passed a mug to the pilot and all three men turned their attention to Kurtz.

"What have we got?" asked Kruger. The South African had donned a skin-tight Under Armor shirt.

"Krenich has a house in Kampala." Kurtz gestured to the screen where a satellite image of the target building appeared.

It took the team a little over half an hour to work through the package that Chua had built them. Once they'd reached the last of the twelve slides they had a comprehensive picture of their new target.

"OK, so what do you guys think?"

"I say we bang it in and work the fucker over." Kruger sipped from his mug. "Trust me, I've seen pricks like this before and he'll talk once we apply a little heat."

"Fok yeah," agreed Toppie.

Booyah nodded.

Kurtz frowned. "This isn't another rag-tag rebel gang. Just this once I think it might be better to employ stealth and guile rather than brute force."

"That's no fun," said Kruger.

Kurtz shot him a shark-like grin. "Trust me. This will be very fun."

REQUENA, SPAIN

A stone cottage on a flinty hillside overlooking rows of green vines was Aden Bishop's place of solitude. The residence on the outskirts of Requena had belonged to his parents, and he'd been coming here since he was a boy. In recent years the original single room structure had been renovated and he'd once dreamed of settling here with Saneh to start a family.

He sat on a low stone wall gazing out over a valley of vineyards. A warm breeze caressed his face as he considered the tension that had been mounting between him and Saneh. It had started months earlier. She'd continually pushed him away, becoming more and more distant as the days wound on. For a man who loved his partner more than life itself, it was heartbreaking. Nothing he did seemed to fix the problem. He hoped that time apart would give her the space she needed to deal with whatever it was.

A nudge against his leg told him that Daisy, his Border Collie, had returned from sniffing around the perimeter of the two-acre property.

"No squirrels?" he asked as he ruffled her ears.

The dog looked up at him with bright eyes and nuzzled his hand with her snout.

He tapped the wall next to him and Daisy jumped up alongside. Then he threw an arm around the dog and pulled her in close. "You always know how to make me feel better, don't you?"

She let out a bark.

"OK, I hear you. Let's get inside and get something to eat."

As Bishop rose and the dog jumped down from the wall he had no idea that he was being watched by a sophisticated electro-optic sensor. The high-tech camera was hidden in a distant vineyard. Connected to a powerful battery and a short-range data transmitter the device was being monitored remotely by two men sitting in a hired sedan.

One of the men sat in the passenger seat cradling a tablet that displayed images from the camera.

"Is that him?" asked the driver.

"Yeah, we've got PID," said the second man.

The driver took a phone from his pocket and typed a message into a secure chat application.

Target located and identified.

It was a matter of seconds before the device pinged, announcing a response from their mission director, Avi.

Continue to monitor. Be prepared for rendition.

———

NYAGATARE, RWANDA

It was Saneh's second night staking out Pepe's sports bar in Nyagatare. She'd made a few subtle enquires as she evaded the approaches of no less than a dozen men. Eventually, someone had confirmed that Bianca did, in fact, drink at the bar, but hadn't been around for the last few days.

As she sat drinking a beer in the corner of the dingy watering hole her thoughts strayed from the mission, to Bishop. She wondered what he and Daisy were doing. Knowing him, he'd be in front of a crackling fire with a whisky in hand, Daisy curled at his feet. What she wouldn't give to be there with them.

She sipped her beer and was considering leaving when a woman entered the room and made for the bar. She instantly recognized Bianca Paquet. The blonde Canadian ordered a drink then turned to scan the room. Saneh dropped her head to avoid eye contact.

"Mind if I take a seat?" The accent was uniquely French Canadian.

Saneh looked up and smiled. "Sure, why not." It was just her luck that Bianca was the type of person who was comfortable enough to approach a complete stranger in a bar.

"So what brings you to Nyagatare?" asked the former Canadian Special Forces operator as she placed her drink, what looked like a whisky on the rocks, down on the table and sat.

"I'm working a contract for the UN."

"Human rights?"

"No, medical supplies," replied Saneh.

"That's a pity." Bianca raised her glass. "Well, here's to meeting another English speaking woman in the armpit of the world. Bianca, nice to meet you."

"I'm Sarah." She touched her beer to Bianca's glass. "So, what are you doing out here?" She instantly regretted asking the question. She'd broken the first rule of assassinations. Never make it personal.

"I'm doing some investigation work."

"You're a journalist?"

Bianca laughed. "No, far from it. I'm a concerned citizen trying to right a wrong."

The phrase sounded exactly like something that Bishop

would say. It could also go a long way to explain why Lisker wanted this woman dead. "Wrong?"

Bianca nodded and sipped her drink. "I found out there's a medical research facility here that's testing on children."

Her first thought was that Bianca was some kind of conspiracy nut job and possibly an alcoholic. However, the fact that Mossad's Director of Special Operations wanted her terminated added a level of credence to what she was saying.

"And you've got proof?"

The Canadian glanced around the room. "I heard rumors and then I connected the dots. Look, I don't want to say anything else here. The guys running security on the facility have ears everywhere. If you're interested, we can meet tomorrow and I'll give you the details. You might have an idea on how to help."

The investigation was something that Bishop would have leaped on, but Saneh already had a mission of her own and his survival depended on it. "Sounds good. I've got a few contacts that might be useful."

"Don't bother with the UN. I've already tried the human rights office."

Saneh smirked. "Weren't interested?"

"Let's just say that it didn't fit in with their agenda."

"Doesn't surprise me, can I get you another drink?"

For the next hour Saneh kept the booze flowing and Bianca kept talking. It was a tactic that she'd employed previously. The alcohol would slow her target's reaction time, making it easier to deliver a lethal strike with the stiletto blade hidden in her cargo pants. Or so she thought. The problem was how much she and her target had in common. Bianca, like her, had come from a broken family and had escaped into government service. And, despite being security savvy, had let slip a few comments that made Saneh think she was most likely from a 'special activities' background. As much as she tried to dehumanize her target, she couldn't.

"Well, I'm going to get out of here, eh. I'll see you tomorrow," said Bianca. "Been real nice talking to you."

"I think I'll go too. Did you need a lift anywhere?"

Bianca shook her head. "No thanks, I'm walking distance."

As Saneh followed her out of the bar into the dingy street she slid her knife from its sheath and palmed it. Guilt assailed her as she mentally rehearsed driving the thin black blade into the woman's neck and leaving her crumpled corpse by the road. It was something she'd done half a dozen times previously at the behest of her masters. However, things were different now. Now she'd do it for Bishop and the rest of the PRIMAL team, her family. She let the blade slide through her fingers and gripped the handle. Bianca had to die so that she could protect the ones she loved.

She spotted the threat a split second before her target did. Three Caucasian men appeared from the shadows cast by a flickering street lamp and made a beeline for her target. Saneh ducked in behind a parked car and watched.

One of the men grabbed Bianca from behind, clamping his hand over her mouth. The Canadian ducked and spun, driving her elbow into her assailant's flank. She moved with a level of expertise that implied hours of training in self-defense.

Saneh caught a glimpse of a flash of steel as one of the men pulled a knife from his jacket. With one man winded it was still two to one, a fight that Bianca was never going to win. Her mission was about to be completed for her, and yet she felt nothing but regret and anger.

One of the other men punched Bianca in the stomach and she doubled over. The man with the knife stepped in for the kill as Saneh leaped into action.

"Hey asshole," she yelled as she sprinted toward the assailant, her own blade ready.

Knife guy turned and she caught a glimpse of a face twisted with hate as she ducked under his wild slash and punched her stiletto into his thigh. He screamed in agony as she snapped her elbow up into his jaw, dropping him like a sack of potatoes.

Spinning she sized up her next opponent and strode toward him. The thick-necked, muscle-bound thug whipped a baton from under his jacket. "You're going to regret sticking your nose into this, bitch." He swung the length of tensile steel at her head.

Saneh slipped the strike and lunged forward with her blade, stabbing for his torso.

He was quicker than the other man and slid backward, directly into a devastating sidekick delivered by Bianca. His head snapped forward and he collapsed to the ground.

"Come with me!" Saneh grabbed Bianca's arm and dragged her to her SUV. "There could be more of them."

As the two women climbed into Saneh's car, neither of them noticed a figure watching them from another vehicle. The man inside waited till they'd pulled out onto the street before following them from a distance.

Chapter Twelve

TEL AVIV, ISRAEL

MANFRED LISKER WAS SIPPING from a fresh cup of tea in his favorite café when one of his mobile phones rang. He checked the screen before answering the call.

"Are you trying to fuck me?" said the voice on the other end. It was one of his men, currently on assignment in Egypt.

"What are you talking about?"

"Where the hell is my equipment?"

Lisker's eyes narrowed. "The shipment didn't arrive?"

"Oh it arrived all right. Two crates of god damn bandages and not a fucking rocket launcher among it."

"What? Are you sure?"

"I unpacked them myself. How the fuck am I supposed to run a covert war without any weapons?"

"I'll sort it out."

"Make it fast. My people here are getting nervous."

Lisker terminated the call then removed the sim card

from the phone. Paying for his drink he left the cafe, dropping the phone into a trashcan on the way out. His driver spotted him as he approached and opened the rear door of the armored Mercedes. Once inside he dialed Avi on a secure phone.

"Tariq didn't deliver the last shipment," he said when the call connected.

"And Mantis didn't kill her target."

"What?"

"The head of security for Lifebright took it upon himself to try and erase her. Mantis intervened."

Lisker gazed out of the inch thick glass at the distorted landscape beyond. "We need additional leverage over them both. I want your people to pick up the boyfriend."

"You want him brought here?"

"No, keep it local. Use the Sakkin fund to establish a safe house and have your people standby. If she pushes back on your direction feel free to motivate her. Where are we on the rest of Tariq's network of operatives?"

"Close. We've identified several possible locations. The properties belong to shell companies associated with Lascar. I'm waiting on 8200 for target fidelity."

"Plan for a contracted solution to neutralize it."

"That has potential for unintended collateral."

"Correct. We'll make it look like one of Tariq's shady dealings has gone south. Once we're finished, Lascar Logistics is going to be looking rotten to the core. The Sheiks will want nothing to do with Mr. Ahmed."

"Giving Sakkin the opportunity to acquire his aviation assets."

Lisker contemplated the thought. "Enabling future operations. I'll discuss it with Ginsberg. Let me know when you have Bishop."

"Will do."

Lisker ended the call as his car passed through the security gates at Mossad's headquarters and descended into the underground parking lot. In his profession things didn't always go to plan. The key was to run multiple lines of operation with enough flexibility to adapt to change. That's what made him a master at the game.

———

NYAGATARE, RWANDA

"We should move," said Bianca as she peered out the window of Saneh's hotel room. "Everyone will know you're staying here."

"Good point," replied Saneh as she gathered the few things she'd unpacked and stuffed them into her bag.

"Thank you again for helping me."

Saneh managed a nod. "Those men, are they from the medical facility you told me about?"

"Yeah, kinda confirms my story, right?"

"They're definitely pissed about something. Look, I've got to make a few calls." She threw Bianca the keys to her SUV. "Do you want to wait in the car? It's parked outside. I'll be two minutes at most."

The Canadian nodded. "I've got a place just out of town that we can use."

As the door snapped shut behind Bianca, Saneh dialed Bishop's number on a phone she'd bought with cash at the airport. She paced the room as the number rang and rang. After thirty seconds she ended the call before trying again. The outcome was the same.

"Bishop, where the hell are you?" For a split second she

considered calling the Sandpit and talking to Chua or Vance, but that would put even more of her friends in danger.

She tried again.

Still nothing.

Stuffing the phone in her pocket she grabbed her bag and slung it over her shoulder. She'd try again later. If Lisker wasn't already aware that she'd saved Bianca from a hit squad then he soon would be. When that happened he'd send his best people after her and Bishop, unless she assassinated Bianca and sent Lisker the evidence. But, that wasn't an option now. The Canadian was too much like Aden; hotheaded, altruistic and wanting nothing more than to bring a little justice to the world. If Saneh killed her she'd be destroying everything that she believed in.

She left the room, departed the hotel via a fire exit and joined Bianca in the SUV.

"OK, so what's the course of action?" asked Bianca. "You going to help me deal with these assholes?"

"Let's start with getting somewhere safe. Then we can come up with a game plan."

TEL AVIV, ISRAEL

"This another of your secret spots?" asked Keila when she spotted Asher in the lineup at the takeaway window of a trendy café. He'd called her at work and she'd driven across town to meet with him.

"This one isn't much of a secret." He smiled. "Everyone in the organization gets their coffee here."

She glanced through the window at the crowd in the cafe. "I hope you guys sweep the place for bugs."

He laughed. "We probably should. What are you having?"

"We doing takeaway?"

"Yeah sorry, I've only got a few minutes."

"Soy latte then."

Asher placed the order then they stepped away from the line to wait.

"So, I wanted to give you a quick heads up," he said quietly. "We broke the network."

"Does Lisker know?"

He shook his head. "Not yet."

She leaned forward and kissed him on the cheek. "Appreciated."

"So, does this get me a second dinner date?" he asked as they waited.

"Definitely."

The barista announced their order and they took the cups from the window.

"You free tonight? I know a great little place a half hour out of town. Best Greek you've ever tasted. I could pick you up at eight."

"Sounds great." She smiled coyly as she left him and started back to her car. As soon as she was in the driver's seat she opened the glove compartment and selected a phone from the dozen inside. What she was about to do was utterly against all protocols and could be construed as treason. She paused with her finger hovering over the keypad. Screw it, she couldn't let Lisker win them all.

———

REQUENA, SPAIN

Bishop had only just kicked a pair of battered work boots from his feet when he heard his burner phone ring from the kitchen table. He lurched inside, stepped over Daisy who was stretched out on the floor, hit answer and pressed it to his ear.

"Aden, your secure comms have been penetrated. You need to warn your team."

He instantly recognized the voice as Keila's.

"What…?"

The call ended and he glanced at the screen. He had three missed calls from a number that he didn't recognize.

Daisy let out a bark. He opened the cupboard under the sink and tore a Glock 19 from where it was taped. The dog's barking gained in intensity as he press-checked the pistol, confirming there was a round in the chamber.

A gas grenade smashed through the window and bounced off the far wall. The smell caught him by surprise; he expected the sting of tear gas not the bitter sweetness of a sedative. "Daisy, come."

Staying low he held his breath and grabbed the dog's collar, dragging her out of the kitchen into the bedroom where there was a door out to a patio. He'd left it open a few inches to let the evening breeze in. He pushed the dog toward the opening. "Daisy, go run."

She let out a low whine then nosed the door open and disappeared outside. A split second later Bishop heard her bark followed by the snap of a suppressed weapon. Diving through the gap, he rolled, raised his pistol and fired four rounds in the direction he'd heard the shots. Bullets hissed past him as he scrambled for the cover of a low stone wall.

Rounds ricocheted off the rocks and snapped through

the bushes. Bishop recognized it as suppressing fire and reoriented. The assault force came from around the corner of the cottage. He hit the lead operative with two rounds to the chest, bowling him over. Another back-peddled as he fired and Bishop hunkered below the stone wall.

A third man appeared in the doorway that he and Daisy had escaped through. Heavily clad in dark green armor with a riot helmet, he raised a shotgun. Bishop rolled onto his back and fired at the figure's head. His volley of 9mm bullets slammed into the heavy polycarbonate face shield.

The figure staggered and the shotgun boomed. Bishop flinched as a baton round bounced off the stone pavers. He fired another two shots then dove over the wall into the orchard below. Bullets slapped the olive and almond trees as he climbed to his feet and sprinted away from.

"Daisy!" he yelled frantically between breaths as he crashed his way through the orchard. A bullet nicked his thigh and he staggered. Falling he threw out an arm and grabbed a tree trunk.

He could hear footfalls as he checked his leg. The bullet had gone straight through the meaty outer of his thigh. He ignored the searing pain and pulled out his phone. Punching a memorized number into it he waited for the call to connect before uttering a single word. "Exodus!"

"Get your hands up!" The shout came from the top of the orchard. Bishop considered making a run for it but didn't think he'd get far. He pocketed the phone and let the Glock hang from his finger.

"Drop it."

The pistol fell to the ground as a second and third man appeared, all armed with suppressed assault rifles.

"On your knees, hands behind your head."

Bishop winced as he followed the directions.

"There's that fucking dog," one of the men said as they approached.

"Daisy go!" Bishop yelled.

"Shut the fuck up!" was the last thing he heard before something hit him in the side of the head and his world went black.

TEL AVIV, ISRAEL

The Sakkin Industries private jet banked gently as it left the runway at Tel Aviv international airport and climbed toward its cruising height. In the main cabin Manfred Lisker sat in a comfortable armchair with a touch screen extended. Behind him a pair of Sakkin technicians sat with their own screens wearing headsets.

"Manfred, I hope you're making good use of the jet," said Ginsberg from the screen. His voice was being projected over a pair of noise-cancelling headphones that the Mossad officer was wearing.

"Thank you for making it available."

"My pleasure. I've considered your proposal regarding Lascar Logistics' specialist fleet."

"And?"

"I did not realize their Priority Movements Airlift wing was so well equipped. I think it would serve Sakkin's interests perfectly."

"My thoughts exactly."

"Indeed. However, the price would have to be right."

"It will be."

"Excellent, I'll be in Tel Aviv in a week. We can iron out the details." Ginsberg's face disappeared.

As the aircraft reached cruising height Lisker's secure phone rang. The aircraft's techs had linked his devices to the onboard network.

"Avi, tell me good things."

"They've broken the network. The location in Abu Dhabi matches up and I've got a contracted asset standing by. I've also locked down the 8200 team."

"And Bishop?"

"We've got him detained."

He checked his watch. "I land in Abu Dhabi in twenty minutes. Is everything in order?"

"They're ready for you."

"Launch on my command." Lisker ended the call and eased back into the chair with a smile. The pieces were all in place. Soon Tariq Ahmed and Mantis would both be realigned to his objectives.

Chapter Thirteen

HANGAR 12A, ABU DHABI

TARIQ AHMED STEPPED from the side door of the Lascar Logistics Iluyshin-76 dressed in his usual three-piece suit. The instructions from Lisker had been specific. He was to bring a cargo jet to hangar 12A at the international freight terminal and enter alone.

He stepped through the hangar door and immediately noticed the private jet parked to one side. Opposite it a cargo lifter waited with two crates atop it.

"Tariq Ahmed, a pleasure to finally meet you in the person." A figure stepped from the jet.

Tariq knew from his research that it was Lisker, head of special operations for Mossad. "All mine." He extended his hand as they met and matched the man's icy stare.

Lisker's hand felt cold as they shook.

"Thank you so much for meeting me here," said the Mossad officer as he walked toward the crates on the lifter.

"I thought it important to discuss in person the issues with some of the previous shipments."

Tariq's phone vibrated inside his jacket but he ignored it. "What issues are they?"

"Certain shipments have not reached their destinations."

He feigned surprise. "I find that hard to believe."

They reached the crates and Lisker stopped to face him. "You either deliver what I tell you to, or there will be grave consequences."

Tariq glanced at the open boxes and saw they were filled with 107mm rockets in metal tubes. "My aircraft don't deliver weapons."

Lisker chuckled as he reached the bill of loading from the crate and handed it to him. "If you don't smuggle what I want I'm going to ship these rockets into Lebanon and hand them over to Hezbollah. Then I'll make sure this paperwork hits the Counter-Terrorism desk of every major agency in the western world."

He glanced at the paperwork and saw Lascar Logistics details marked from top to bottom.

Lisker smirked. "It doesn't get more damning than that."

Tariq tossed the bill of sale back on the crates. "What can you possibly hope to gain from destabilizing Egypt? Your country wants secure borders, not another Syria or Libya."

"Just do what I tell you and your loyal employees get to keep their jobs." He took a phone from his pocket and hit a button. "Oh, and your private little army. They're finished."

"Army?"

Lisker raised the phone to his ear. "Don't act coy Tariq.

I know all about Priority Movements Airlift and your hit squad."

Tariq felt his heart drop. "Priority Movements Airlift specializes in delivering aid to war-torn regions. They're not–"

Lisker interrupted him with a raised hand as his call connected. "Kill capture is approved, execute," he spoke into the phone then pocketed it. "I'm sorry. You were saying?"

Tariq swallowed. "The deliveries will be made."

"Excellent, I'm glad we could come to an arrangement. I'll have my people load these and you can get on your way. Now, if you don't mind, I've got some other pressing matters to attend to."

Tariq watched the Mossad officer climb into the business jet and the door closed. Then he dug his own phone from his jacket. A single word flashed on the screen.

Exodus.

THE SANDPIT, ABU DHABI

Bishop's initiation of the Exodus protocol had already triggered a flurry of activity. Chua had killed the iPRIMAL servers and triggered a shutdown of their global infrastructure. In multiple locations programs wiped their communications and intelligence servers, destroying every trace of the sophisticated network that had served the vigilante organization for nearly a decade.

Now he, Ice and Vance took care of the physical evidence. They doused every surface with a DNA destroying solution that dissolved the grease associated with finger-prints. Each man had a grab bag ready, a backpack containing cash, cards, passports and phones. Ice took them from the storage cabinet and carried them through to the operations room.

"We going to burn this joint down?" he asked as he handed Chua his bag.

"Just the laptops and iPRIMALs," Chua replied as he lifted each of the portable computers from their cradles and placed them in a purpose-designed bag. Finally, he dropped in his iPRIMAL and passed the duffel to Ice.

Ice hefted the bag over his shoulder and crossed the living area to the swimming pool. There was a shovel leaning against the pool's pump house and he grabbed it on the way to the beach. The sand was damp and he quickly dug out a pit. Then he yanked the igniter sewn into the bag and tossed it inside.

Mitch Freeman, PRIMAL's chief technician, had designed the burn bag. Its lining contained thermite, a powder that burned at close to five thousand degrees. In a matter of seconds the laptops and phones were consumed in a brilliant white flame that melted the surrounding sand to liquid glass.

Ice turned away and checked his watch as the tech burned. It was ten minutes since Bishop had initiated the Exodus protocol and in that time they'd purged any evidence of PRIMAL's existence. To an outsider the Sandpit was nothing more than a luxury residence housing a few expatriate businessmen. No weapons or suspicious equipment, nothing to compromise Tariq Ahmed or Lascar Logistics.

Shielding his eyes he glanced at the pit in the sand. The thermite had reduced the bag to a flaming puddle of metal and plastic. He'd give it a minute more before burying the remains. As he waited he took a moment to consider why Bishop had called Exodus. He assumed that it had something to do with his Israeli contact, Kelia. It would make sense that she'd tip him off to any compromise of their network or systems. Ice just hoped that nothing had happened to him or Saneh.

Once the thermite had sizzled out Ice filled the hole and returned to the villa. As Ice made his way back through to the living area he thought he heard a noise from the corridor that led to the entrance. He paused alongside the reinforced front door and listened. There was a scratching noise coming from the handle followed by a loud click. He felt a kick of adrenaline; there was no way someone should have been able to bypass their security system.

The door slowly opened inward. Ice stepped behind it and watched the shadow thrown up against the wall. A single figure crossed the threshold with a submachine gun held ready.

Ice shouldered the door, smashing it shut on a second intruder. His palm slapped the deadbolt closed as he grabbed the first man with his robotic hand and hauled him rearward.

The man was strong but didn't stand a chance. Ice slipped an arm around his throat and cut off the blood flow to his brain. A split second later he was dragging the limp body into the kitchen. "We've got company," he bellowed.

Vance and Chua appeared as Ice stripped the man's assault vest. He checked the submachine gun before stuffing spare magazines in his cargo pockets and handing a pistol to Vance. "We need to go."

The sound of a sledgehammer on the front door spurred Vance into action. "We'll get out by boat."

Ice aimed his newly acquired submachine gun at the front entrance while Vance led Chua to the floor-to-ceiling glass doors that separated the house from the pool and dock.

Vance caught a glimpse of armed men through the glass and skidded to a halt. "Upstairs! Upstairs!"

"Mousehole!" yelled Chua as an explosion at the front door announced the assaulters were inbound.

Ice's submachine gun snapped as he fired at the entrance. Weapons crackled in reply and bullets shattered the glass windows.

Chua grunted and staggered, but continued to the stairs.

A grenade skidded across the tiles toward Ice. He booted it back down the corridor and fired the last of his magazine.

Vance lumbered up the stairs following Chua. At the next floor they continued down a long corridor that finished at the building's outer wall. A seascape print with a thick frame adorned the wall. Vance dashed to the picture and ran his fingers around the frame. He found the tab that Mitch had built into the design and gently eased the igniter from its recess.

"Ready?" He turned and saw Chua, a few yards away clutching his side, his shirt drenched with blood. "Chua?"

Chua staggered forward and Vance caught him. "Blow the hole," he managed.

Ice appeared and ducked into the hallway as bullets slapped into the plasterboard behind him. "What's the holdup?" he asked as he held the submachine gun out over the stairs and hosed the landing with lead.

"Chua's hit."

"It's nothing," said Chua. "Blow the damn wall."

Vance yanked the igniter. The fuse hissed and smoke filled the corridor as they ducked into the adjacent room.

The charge detonated with an ear-splitting boom that shook the house to its foundations. Dust billowed into the room as Ice took up position near the staircase. "Get Chua out of the building."

Vance threw the wounded man's arm over his shoulder and dragged him through the gaping hole the charge had blown, and into the adjoining construction site.

Behind him Ice's submachine gun spluttered as he kept the assaulting force at bay.

The house that butted up to the Sandpit was a mirror image and also owned by Tariq. Incomplete, it offered the PRIMAL team an alternative avenue of escape and somewhere to stash a boat and a second vehicle.

Vance paused alongside a pair of welding bottles. "You doing OK?"

"Yeah, I'll live."

Ice emerged through the wall. "What the hell are you guys waiting for?" He turned and fired a burst back through the jagged hole.

Vance hefted Chua over his shoulders and lumbered down the stairs. Behind him he heard a loud clang as Ice tossed the welding set into the wall breach.

As they reached the lower floor and headed toward the garage the building shook with another massive explosion. Flame and dust washed over them, tossing the two men like rag dolls.

A moment later Vance rose to his knees. "Chua you with me?" he bellowed over the ringing in his ears.

Chua coughed from beneath a sheet of plasterboard. "Yeah, yeah, I'm OK."

As Vance cleared the debris he could hear the distant wail of sirens.

"Where's Ice?"

Vance climbed to his feet and searched the stairwell. The narrow opening was blocked by shattered cinder blocks and a mangled cement mixer. "Ice!" he bellowed.

There was no response. The sirens grew louder.

"Ice!"

Chua coughed again and Vance turned to see his friend propped against a wall clutching the wound in his side. He was torn between getting him to safety and looking for Ice in the rubble above. The wailing sirens made the choice for him. If he stayed Chua and he would be taken into custody or worse. Whoever had authorized the attack on the Sandpit had to have influence and resources.

He helped Chua to his feet and they made their way into the garage where a plumber's van was parked. Once Chua was lying in the back he shut the doors and rechecked the stairwell for any sign of Ice. There was no sound or movement. He tried hauling a chunk of wall out of the walkway, but it was lodged firm. "ICE!"

With no reply he returned to the van and activated the roller door. As he pulled out of the building he glanced in the rearview mirror. The garage was empty. He continued up the driveway, concealed by the tall wall bordering the property.

As he pulled out on to the road shared with their former headquarters Vance glimpsed a team of men dragging their wounded and dead teammates into a waiting van. At least Ice had made them pay with blood. "Chua, how you doing back there?"

"I'll live." His voice was faint. "Where's Ice?"

A ball of grief in Vance's throat almost choked him. "We had to leave him behind."

———

THE SANDPIT, ABU DHABI

A silver Range Rover wound its way past an ambulance and came to a halt in front of a police barricade. Tariq alighted from the rear of the car, having come directly from the airport.

As he approached the barricade an officer raised his hand. "You can't go any further. This is an active crime scene."

"I own the building," snapped Tariq as he peered past the man at the haze of smoke.

"That doesn't matter. You can't go in."

"Call your superior. Tell him Tariq Ahmed wants to pass."

The officer frowned, the name was familiar to him, but he couldn't remember why. Relaying the message he soon found out that Mr. Ahmed was a very influential man.

Tariq moved past the barrier to the front door of the building formerly known as the Sandpit. He ran his fingers along the shattered jamb of the front door. It had been blown inwards by a breaching charge. The people Lisker had sent were capable. As he entered the hallway he noted the bullet holes that pocked the plasterboard. There was blood on the white tiles, revealing that the PRIMAL team had made a good account of themselves.

"Is anyone there?" he yelled.

Moving into the living area he noted the shattered glass that was once the doors to the pool area. If the team were as good as he suspected they would have hit the building from more than one direction, forcing Vance and his team upstairs.

On the upper level he found more blood and drag marks on the dust-coated floor. At the end of the corridor a gaping hole led into the adjacent building site. He wasn't privy to the Sandpit's emergency procedures but he assumed the mouse hole was part of it. The building next door was one of eight that a proxy company of Lascar Logistics owned in the area. It had been kept underdeveloped to enhance the Sandpit's security.

He stepped through the breach into what looked like a war zone. An explosion had knocked out internal walls and collapsed a section of the ceiling. There were still smoking remnants of what looked like a gas bottle embedded in a steel pylon.

Tariq nearly leaped from his skin when a pile of debris moved. There was a loud groan and a metallic fist punched up through a block of concrete splitting it in half. Then, like something out of a movie, a figure appeared from the debris.

"Ice, you scared the life out of me," said Tariq as he helped the PRIMAL operative to his feet.

"Where are the others?" Ice asked. Dried blood matted his short blonde hair and dust covered every inch of his body.

"I was going to ask you the same." Tariq took out a phone and dialed his driver. "I need you to box around and pick us up from Al Saduk road." He turned his attention back to Ice. "Are you injured?"

Ice flexed his robotic hand as he checked his torso with the other. "I'm good."

"We need to get out of here. Police have cordoned the

street. They're most likely awaiting a tactical response element. We can get out on the other side of the island if we move fast."

"Any sign of the attackers or Vance and Chua?" Ice asked as he found his go bag and inspected the blocked stairwell to the lower floor.

Tariq shook his head. "No, is there another way down?"

"Back through the Sandpit and through the fence."

"Lead the way."

They jogged down the stairs, out through shattered windows and through a loose section of fencing into the adjoining yard. Ice checked the garage as they passed. "They took the van," he said with relief. "Vance and Chua got out."

Tariq nodded and led them across the building site and out a side gate. His Range Rover was parked on the street, engine running.

"POLICE, POLICE, POLICE!" a megaphone blared as he and Ice climbed inside and the driver smoothly accelerated away.

"Exodus has already been called," said Ice. "Chua and Vance will be carrying out their E and E plan."

"I'm aware."

"According to protocol we shouldn't be together." Ice paused before continuing. "What made you come to the Sandpit?"

Tariq gazed out the window as they crossed a land bridge flanked by palm trees. "When Exodus was called I monitored the police net."

Ice seemed to accept the explanation. "So any idea who hit us? Bishop made the call, he might have got a tip-off from his contact in Mossad."

Tariq didn't respond. Keeping his dealings with Lisker private was the hardest decision he'd ever made, and now he realized he should have closed the Sandpit weeks ago.

Ice continued, "They looked like contractors to me. Whoever they were, we got damn complacent, Tariq. The old PRIMAL wouldn't have let those assholes jump us."

Tariq shook his head. "Violence isn't the solution here, James. You need to continue your Exodus protocol. Can I help in any way?"

Ice shrugged. "I was going to jump a Lascar Log flight out of town and make my way to Spain."

Tariq pulled a tablet from behind the seat to his front and checked the aircraft movements application. "We've got a cargo jet heading out to Lisbon in twenty minutes. I can have you on it."

"Perfect."

His driver registered the plan with a nod in the rearview mirror. It was only a short distance to the Lascar Logistics cargo terminal. For the entire ten-minute drive Tariq battled with the torment inside. He wanted, more than anything, to tell Ice that he, Tariq Ahmed, was the reason that the Sandpit had been raided. But, that would only send Ice after Lisker and ultimately that would destroy him and the rest of PRIMAL.

When they arrived at the airport the driver swiped through the cargo terminal security gate and drove them directly to the hangar where the flight was scheduled to depart.

Tariq got out of the vehicle and walked Ice directly to the waiting Lascar jet. "Thank you for everything, James."

Ice turned and wrapped him in a bear hug. "No, thank you, Tariq. You made it all possible. And god knows it ain't over yet. Not by a long shot." He turned and boarded the jet.

"No, it most certainly isn't," murmured Tariq.

Chapter Fourteen

SAFEHOUSE, DUBAI

THE SAFE HOUSE was a nondescript residence in a suburb on the outskirts of Dubai. It was the first stop in a series of locations that would enable Vance and Chua to exit the Emirates covertly and establish themselves at their final destination.

Vance backed the van into a garage and waited as the roller door dropped. Once concealed he helped Chua from the back of the van and into the kitchen where he sat him in a chair. A quick inspection of a cupboard under the sink revealed a comprehensive trauma kit.

Using a pair of medical shears he cut Chua's Rogue Fitness shirt up the side.

"Hey, that was my favorite." Chua grimaced as Vance inspected the wound in his flank.

"I'm sure you can get another one online. It's a clean shot. Straight in and out."

"There is no online, Vance. That's why I've got no idea who just fucked us."

"You don't think it was Mossad?"

Chua shook his head. "It's possible that 8200 compromised iPRIMAL, but the Israelis have no reason to move against us. Not like this."

"Hang on, I've got to close this." Vance took a plastic spray from the med kit and sanitized the wound.

Chua flinched.

He took a medical stapler from the pack and pressed the sides of the wound together.

"It just doesn't make sense," Chua continued.

The stapler let out a loud clack and banded the wound.

"Holy shit!"

"Oh come on Pogue Fitness, it's not that bad. Now lean forward so I can fix the other side."

Chua did as he was told and Vance finished the procedure. He took an antibiotic injector and shot it into his friend's arm. "Oh look, there's a local anesthetic in here," he teased as he packed the stapler and shears away.

"You're an asshole." Chua grunted as he slumped into the chair. "How long have we got till we need to move?"

"You can rest up for a bit. We'll leave tonight."

Chua exhaled. "Do you think Ice got out?"

"Yeah, it would take more than a few hired goons to get the better of him," he replied, unconvincingly.

Chua inspected his wound and winced. "I hate not knowing what's going on."

"That's kind of the point of the Exodus protocol," Vance said. "Now get some rest. We've got a long journey ahead of us."

———

ABU DHABI

With Ice on his way out of the country Tariq had his driver take him directly to a secure software development facility he owned. The company was responsible for all of Lascar Logistics and affiliate's data storage and recovery. It was also the firm that had offered employment to a former member of the PRIMAL team, their chief hacker, 'Flash' Gordon.

The systems engineer and code genius was responsible for attempting to penetrate Lascar Logistics networks, enabling other engineers to patch the weaknesses he found and keep their data secure.

Tariq met him in the ultra-secure room where Flash now worked. The software engineer spun from his terminal, acknowledging Tariq with a cock of his head.

"Hey boss, you here about the Exodus protocol?"

Despite the sterile corporate workplace Flash was dressed in a trucker cap and vintage T-shirt emblazoned with, *Zero Fucks Given*.

"You're supposed to be clear. How do you know about Exodus?" As a former PRIMAL director, Tariq was the only retired member who was supposed to receive the notification.

Flash shrugged. "I built the system. Only seems fair that I know when you guys mess up and it gets compromised, right? You know who hacked it?"

"From what I understand there are only two organizations that could."

"Yeah and we didn't piss off the NSA."

Tariq pulled an office chair from an empty desk and sat, clearing his throat. "Flash, they hit the Sandpit today. Professionals. They got the drop on the team. Somehow they bypassed the security systems."

Flash's features hardened. "How bad?"

"Vance and Chua got away. I managed to get Ice out, but I fear the others may be in imminent danger. Which is why I'm here."

"What can I do?"

"Mossad has a senior agent who goes by the name Manfred Lisker. He's been using Lascar Logistics to smuggle shipments of weapons into Egypt."

"And you think he's the one who compromised PRIMAL."

Tariq looked him square in the eyes. "I need hard evidence linking him to the arms shipments." He handed Flash a secure USB stick. "This is everything I know."

"I'll give it a go, but I don't have all the resources of PRIMAL here."

Tariq nodded as he rose. "That's never slowed you down before."

Flash watched as his boss disappeared out the door. He'd already made plans to skip out to Hong Kong where he'd kick off a startup that he'd had in the works. However, he had a feeling the PRIMAL team needed all the help it could get. Hong Kong could wait.

———

KAMPALA, UGANDA

"So let me get this straight. Exodus means that PRIMAL is shut down and we're supposed to run away and hide under a rock?" asked Kruger as he racked the slide on his pistol.

Kurtz nodded. "That was always the plan."

The two men were sitting in the back of a delivery van

on a dark street in one of the wealthier suburbs of Uganda's capital.

"Sounds like a shit plan. I mean what do we need them for?"

"That's not the point. The system has been compromised. Someone could be trying to hunt us down."

Kruger grinned as he holstered his pistol. "I'm cool with that." He unzipped a bag and folded back the sides, revealing a battery-powered demolition saw. "So, my main man, are we going to do this? Or is this Krenich piece of shit going to get away with trafficking girls?"

Kurtz took his suppressed AK from the bag under his seat, unfolded the stock and cocked it. "We're going to see it through."

His partner thumped his shoulder. "Fuck yeah we are."

The two men donned equipment-laden vests, balaclavas and night vision then stepped out of the van. Hidden in the inky blackness of a moonless night they slipped through a hole in a chain fence that they'd cut previously. Advancing stealthily they made their way across a manicured lawn toward a modern two-story home of concrete and glass.

A dozen feet from the illumination cast by an array of security lights Kurtz thumbed a remote control. Small explosive charges, already placed on a power distribution box and data hub, detonated with a soft thud plunging the building into darkness. A cell phone jammer in Kurtz's backpack would further isolate the occupants from emergency services.

When they reached the front door Kruger attacked it with the portable saw. The diamond blade sliced through steel in a shower of sparks. With deft cuts he removed the hinges and kicked it open.

Kurtz made entry as his partner killed the saw and

followed him into the house. IR lamps on their night vision goggles cut through the darkness as they moved through a landing to the building's stairwell.

"Mukisa! Is that you?" The voice came from the second floor. "Bloody African power cuts. Where the hell is my phone?"

A light flashed on and footsteps thumped down the stairs.

Kurtz gestured for Kruger to hide on one side of the stairwell as he moved to the other. They waited till Krenich reached the landing. When he made for the front door Kruger stepped in behind and looped a powerful arm around his neck, forcing his pistol into the man's temple. "Don't make a sound."

Krenich let out a pathetic moan and dropped his phone. Kruger dragged him into the dark living area and forced him to his knees. "Hands behind your head."

"There's a safe upstairs. You can have all the money in it," said Krenich as his hands were fastened with a cable tie.

"We don't want money," snarled Kurtz as he slid a knife from his vest. The stainless steel edge glinted in the light cast from the phone still active in the landing.

"There are cars in the garage and the girl upstairs. They're all yours if you don't hurt me."

"What a piece of shit," said Kruger as he stepped away from their captive and raised his pistol to cover Kurtz.

"You sell out on a lot of girls, don't you Mr. Krenich," Kurtz said dragging out the last letters of the man's name. As he finished speaking he heard the faintest sound from behind, a footfall on the polished hardwood floor. Spinning he spotted a figure through his night vision goggles. A submachine gun stammered as he threw himself sideways, narrowly avoiding a stream of bullets.

"Where the hell did that come from?" yelled Kruger before returning fire.

"That must be Mukisa," replied Kurtz as he fired his AK into the room.

"Who the fuck is Mukisa?"

"You'd have to ask Krenich that. Grenade!" Kurtz lobbed a stun grenade into the room before hugging the wall. The charge detonated with an ear-splitting boom and a bright flash. His night vision goggles blanked for a split second and then he charged toward the doorway. He didn't make it far. A massive shape appeared and slammed into him before he could get a shot off.

Mukisa roared like a wounded rhino as he shunted Kurtz out of the way and slammed into Kruger. The former South African mercenary managed to hold his ground despite the sheer mass of his attacker. Kurtz watched from the ground where he'd fallen as Kruger and Mukisa wrestled.

"Mukisa, kill them!" screamed Krenich from where he cowered a few feet away.

Kurtz lashed out with a kick and silenced the trafficker with a boot to the chest.

Kruger, with his pistol pinned against him by the bulk of his opponent, was forced to attack with his right elbow. Using his height advantage he drove it down into the meat of the man's neck.

Scrambling to his feet Kurtz tore a Taser from his rig and lunged into the fight. Plunging the device into Mukisa's back he thumbed the trigger.

"Son of a bitch!" bellowed Kruger as he caught a partial charge.

Their attacker managed to remain standing as Kruger broke away and Kurtz hit him with another dose of voltage.

The last jolt did the trick and Mukisa went over like a felled tree, cracking his head on the ground.

Kruger pounced, securing his hands and feet with cable ties before checking his vitals. "He's out cold."

"I want my lawyer," croaked Krenich from where he lay.

Kruger laughed between breaths. "Oh, you couldn't be more wrong if you fucking tried. We're not law enforcement dickhead. We're here for justice."

Kurtz cracked a chem light and tossed it on the floor. "The girls you bought in Somalia, where are they now?"

"Girls, what girls? I don't know what you're talking about."

He squatted in front of the human trafficker and slid his blade across Krenich's bald head before aiming the knife point at the man's eyeball. "Tell us what we want or I'm going to cut out your eyes."

The smuggler swallowed. "OK, OK, I can tell you everything, names, places and routes. But, you have to promise to let me go."

"Deal, start talking."

"Fucking pussy," growled Kruger. "I was looking forward to taking this piece of shit apart."

For the next few minutes Krenich divulged the information they needed. He'd transported twelve of the healthiest girls across the border into Rwanda and delivered them to a medical facility.

"What are they doing to them there?" asked Kurtz.

"I don't know," Krenich replied. "I guess they're testing drugs on them or something. Listen, if you let me go I can find out more."

Kurtz gestured for Kruger to join him behind Krenich

on the other side of the living room. "Do you think he knows anything else?"

"Nah, he's a trafficker. We know his source and now we know his client. He's useless to us now."

"Agreed."

"What do you want to do with him?"

Kurtz turned and stared at the human trafficker where he knelt on the floor. "I promised I'd let him go." He raised his pistol and fired. The bullet hit Krenich in the back of the head with a wet thud and his body slumped forward. "I didn't say where. Hell seems like the right place."

Moments later they were back in the van and driving across Kampala toward the airfield where Toppie and Booyah were waiting with the helicopter and the rest of the gear.

"What's the plan?" asked Kruger.

"We're going to Rwanda."

NYAGATARE, RWANDA

The call came at a little past midnight. Saneh took it in the kitchenette of the tiny apartment that Bianca had rented from a local taxi driver's brother. The number was blocked, but she knew exactly who it would be.

"I hear you've made a new friend," said Avi.

It confirmed Saneh's worst fears. Mossad had someone watching her. "I wasn't about to let some half-wit street thugs claim my kill."

"Oh, you anticipated I'd be watching?"

"I got an inkling that there wasn't a lot of trust between us."

There was a pause on the other end of the phone. "Well I had an inkling that you might require a little more motivation to complete this task."

Saneh's stomach lurched.

"Which is why I had some of my people pick up your boyfriend."

"If you hurt him I'll—"

"You'll what? Get the job done and you can have him back. Cross me and I'll put a bullet in his head."

Saneh knew by the tone of his voice that he wasn't bluffing. If she didn't kill Bianca then Aden's life was forfeit. She ended the call, fighting to keep her panic under control.

"You want to tell me who the hell you really are, and what's going on?"

She spun to face Bianca who was standing in the doorway with a knife in her hand. Saneh's own blade was strapped to the inside of her leg. Throwing a chair would buy her the time she needed to draw it. The dilemma was whether to throw the blade into her target's throat or engage the Canadian in a knife fight.

"I'm waiting," said Bianca.

"My name's Saneh. I came here to kill you."

"For who, Lifebright?"

"No." Saneh pulled out the chair, but instead of throwing it she sat. She literally felt like the walls were closing in on her.

"Then who?"

She looked up at the woman who she'd been ordered to assassinate and fought the urge to burst into tears. "An Israeli."

Bianca shook her head. "Mossad, why the hell would Mossad want me dead?"

"I don't know."

"No, of course not. You just do the wet work." The Canadian's eyes narrowed. "What are you? An assassin for hire or are you one of them?"

Saneh took her personal phone from her pocket and was about to dial Bishop's burn number when she realized that it was now in Avi's possession. Instead she rang the dial-in number for the Sandpit. She needed to come clean to Vance and Chua. At least then she wouldn't be dealing with this alone. The number redirected and a digital voice uttered a single word. "Exodus."

For the second time that night Saneh thought she was going to be sick. Bishop was being held and PRIMAL had been compromised.

"They've got serious leverage on you, don't they?" asked Bianca.

She nodded. "They've got my partner. If I don't kill you, they'll terminate him."

Bianca's knife disappeared into a sheath. "Yeah, but you're not going to do that, right?"

She exhaled. "No. You're too much like Bishop. I know what he would say if he knew the circumstances."

"Good guy, eh."

"The best. He'd give his life for yours in an instant."

"Then I guess we'd better work out how to get you and him out of this fix."

Saneh's eyes narrowed. "You'd help me. Even though I was sent here to kill you?"

"Only seems fair. I mean you saved my ass back at the bar."

"Something tells me you could have handled that on your own."

Bianca winked. "It's the thought that counts." She moved across to the apartment's tiny refrigerator and removed two beers. Twisting off the tops with a deft move she placed one in front of Saneh and took the seat opposite. "So, how good are you with makeup?"

"Mascara and lipstick?"

She took a swig of her beer then wiped her mouth. "I was thinking of something a little more hardcore."

UNKNOWN LOCATION, SPAIN

As Saneh and her new comrade Bianca schemed, Bishop sat cuffed to a steel-framed chair in one of the drabbest rooms he'd ever seen. The walls were covered in khaki brown paint that he swore was reserved for military vehicles. The floor was faded green carpet that looked like it would be at home on a miniature golf course. His chair seemed to be screwed directly into the floor. High-quality handcuffs joined each of his ankles to the thick chair legs.

He estimated that he'd spent less than an hour blindfolded in the back of a van before being brought to the room. That meant he wasn't far from the cottage, probably near Valencia.

The door to the room opened and man in a balaclava entered, carrying a plastic tray.

"Hello," Bishop said pleasantly as he studied every detail of the man. He was dressed in cheap grey slacks, expensive black trail runners and a polo shirt that was a little tight around the biceps. Tall with an athletic build the man moved with a deliberateness that suggested he had a military background. Bishop had him pegged as a contractor who'd purchased everything but his shoes at a local store, standard for a cross border intelligence operation that gave the sponsor deniability if it all went south.

Biceps, as he'd nicknamed him, placed the tray on the floor in front of Bishop and moved behind him. There was the rattle of a key and he felt his cuffs being released. Bringing his hands around to his front he rubbed his wrists before gently touching the wound to his leg. He could feel a firm bandage and see the cloth through the rent in his jeans. The lack of blood told him it had been treated effectively. Glancing down at the tray he saw that lunch consisted of a sandwich and pieces of apple.

"Eat," grunted Biceps.

Bishop didn't have to be told twice. He stuffed the sandwich into his mouth and chewed it hungrily. "So, you guys going to tell me what you want?" he asked between mouthfuls.

Biceps remained directly behind him as he ate.

"I think we might have gotten off on the wrong foot." He swallowed. "My name's Aden, what's yours?"

There was no response.

"Good sandwich by the way." He finished the bread and started on the apple. There was no reason not to eat. If these guys wanted to feed him and keep his strength up he was only too happy to oblige.

"Hands behind back," Biceps said as Bishop finished.

"Look, is that really necessary? I mean we're all professionals here. I'll stay put if you just let me know what you want."

"Hands behind back."

The man's tone told Bishop that failure to comply was

going to result in a beating. That would result in further injuries that may impact his ability to escape later.

"OK, OK." He placed his hands behind his back and the man cuffed them before picking up the tray and leaving the room.

Once the door was closed he returned to investigating every inch of his bleak cell. Glancing over his right shoulder he spotted a remote camera taped into the corner of the ceiling.

All in all, he was impressed by the conduct and setup of the operation. The snatch had been fairly slick and the prisoner handling was efficient. The fact that none of the usual shock after capture techniques had been employed told him this wasn't an interrogation. Nope, he was being held as collateral; most likely by Mossad so they could put the squeeze on Tariq, or maybe Vance and Chua.

The fact that Keila had warned him implied that she wasn't involved. Perhaps she'd been forced to hand over her relationship with Bishop. Either way, it was unlikely the Mossad snatch team would execute him anytime soon. That gave him time to develop rapport and look for an opportunity to escape. Hopefully Saneh and the others had gotten the Exodus call and enacted their own plans. Unfortunately, that also meant they wouldn't be trying to contact him or much less rescue him. Unless Keila could pull something off, he was on his own.

TEL AVIV, ISRAEL

Lisker was at his desk enjoying his morning cup of green tea when Avi dialed in over a secure app. "Tell me something good," he said.

"Mantis has completed her mission."

"Has your man confirmed?"

"Not as yet. She did send through some very graphic images. She hasn't lost her touch."

"Send them through." He took a sip of tea. "And Dubai?"

"That didn't go so well. The team had several wounded and failed to detain any of the residents of the facility."

"What?"

"The building detonated killing at least one hostile. UAE authorities responded immediately. The team was lucky to avoid being caught."

"So no evidence against Tariq?"

"No, but the facility has been neutralized. Tariq Ahmed will be feeling the squeeze."

"It's a start."

"What do you want me to do with Mantis and her boyfriend?"

"I'm not done with them yet. Have her return to the UAE."

"You ordered me to terminate her." Avi's tone told him how much the man was anticipating killing the former Iranian assassin.

"Patience, you'll get your chance." He ended the call and by the time he'd finished his tea Mantis's confirmation images were on his phone. They showed a blonde woman lying sprawled on what he looked like a kitchen floor with her throat cut. She stared lifelessly at the camera in a pool of thick red blood. It wasn't the cleanest of kills, but it was certainly thorough. He forwarded the image to Ginsberg with a short message.

Mission complete.

The response was quick.

Excellent, I'll be in town on Thursday. We need to discuss Egypt.

Chapter Fifteen

LISBON INTERNATIONAL AIRPORT, PORTUGAL

THE LASCAR LOGISTICS air freighter had only taken Ice as far as Lisbon, Portugal. Now, waiting for an Iberia Airlines flight to Barcelona, he sat in a café nursing a can of energy drink. He watched people stream by, excited by the prospect of travel or a reunion with loved ones. Usually he got a buzz from the energy of the airport, but today it had no impact. Ice was overwhelmed by a sense of loss not dissimilar to when he'd left the Marine Corps many years ago.

For the last eight years the PRIMAL team had been his family. He'd been there from its inception. He and Vance had faked their deaths to leave the CIA and work with Tariq to bring a little justice to the world. He found it hard to believe that it was all over.

His Exodus plan, every active member of the team had one, was to meet up with two other PRIMAL operatives who lived in Spain. Pavel and Miklos were not on the 'full-time' squad but subbed in when heavy hitters were needed.

They'd opened a lodge for travellers, near Barcelona, where Ice could regroup and plan the next stage of his life. Mitch, previously PRIMAL's chief pilot and technician, had invited him to join his Special Effects lab in California, but Ice wasn't ready to join the regular workforce just yet. He was contemplating seeing what Kurtz and Kruger had going on in Africa.

He reached for his drink with his artificial hand and remembered that he'd put the robotic one in checked baggage. The prosthetic he traveled with was far less capable but also garnered less attention from airport security. The missing limb, along with the heavy scarring that marred his torso and face was a brutal reminder of the sacrifices he'd made for PRIMAL. Yet, if he could do it all again, he wouldn't change a thing.

A buzzing noise from his carry-on satchel triggered a frown as he dug into the leather bag for his E&E phone. He'd purchased the device locally and the only app he'd loaded was a straightforward, but very secure, messaging service. It wasn't supposed to be used until forty-eight hours after Exodus was initiated.

He used the thumb on his real hand to unlock the device and then entered a number to open the messaging application. There was a single message from a user called Yogapants77.

Keila type team has B. Last known location was his parents. His device is compromised. Please help me find him.

Ice thumbed a reply.

Where are you?

The application let him know that she was typing a response.

Rwanda, I'm heading back to Dubai soon.

What the hell was Saneh doing in Rwanda? he thought as he entered a message of his own.

K2 are heading that way. Get in touch with them. I'll find B.

She replied with a single letter.

K

Ice slipped the phone into his pocket, grabbed his bag and headed straight to the Iberia airlines lounge. A service assistant greeted him with a broad smile. "Do you speak English?" he asked.

"Yes, how can I help?"

"I need to cancel my flight and rebook to Valencia."

———

DOHA, QATAR

Vance held the door of the luxury suite as the bellhop pushed a luggage cart inside.

"Would you like me to unpack, sir?" the man asked.

"All good, bud." He handed him a crisp twenty-dollar bill as Chua entered the room.

"I'll be up for your luggage tomorrow morning at nine sharp. It will be checked all the way through to your destination. If there is anything else you need, feel free to call." The man gave a curt nod and departed.

Chua exhaled as he slumped into one of the room's leather armchairs. "I could get used to this."

"How you feeling?" asked Vance.

They had left the safe house outside of Dubai and driven the four-hundred miles to Qatar in a single day. With Chua still recovering from his injury it was Vance who'd been at the wheel the entire time.

"A little better."

Vance grabbed the room service menu from the dining table and donned a pair of reading glasses. "I'm starving, let's eat and hit the hay. Our flight leaves early tomorrow."

"Sounds good. Is there a Wi-Fi password on there?"

Vance's eyes narrowed. "And what would you need that for?"

"To check up on world events."

"I'm sure there's a TV in the living room. They'll have BBC, CNN and all your other favorites. You'll be able to get your fix."

"You're killing me."

"No, I'm keeping you alive. Seriously, you're worse than a tween. Can't you go without the internet for just a few days?"

Chua shook his head. "I'm an intel guy. I need my information."

"You're a grown man. You can go without Wi-Fi for at least another 24 hours in accordance with the protocol that you established."

"Yeah, yeah, whatever."

"You know there's no internet where we're going," Vance added as he thumbed through the menu.

"What?"

"Yeah, Mitch was saying the place is a real black hole. Totally off the grid."

"You're telling me you organized a new base of operations that doesn't have any connectivity?"

"Relax, it's got hunting, fishing and heaps of mountain biking. You're going to love it."

"Yeah sure, and how are we going to run PRIMAL operations?"

"Well, I thought we might slow things right down." Vance placed the menu back on the table.

"You want to retire?"

"I was thinking more of a change in role. More advisory over hands on."

"But who would run PRIMAL?"

Vance frowned. "Chua, Exodus has been called, there is no PRIMAL anymore. They're going to have to rebuild from the ground up."

"They?"

"Bishop, Ice, Saneh, Mirza, Mitch, whoever wants to."

"And we fall into more of an advisory role?"

Vance nodded. "I don't know about you, but I'm a little burnt out."

Chua gestured to the wound in his side. "And I'm shot out."

He laughed. "Yeah, well it's something to think about." He turned his attention back to the menu. "I'm going to have the burger. You want one?"

———

179

RWANDAN BORDER

Kurtz swirled the takeaway coffee he was holding and peered absently into it as the liquid spun. He wondered what the other members of the PRIMAL team were doing as he and Kruger continued their odyssey to recover the kidnapped girls. Mirza and his girlfriend would still be in London, Vance and Chua had probably escaped to somewhere in South East Asia, Mitch would be in America with his new company, and Bishop and Saneh were most likely in Spain. He wondered if there was a chance that the team would ever get back together or if this was it, the end of PRIMAL.

"Tank's full," said Kruger as he joined him at the rear of the truck stop near the Rwanda-Uganda border. "You want a refill coffee?"

"*Nein*, it tastes like shit."

Kruger laughed as he strolled across to the diner, leaving Kurtz to walk back to their pickup parked at the gas pumps. They had hired the truck in Kampala and driven south six hours toward Nyagatare, Rwanda. Booyah followed them on a motorbike before peeling off to recon a refueling point for their Mi-17.

As Kurtz climbed into the passenger side of the pickup his phone rang. He checked the screen. The number wasn't one that he recognized, however, he could tell it was local. He answered it. "Hello."

"Shorty it's me. A little bird told me you were heading my way."

He instantly recognized the voice as Saneh's. Shorty was the English translation of his nickname Kurtz. "Not unless you're in Rwanda."

"I am. Look, there's no time to explain. I'll send you a location where we can meet."

"*Ja*, OK."

The call ended leaving Kurtz somewhat confused.

"Who was that?" asked Kruger as he climbed into the cab with a can of energy drink.

"Saneh, she's in Rwanda."

"With Bishop? Is this part of her Exodus plan?"

"She didn't say."

His phone chimed. "This will be our RV." He took out a notebook and scribbled down the coordinates. Then he swapped the minutes in the latitude with the degrees in the longitude and vice versa. It was a simple technique they used when transmitting a location over an insecure net. Then he punched the coordinates into his GPS.

The position that Saneh wanted to meet them was less than twenty miles away outside a small town called Tabagwa. He noted that it was less than an hour from the location that Krenich had given them.

"What do you think she wants?" asked Kruger.

"I'm not sure. But from the tone of her voice, I'd say it's important."

"So is rescuing the last of the girls."

"Family comes first," said Kurtz as he started the truck.

Kruger raised his can of energy drink in a mock toast. "Amen to that."

TEL AVIV, ISRAEL

Keila caught Abel's eye as she entered the *Kidon* office and gestured for him to join her at the corner kitchenette. "I can't get hold of Bishop."

Her lead analyst shrugged. "That's not unusual, right?"

"I'm worried something has happened to him. You heard anything on the grapevine?"

He frowned. "I heard a rumor that Lisker's guys had made a move on one of their target sets. You don't think they've grabbed him and the others?"

"I'm not sure."

"Can't you ask your guy at 8200?"

"I tried. He's not answering my calls either."

"Gaslighting, or do you think he knows something?"

Her eyes narrowed. "He may be on lockdown."

"Which would imply that something big is going on. I'll reach out to some of the other analysts and see what I can dig up."

"Appreciated, I'll try Asher again."

"Be careful with him. If Lisker puts the squeeze on him, he might give you up, and the word on the street is he's heading all the way to the top."

"Are you kidding? He's a borderline criminal with his own personal hit squad. If he becomes the director of Mossad he's going to do whatever he wants. There will be no oversight of his actions."

"You seriously think there's any oversight now? Director Atzomi doesn't know half the crap that Lisker has going on. I heard he's in bed with Sakkin Industries."

"What evidence is there of that?" she asked.

"I've got a buddy in the Pretoria Embassy. Lisker attended a symposium they put on. He saw him talking to Daniel Ginsberg, the CEO of Sakkin."

"That doesn't mean they're working together."

"My friend saw Lisker leave in one of Ginsberg's cars. He tailed it to the heliport where he took off in a chopper."

"Slow day in Pretoria?"

Abel shrugged. "Every day's a slow day according to him."

"Does Sakkin have many interests in South Africa?"

"Yeah, they're building a massive headquarters in Cape Town."

"Well, it's no secret that Lisker wants to expand into Africa. He's been pushing for an increased presence from Egypt to Rwanda." She paused in thought. "Abel, the guy that was assassinated in Dubai."

"Jarvis, the head of Intelligent Responsive Systems."

"Yeah, are there any links to Sakkin Industries there?"

"Not sure, I'll check it out."

"Do some digging and see what else you can find. I'm going to corner Asher."

She left Abel and the rest of the team in the office and drove the two blocks to the 8200 complex. If she was to storm into Asher's office and cause a scene word would get back to Lisker, however, it was nearly ten o'clock, so she had a feeling he wouldn't be at his desk.

She got a park opposite the hole in the wall where she knew he got his coffee and waited. Sure enough, within half an hour he appeared and placed his order.

Keila exited her vehicle and approached where he stood waiting, checking his phone. "So you've definitely seen my messages, right?"

"Keila, look—"

"Hey, I get it. Lisker can end your career with a snap of his fingers. All I need from you is a couple of yes-no answers."

The barista announced Asher's order and he collected it from the window with Keila in tow.

"You already know what I'm going to ask," she persisted.

"Walk with me."

They set off down a street that didn't lead directly back to his building.

He sipped his coffee before speaking. "I know what you're going to ask and you already know the answer. Shortly after we broke their network it went dark, and I mean pitch black. No activity on linked devices, nothing."

"You think Lisker's team went in hot?"

"It happened ten minutes after the network was shut down. I think that you tipped them off."

Keila's silence all but confirmed the statement.

"Did they get anyone?" she asked, quietly.

"I don't know for sure. But, I do know they were tracking a couple of handsets outside of the secure network. One of them was in Spain, just outside of Valencia in a little town called Requena."

"Shit!"

He stopped and turned to her. "What's wrong?"

"That asshole Lisker is wrapping up my contacts."

"Look, I wish I could do more."

She leaned across and kissed him on the cheek. "You've already done enough. Look, when the dust settles dinner's on me. In fact, I'll cook at my place."

Asher grinned. "Brilliant, I'll wait for your call."

"Better pick up this time," quipped Keila as she walked away. En route to her car she rang Abel.

"Any luck?" he asked.

"Our boy was in Spain. See if you can locate his burn phone."

"OK, when are you leaving? Did you want me to see if Dan is free to go with?"

"Am I that predictable?"

"Nope, but I know how you think."

"Don't worry about Dan, we need to keep this lower than low. I'll go and sniff around by myself."

"Stay out of trouble."

"Will do."

Chapter Sixteen

TABAGWA, RWANDA

THE LOCATION that Saneh had sent Kurtz was an abandoned building a few miles out of a dusty Rwandan village. Judging from the amount of garbage strewn through the surrounding thorn bushes and trees it had probably been a general store.

"You think this could be a setup?" asked Kruger from where he was laying behind his PKP machine gun.

Kurtz lowered his binoculars and glanced across at him. "She didn't use any of the duress phrases."

"Better safe than sorry, eh."

They'd parked their pickup in the scrub and walked in to observe the location. Kurtz had already flown a small drone in a full loop around it and seen nothing of interest.

"Vehicle inbound," said Kruger, peering through the scope on his machine gun.

Kurtz focused on the road and saw the dust cloud. It grew in size until he could make out a white SUV at its head. The vehicle slowed as it approached the store before turning into a clearing to its front. He checked his watch; it was eleven minutes to the hour, standard RV window.

Kruger let out a low whistle as two figures emerged from the vehicle. "Saneh's got a lady friend."

Kurtz identified Saneh but didn't recognize the second woman. She was taller than Bishop's partner, with broader shoulders. She wore sunglasses and a cap pulled low. Saneh turned and faced directly toward him with her right hand tucked into her pocket, signaling that it was all clear. "I'm going in."

"I'll cover."

Kurtz climbed to his feet, taking up his customized AK as he tucked the binoculars into a pouch. Walking through the scrub he removed his cap and held it low in his right hand; a predetermined signal. It took him less than a minute to cover the few hundred yards and join the two women.

"Kurtz, it's so good to see you." Saneh threw her arms around him.

"You too. Is Bish here?"

"No, he's in Europe."

They broke and Saneh gestured to the second woman. "Kurtz, this is Bianca. Is Kruger in overwatch?"

"*Ja.*" He offered his hand to the other woman.

Her grip was firm as she removed her sunglasses and smiled warmly. "Kurtz, it is a pleasure to meet you." The accent was French with a hint of something else. She had defined angular features and held his gaze with bright blue eyes.

"You too, Bianca."

"All right, let's move inside and bring everyone up to date," Saneh said as she led them into the building.

He nodded and thumbed the mike switch on his rifle. "All clear, bring it in."

Kurtz wasn't surprised to find that Saneh and Bianca had already been to the abandoned store and tidied it up. They'd added stretchers under mosquito domes, a gas burner and jerry cans of clean water.

Kruger joined them after parking alongside Saneh's SUV. Once he'd been introduced to Bianca they sat on camp chairs around a table laid with butcher's paper.

"So what's this all about?" Kurtz asked Saneh. "Why are you in Africa without Bishop?"

"It's a long story. Putting it simply, I was sent here to kill Bianca."

Kruger's brow shot up. "Come again?"

"Like I said, it's a long story. Basically, Bianca stumbled on something sinister and in trying to do something about it she angered the wrong people. However, unfortunately for them, I was tasked to neutralize her."

"We staged my death," added Bianca.

"And it looks like they bought it. Which means we've got a very small window to deal with the Lifebright Foundation."

"Say that again," said Kurtz.

"What, Lifebright?"

"The Lifebright Foundation hired you to kill Bianca?"

Kurtz noted the sideways look that the French Canadian shot Saneh as she spoke. "In a roundabout way, yes."

"We're here for the Lifebright Foundation," said Kruger.

Saneh's eyes widened as she connected the dots. "Of course, the missing Somali girls."

Kurtz nodded. "We've been tracking them across three countries. Our last point of call was a people smuggler in

Uganda. He confessed to delivering the girls to the Lifebright Foundation here in Rwanda."

"You got a confession?" asked Bianca. "That's awesome. We can take that to the UN and try to get them shut down."

All three PRIMAL operatives stared at her.

"That's not really the way we do things," said Saneh. "Plus, you're supposed to be dead, remember."

"We're thinking a raid," said Kurtz.

Bianca nodded vigorously. "Hell yeah." She gestured to Kurtz's assault rifle. "Can you get more hardware?"

Kruger laughed. "It's Africa, we can get anything you want."

While Kruger and Bianca discussed weapons and an assault on the Lifebright facility, Saneh led Kurtz outside.

"I've got to head back to the Emirates," she said as they made their way to the vehicles.

"OK."

"I need you to look after Bianca."

"She seems capable."

"She is. Will make a good addition to K2, you guys need a little less testosterone."

Kurtz laughed. "Does she know you're leaving?"

"Yeah."

"What does she know about PRIMAL?"

"Nothing. I told her you're a couple of guys working a contract for a Somali warlord."

"Not completely untrue."

Saneh hugged Kurtz. "I guess I'll see you when I see you. Give 'em hell." She wiped a tear from her eye as she climbed into her SUV. As she was about to start the engine she paused and lowered the window. "Oh, and Kurtz. When you speak to Chua or Vance, I was never here."

He nodded and shot her thumbs up. "Got it."

As she pulled out onto the dusty African track Saneh kept her eyes on the road. There was no glance in the rearview mirror, no final look at what could be the last PRIMAL mission she was ever involved in. She had a mission of her own and there was every chance it could be her last.

―――

BEN GURION INTERNATIONAL AIRPORT, TEL AVIV

Keila was minutes from boarding her flight to Valencia when her phone rang. It was Abel with an update. "You're not going to believe this, but Sakkin Industries just procured Intelligent Responsive Systems, the company of the guy who was murdered in Dubai."

"Allegedly murdered."

"Yeah, right. I found an interview with Isaac Jarvis in a business magazine from three months ago. He mentioned that IRS was under attack from an entity attempting a hostile take over. Jarvis mentions that he was fighting it with everything he had."

"And you think it was Sakkin trying to seize control."

"Without a doubt."

"To what ends?"

"Autonomous systems. IRS is the leading developer of the AI required for autonomous robots. Robots that can make educated decisions."

"Perfect for security?"

"Yep and Sakkin already have several platforms capable of providing autonomous border protection."

"But what does this have to do with Lisker? Have you found anything tying him directly to Ginsberg or Sakkin?"

"Not yet, but I'll keep digging."

A first and final boarding call for Keila's flight sounded.

"Keep at it. I've got to run." As she cleared the gate and entered the air bridge to the aircraft her mind was racing. What 'skin' did Manfred Lisker have in the game with Sakkin? Was he a silent partner or was Ginsberg backing the head of Special Operations for a higher position? If Lisker became head of Mossad then contracts would flow to the security contractor. Whatever the relationship, she was sure that Bishop could shed some light on Lisker's non-sanctioned activities.

————

LASCAR TOWER, ABU DHABI

Emily glanced up as the door to Tariq Ahmed's office hissed open and her boss appeared. "Emily, can you please join us."

She frowned as he turned and reentered his office. She was rarely invited into the penthouse office from which Tariq Ahmed ran his empire, and never had she been asked personally. Tariq was a great boss, but he was also intensely private and the office was his inner sanctum. She was always summoned via intercom and always for a specific task.

Following him into the office she noted that Tariq's lawyer, who had arrived earlier, was standing alongside the conference table on the far side of the room. There was an array of paperwork neatly collated on the black glass.

"Hello, Emily," the lawyer greeted her.

"Ali." She turned to her boss. "Did you need something, Tariq?"

"Please take a seat." He waited for her to sit before joining them at the table. "Emily, Ali and I have been going over the succession plans for my holdings."

She nodded, they'd brought her in to witness changes to Tariq's will.

"As you already know in the event that something happens to me, all my holdings go to Fatima."

Fatima was Tariq's wife, an intelligent and beautiful woman who Emily had met less than a half dozen times. She had her own company, a tech firm that specialized in web marketing software.

Tariq straightened his suit jacket. "However, what concerns me is that she doesn't actually have any experience with the firm. As such I would like to appoint you and Ali as her special advisors."

"That goes without saying, Tariq. Of course, we would help her make the transition."

"I want a little more from you than that. I am going to allocate you five percent of the holdings, each."

She could tell by the surprised look on the lawyer's face that this was the first she had heard of it too. "Tariq, that's literally hundreds of millions of dollars worth of stock and a significant amount of control. You pay me more than enough for my services. There is no requirement for anything of this scale."

"I agree, this is beyond generous," added Ali.

"This isn't about generosity. It's about trust and, along with my wife, there is no one I trust more to steer Lascar in my absence and ensure the prosperity of our employees."

Emily's brow furrowed. "With all due respect, you're sounding a little fatalistic. Is everything OK?"

"Fine. I'm simply reviewing my succession plan. It's something I do annually. All I need is for you and Ali to review the documents and sign them. Then we can all get back to work."

She shot Ali a sideways glance and the lawyer shrugged. Taking the folder that Tariq handed her she began to read the twenty-page document. Having studied law at university it didn't take her long to review and sign the papers. Then she excused herself and returned to her desk.

A quick scan of her calendar confirmed her fears. Succession planning had occurred only a few months earlier in June. For a man who stuck to timings almost religiously, this was out of character. Something was going on.

Chapter Seventeen

REQUENA, SPAIN

AFTER AN HOUR of watching Bishop's cottage Ice was confident that it wasn't under surveillance. However, he also knew that the residence was empty and professionals had hit it.

Through binoculars he'd spotted a broken pane in one of the windows and splintered wood around the door jamb. Someone had launched gas or a flashbang through the window and mechanically breached the front door.

He scanned the hillside opposite for any sign of a stay-behind surveillance team, but couldn't see anything out of the ordinary. As he lowered the binoculars he spotted a white hatchback driving slowly along the road that passed the cottage. It was the first vehicle he'd seen since arriving.

The car parked a few hundred yards short of the cottage and a person emerged. Adjusting the focus of the binoculars brought the athletic figure of Keila Bachman into focus. Ice had never met the Mossad operative but he'd read her file and knew her from photos taken by Bishop. Her presence implied that Mossad was definitely involved in the abduction.

He watched as she observed the cottage, then returned to the car and continued her approach. The limited surveillance indicated she had insider information and that the threat had long passed. Returning to his own vehicle, a rented SUV, he drove the half-mile to the cottage through the haze of dust from where Keila had passed.

Sure enough, when the building came into view her car was already parked with the driver's door open. He stopped alongside her vehicle and stepped out. As he approached the residence she appeared in the doorway, one hand on the splintered frame the other hidden behind her leg. Ice assumed she was concealing a pistol.

"My name's James." He stopped a few steps from her. "I'm a friend of Bishop."

Her eyes narrowed. "James Castle, Ice?"

"My friends call me that."

"Have you seen Bishop?"

"No, but I'm guessing you know who has, Keila."

She shot him a hard stare before backing away from the doorway. "Come inside, we can talk there."

Ice was confident that even if she pulled the weapon he could disarm her without inflicting too much harm. Bishop had reported she was a capable fighter, but his size and mechanical hand would give him the edge.

Inside the kitchen Ice detected a faint smell, inhaling deeply he tried to place the sweet odor.

"I'm guessing it's a sedative," said Keila as she surveyed the quaint stone-walled kitchen.

"Standard Mossad procedure?" Ice said with a smirk.

"Not particularly. Did you use it in the CIA?"

"Touché," he murmured as he left the kitchen and stepped into the bedroom where a sliding door was open. Stepping outside he noticed pistol casings strewn across the flagstones. It looked as if Bishop hadn't gone down without a fight.

There was a rustle in the bushes behind a low wall.

Keila raised her pistol as she entered the room.

"No need for that." Ice whistled and the noise stopped. He whistled again and a bolt of black and white fur leaped the wall and dove for his legs. "Daisy, good girl." Ice bent and scooped the dog from the ground.

The Border Collie ravaged his face with licks and snuffles as he struggled to hold her. "It's OK, it's OK."

"Is that Bishop's dog?"

"Yeah, she's an Explosive Detection Dog."

Keila patted Daisy's head and was rewarded with licks.

Ice held her till she had calmed slightly then lowered her to the ground.

"So you've got no idea where they took Aden?" asked Ice as he resumed his inspection of the property, with the dog and Keila following.

"No, I think he may have been snatched by a contracted team."

"But you're not going to tell me why."

Keila shrugged. "I'm here to get him back."

Ice's brow rose. "Right, well I guess we should start by reviewing the surveillance footage."

"I didn't see any cameras."

"There are always cameras." Ice led her and Daisy back into the kitchen and began inspecting the walls, benches and refrigerator. After less than a minute of searching he paused at an antique wooden drinks cabinet next to the fireplace. The door creaked as he opened it. Removing a dozen bottles of whisky he pressed on the wooden paneling behind them. There was a soft click and the wood slid away. Peering inside he found a thin black box the size of a box of chocolates. It sported an array of stubby antennas. "You got a laptop?"

"Yes, in the car."

"Get it."

He disconnected the covert server from its power source as Keila retrieved her computer. When she reappeared he plugged the router into her laptop and accessed the internal drive through a web browser.

"You all use these?" She watched over her shoulder.

"It's equipment I'm familiar with."

"And passwords?"

He ignored the comment and checked what covert cameras Bishop had installed as Daisy rested her head on his leg. There were three. One watching the driveway, one covering the back of the house and another located a little over a mile away on the road that led to the cottage.

"The driveway feed will show us any vehicles they used."

Ice opened the file and scanned through footage at high speed. It didn't take him long to find a shot of a van arriving. It was white and didn't have any plates.

He checked the time stamp and switched to the camera covering the front of the cottage. Sure enough, men clad in tactical gear dragged a hooded and cuffed figure into the van before driving away.

"Without plates we haven't got a hope in hell of finding them," said Keila.

"Hmmm," murmured Ice as he switched to another of the cameras. "No one drives around without plates, especially not with a prisoner in the back. If they didn't have enough time to acquire alternatives they'll put the old ones back on."

He found a frame where the van was in the shot. Sure enough, as he had predicted the van was now sporting registration plates.

"Can you use your assets to run it?" asked Ice.

"I can." She thumbed a message on her phone.

As she did, Ice rose from the table and walked into the kitchen. He scanned the appliances, then turned on a large coffee machine. "How do you have it?" he asked Keila.

"You don't already know?"

He laughed. "Look, if we're going to be working together, I need to know how you have your coffee."

"Working together?"

"Yeah, working together to recover Bishop. I mean that is why you're here, right."

"He saved my team in Syria."

Ice nodded. "Yep, so we're working together."

As she continued messaging on her phone he made them both lattes and poured the remaining milk into a saucer for Daisy. "How long will it take your people to track the van?"

"I'm not sure. Depends on how secure the servers are." She took a cup from Ice. "Thanks. How did you know that Bishop was missing?"

"Saneh called me."

"Where is she?"

"Taking care of something else."

"Must be pretty serious if she prioritized it over Aden."

"She sent me."

"Did she pull you out of retirement?"

Ice ignored the comment. "So, any idea why a rogue

Mossad team snatched a security contractor from his holiday home in Spain?"

Her eyes narrowed. "I'm not discussing company business with you."

"Fair enough." Ice sipped from his coffee. "Do you play cards?"

INTERNATIONAL AIRPORT, DUBAI

"You sneaky bastard," said Flash Gordon as he sat behind his laptop in a café at Dubai international airport. After days of hacking into what seemed like a hundred different servers and scrolling through thousands of pages of company and banking details, he'd finally found the piece he was looking for. A loophole in the South African taxation system had allowed him to trace the flow of money through several shell companies into the structure that Manfred Lisker was using to pay Lascar Logistics for airfreight services.

The evidence he'd found wouldn't hold up in a court of law, there was nothing directly tying Lisker to any of the accounts. However, it did show that a single corporate entity was supplying the funding and now he knew what that entity was.

Flash finished collating his findings in a single encrypted PDF then signed onto a one-time use cloud drive and uploaded it. The highly secure program would alert Tariq that the file had been sent.

He clicked on a purge program he'd engineered and watched as the software wiped the hard drive and then corrupted the operating system. Confident the laptop was clean he slid it into his backpack and left the café.

Checking the departure screen he saw his flight to Los Angeles had commenced boarding. Now that his job for Tariq was complete it was time to start a new chapter. Mitch Freeman had offered him a role establishing a special effects company in LA and the film industry seemed intriguing. His Hong Kong plans would have to wait.

Walking through the airport he wondered what Tariq would do with the information he'd uncovered. He hoped it allowed the transport tycoon to squeeze out from whatever leverage Mossad had over him.

NEGEV DESERT, ISRAEL

It was Lisker's second visit to the Sakkin Industries medical facility hidden beneath the yellow sands of the Negev desert. A genetic research laboratory it was the home of the Proteus project, a long-term program that Lisker believed would solve Mossad's manning issues. On his first visit the facility was bustling with activity and he'd been impressed with the progress that Marnisha Copeland, the project head, had made. Today's visit told a very different story.

He frowned as an aide led him through bare corridors past empty laboratories toward the heart of the facility. Stopping in front of a frosted door he gestured for Lisker to enter. "Director Ginsberg and Doctor Copeland are waiting inside."

Lisker entered the sleek office where the Doctor was seated behind a desk with Daniel Ginsberg sitting in the corner. There was an open bottle of expensive whisky between them and three glasses.

"Ah, Manfred, join us for a drink," said the CEO of Sakkin Industries. "Doctor Copeland was just updating me on the progress that has been made."

The attractive elfin-featured geneticist smiled politely.

"There has been progress? Because it looks to me like it's all been shut down."

"Not at all, just moved offshore for security and," he paused, "political reasons."

"You mean ethical reasons."

"Those too."

Lisker sat and Ginsberg poured him a drink. "So, what progress has been made?"

"Dr. Copeland, if you don't mind."

"Certainly, Manfred as you know from your previous visit we were focusing our efforts in two areas, genetic manipulation and artificial birthing. This facility has primarily been focused on genetics with artificial birthing having been moved to another facility under the direction of my associate Dr. Morrison."

"The Rwandan lab?" asked Lisker.

"Correct."

He turned to Ginsberg. "The issue pertaining to that facility has been resolved."

"Excellent."

"There was an issue?" asked Copeland.

"A minor security problem," answered Ginsberg. "Please go on."

"Very well. Doctor Morrison has had significant success in both surrogate and artificial birthing."

"Artificial?" asked Lisker.

"Yes, he has been able to remove a womb from a live

host and provide it with life support. In the next two to three years he is hoping to print a womb and seed it genetically with zero requirements for a surrogate or host."

Lisker was slightly perturbed by the cold manner with which the Doctor discussed what he only assumed was a process that involved live humans. Personally, he didn't care who died to further their agenda, but he expected slightly more from a Doctor and a potential mother. He wondered if the icy scientist had any children of her own. He assumed not.

"My own research has advanced significantly. I have been able to isolate many of the genomes responsible for particular attributes and manipulate them accordingly."

"We've had several fascinating spin-off technologies that include anti-aging treatments and genetic enhancers," added Ginsberg.

"So there's no danger of the Proteus project failing?"

"You kidding? The life-extension technology alone will pay for the project for the next fifteen years."

"Which is how long it might take," added Copeland.

Lisker raised his glass. "The long haul it is. A toast to your work, Doctor Copeland, and your ongoing support, Daniel."

"Appreciated," she replied before they touched glasses and drank. Finishing her whisky in one hit Copeland rose from the desk. "I've got some matters to attend to. Gentlemen, it's been a pleasure."

Once she'd left, Lisker turned to Ginsberg. "That woman is ice cold."

"She's a genius, exactly what we need."

"No doubt about that."

"Well done on having the issue in Rwanda resolved. Were there any difficulties?"

"A clean job."

"Good." Ginsberg refilled his glass and offered to do the same for Lisker.

He nodded.

"My IT security people tell me that someone has been sniffing around in our accounts and shell companies."

"You know who?"

He shook his head and sipped his drink. "I thought you might have an idea"

"No one springs to mind," Lisker lied. There was a high probability that Tariq Ahmed was the man behind the intrusion. He had the resources and the motivation to dig around in Lisker's undertakings. "Could it be related to Intelligent Responsive Systems?"

"Most likely. Since we procured the company, attempts to compromise our servers have doubled."

"But the merger was successful?"

"More of an absorption, but yes, very successful. Which reminds me. I've been meaning to discuss a new position with you."

"Go on."

"I'm looking for someone to head the Global Strategy Branch, assist in driving the company into the future. It's the perfect role for someone with your insight and leadership. The branch is fully funded with complete autonomy."

Lisker nodded. "I have a man who would be highly suitable."

"You wouldn't consider it for yourself?"

"No, I have a path planned."

"Ah, the directorship."

Lisker said nothing and sipped his whisky.

"Let me know if there is anything I can do to assist."

"Everything is in place. It is simply a matter of time."

Their meeting continued for half the bottle of whiskey before Lisker departed the facility. Back in his car, heading across the desert, he phoned Avi. "I'm on my way to Jordan, have Tariq Ahmed meet me there."

"And if he fails to comply?"

"Where is Mantis?"

"Back in the UAE."

"Do I need to paint a picture?"

"No. I'll make it happen."

"We're at a critical juncture, Avi. If the shipments of weapons don't reach Egypt this week the uprising will fail."

"He will be there."

Lisker ended the call and closed his eyes, exhaling. Everything was riding on the next forty-eight hours. If things went well, the conditions would be set for him to assume control of Mossad. Once that had been achieved he could work with Sakkin to establish the intelligence agency as Israel's premier security force.

LIFEBRIGHT FOUNDATION FACILITY, RWANDA

"So you set this up?" asked Kruger as he, Bianca and Kurtz used her hide to observe the Lifebright facility. They'd parked their vehicle three miles away and the former Canadian Special Forces operator had led them through the darkness, directly to the original position from which she'd observed the compound.

"Sure did, you got a problem with it?"

"No," said the South African. "I've never met a female sniper before."

"It's an excellent position," added Kurtz.

"A few things have changed," she said. "Those small buggies are new."

Kurtz adjusted his night vision binoculars and spotted the vehicles. They were the size of an ATV but lacked the cabin where a driver would sit. Instead, they were crowned with what looked to be a remote weapon turret complete with a machine gun and an array of optical sensors. "It's some kind of drone."

"They've enhanced their security. That makes things more difficult," said Bianca.

Kruger snorted. "Nah, we just blow them all to hell. Let's hit this thing hard and leave it a smoking ruin."

"I think, considering the girls, a subtler approach might be in order," she said.

"*Ja*, I agree," added Kurtz. "We can find a gap in their security and slip in. Then we can neutralize their security measures from the inside and escape using a distraction."

Kruger rolled his eyes.

"Sounds good," she said. "We probably need to do a full recon of the facility to confirm nothing else has changed since I was here last."

"You mean since you died," said Kurtz.

"That too."

"I'll do a sweep," said Kruger. "My legs are going to sleep."

Kurtz slid a tablet from his combat vest and activated the screen. "We'll monitor you from here." His tracking device appeared, overlaid on a Google earth image of their location.

"So if I get into trouble we go in guns blazing?" Kruger asked.

"Don't even think about it."

"Got it. All covert 'n' shit."

The big man disappeared into the night without a sound.

"You sure he's not going to start something?" Bianca asked when he was gone.

"He knows a covert approach is our best chance of recovering the girls."

"That means a lot to you both, doesn't it?"

"It's the mission we were hired to complete."

"Yeah, but it's more than the cash, isn't it?"

Kurtz made an adjustment to the night vision binoculars mounted on a tripod in front of him. "Too many innocents have died. I'm not going to let them kill more."

"Have you been doing this sort of thing long?"

"A few years."

"You, Kruger, Saneh and her partner Bishop, all working together?"

"When we need a bigger team, Saneh is a very capable operative."

"Yeah, I picked up on that."

As they talked Kurtz spotted a set of headlights, bouncing as the vehicle approached along the potholed service road.

"That will be the food delivery," said Bianca. "A local guy brings it in every morning at this time. I assume it's for the girls and the staff."

"You know where it originates from?"

"I can find out."

He watched as the truck stopped at the security gate and a guard checked the driver's credentials. A moment later he waved the delivery vehicle through, into the compound. "Then that's our covert means of entry."

Chapter Eighteen

AMMAN, JORDAN

TARIQ AHMED ADJUSTED his waistcoat as he descended the ancient steps of the Roman amphitheater in central Amman, Jordan. It was mid-morning, and despite being a beautiful day, the ancient site was devoid of tourists. Tariq assumed that Manfred Lisker had emptied the attraction as a form of intimidation.

Despite being summoned to meet with Mossad's Director of Special Operations, Tariq was in a good mood. As expected, Flash's information pack was exactly what he needed. He paused halfway down the theater to reflect on the majesty of the structure. In his imagination he could hear the voices of the actors echoing from the rough cut stone as they entertained Amman's elite.

At the rear of the stage he spotted an archway leading into the tunnels where performers once prepared. Tentatively he entered the dark walkway and peered into the shadows.

Lisker was waiting for him, alone. Like Tariq he was dressed in a well-cut suit. However, the Mossad operative wasn't wearing a tie, which Tariq put down to the unusual setting for the meeting.

"Tariq, thank you for coming."

He nodded.

"I'll cut to the chase. I've been less than happy with the services your company has been providing."

"I'm sorry to hear that. Have you lodged a complaint with our customer relations team?"

Lisker stepped forward into a beam of light streaming through the archway. A vein in the side of his head throbbed as he clenched his jaw. "Do I need to remind you what will happen if you fail to comply?"

He shrugged. "You'll destroy my company. Drag my name through the mud. I assure you, Manfred, that any destruction will be mutually assured. I know where your funding is coming from and I know it's unauthorized. I wonder what would happen to your career if Director Atzmoni was to find out." He paused. "Lascar is no longer your plaything."

"You'll fucking regret this," Lisker hissed through his teeth.

"Maybe, but if you come after me, you'll definitely regret it."

Tariq turned and walked back toward the amphitheater. Lisker watched him leave with both hands balled into fists by his side. "You motherfucker," he mumbled as he pulled his phone from his pocket and dialed Avi.

"Boss, did Ahmed make the meeting?" Avi asked.

"Is Mantis back in the UAE?"

"She touches down in two hours."

"Have her kill Tariq Ahmed."

Avi took a moment to respond. "If she refuses?"

"Kill her boyfriend, kill her and have someone else kill Tariq. Use the Sakkin funding and make it bloody."

"I'll get right on it. What do you want me to do about the arms shipment?"

He exhaled. "I'll find another way."

Lisker pocketed the phone as he turned down a side passage then climbed a short flight of stairs to an exit. By the time he reached his car he was fuming to the point of white rage. He was going to destroy Tariq Ahmed's legacy, utterly demolish Lascar Logistics and all of its subsidiaries. But first, he needed to find a way to smuggle missiles into Egypt.

SYDNEY, AUSTRALIA

"You ever been to Sydney?" asked Chua as he and Vance relaxed in the business lounge at Charles Kingsford Smith International Airport.

"Yeah, I recruited Bishop here. Seems like a lifetime ago."

"Right, I remember that." He pointed out the window at the city center a few miles distant. A cluster of skyscrapers rose into the air around what looked to be a central tower with a spire. "Is the bridge out that way?" He referred to the iconic Sydney harbor bridge that featured in almost every Australian tourism product.

"A little past it. When we're settled in our new location you should come check it out. Sydney is a beautiful city."

"I will." Chua moved across to one of the three computer terminals in the lounge. He logged on and checked a digital nomad Facebook page. Whistling as he scrolled through the posts he didn't notice Vance watching him over the top of an airline magazine.

"You breaking protocol?"

"What?" Chua turned and shot him an incredulous look.

"What are you looking at?"

"There's no hiding from you."

"Chua, you wrote the protocols."

"True, but Kurtz hasn't been using iPRIMAL. He's using an older method we established so he could work in Africa offline."

"The Exodus protocol states that you are to have no contact with any past or present members of PRIMAL." Vance paused. "How are they doing?"

"They've located the last of the girls and they're working with a local contact to recover them."

"That's good to hear. Have you been in contact with anyone else?"

"No. But I expect them to start checking in within the next 72 hours. Then I can work out who tried to take us down."

"As per the Exodus protocol."

"Correct."

"And the news?" Vance asked, his brow furrowed. "Anything interesting out of Abu Dhabi?"

"Hang on." Chua's fingers flew over the keyboard as he browsed. "Here it is. Authorities are reporting a gas explosion in the estate. No casualties."

"So Ice got out," Vance said as he tossed his magazine on a table.

Chua nodded as he wiped the browser history and logged off.

"How about you? Your wound need dressing?"

"No, it's actually feeling a little better."

"Good, because I'm over being your nurse."

"But you're so good at it."

A bell chimed and a PA system announced that their flight had commenced boarding.

Vance stood with his bag. "Last leg."

Chua did the same. "There better be a gym at this new location."

"Trust me, you're going to love it," he said as they left the lounge. "It'll be good to put up our feet."

"Yeah, I'm actually enjoying not having Bishop on the other end of a line every ten minutes asking for a new target." Chua paused. "I hope he and Saneh are all good."

"Those two will be onboard their boat making for the French Riviera."

"The kids are all grown up and mom and dad can travel in peace."

Vance let out a snort. "You do know that you're mom."

"Whatever, everyone knows intel runs the shop."

"Keep dreaming little man."

———

LIFEBRIGHT FOUNDATION FACILITY, RWANDA

Jamilah knew something was wrong when the orderlies failed to bring her meal the night before. She'd spent the night awake in terror of what the morning would bring. They had arrived in the earlier hours. She'd put up a fight but was no match for their size and the fast-acting sedative. Once again she found herself strapped to a chair in a sterile laboratory fighting to stay conscious.

Like clockwork the cold-eyed doctor appeared and looked over her charts and the sensors stuck to her skin. Then the freezing showerhead device caressed her stomach and pelvis.

"She's ready, prep her for surgery."

She faintly registered the words but had no idea what they meant. The doctor and two orderlies left the room, and a moment later the orderlies reappeared with a wheeled stretcher. As they slid her from the chair and lifted her onto the gurney she managed to flail her hand across one of their faces.

"Bitch!" He slapped her hard.

The pain cut through the sedative's fog and tears streamed down her cheeks as the men strapped her to the gurney. Fluorescent panel after panel flashed by as she was wheeled deeper into the facility. The stench of antiseptic and medical supplies stung her nostrils as she was pushed through a set of doors. Powerful lights shone down as they brought the gurney to a halt.

The two men who'd taken her this far left her alone in the room. Jamilah raised her head to see what was around her. She'd never been to a doctor's surgery in her life let alone seen a fully equipped operating theatre. The trays of sinister-looking medical tools were terrifying and left her in no doubt that something horrible was about to happen.

In an adjacent office Doctor Morrison sat at his desk reviewing his notes on subject 173X. He was comparing the results with another subject whose womb had not survived being removed. This new subject was more developed and he hoped that maturity held the key to success. Morrison always scheduled his surgeries for first thing in the morning. Rested and caffeinated, he felt it was when he did his best work. Sipping a coffee he glanced up at the bank of screens on his office wall. He saw that 173X was ready in the operating theatre and that his anesthetist was in attendance. On another screen he noted that the food delivery truck was arriving. He made a note to ask Elias if he could source fresh milk, the heat-treated stuff tasted terrible.

———

INTERNATIONAL AIRPORT, DUBAI

No sooner had the flight to Dubai touched down than Saneh activated a fresh burner phone and texted Ice.

Any news on our boy?

As she waited for his response she found a departures board and checked on her flight to Spain. It was boarding in a matter of minutes. Walking swiftly through the sleek modern terminal she navigated her way around large groups of tourists. She was a short distance from her gate when her phone vibrated with a reply.

We've got a lead we're following up.

We? Saneh wondered who else was with him. Joining the line at her gate she was midway through thumbing a response when she looked up and caught the eye of someone she knew, Avi.

He shot her a steely gaze then flicked his head to one side. She glared at him before stepping out of the line and following him.

"I did what you wanted," she snapped when they were out of earshot of the other passengers.

"We've got another task for you."

For a second Saneh considered fly kicking him in the face and strangling him with the strap of her carry-on bag. But, she knew if anything happened to him, then Bishop was as good as dead. Her only hope was to agree to whatever Avi wanted and hope that Ice came good on the recovery mission.

"What is it?"

He smiled. "We want you to kill the man who betrayed you to us."

She exhaled slowly and said nothing.

"Oh come on. You know who I'm talking about. Your old friend, Tariq Ahmed."

Saneh had always assumed that Mossad managed to track her down as a result of a mistake she'd made. She had never considered that someone within PRIMAL could have betrayed her.

"You're wrong."

He smirked. "I was there when it happened. We plucked him from the clutches of an Islamist hit squad and he sang like a canary. Tariq Ahmed was more than happy to sell out an Iranian killer to protect his empire. There's video evidence if you'd like to see it."

Saneh struggled to contain her emotions as her mind raced. Tariq was a close friend and the patron of PRIMAL, but Avi's accusation rang true. Tariq's behavior over the last few months, distancing himself from PRIMAL, it now made sense.

"Of course, he had no idea that you were a double agent. You've got twenty-four hours to complete the assignment. If you're successful, Bishop goes free. If you aren't…" He ran a finger across his throat before turning and walking away.

Was it possible that Tariq had sold her out to Mossad to save his own skin? Even the thought of it was like a punch to the gut. She felt physically sick as she slumped onto one of the bench seats that lined the walkway. Tariq wouldn't have known that she was working with Mossad. He would have surrendered her thinking he was condemning her to death, and now Bishop was facing the same fate. She came to the cold realization that Avi was speaking the truth. Tariq must have sold her out.

She channeled shock and grief into smoldering anger, focused on the man who'd destroyed the life she had created, the life with the man she loved. She was going to kill Tariq Ahmed and then she was going to kill Avi. The plan was simple, she would keep on killing until Bishop was safe and they were free.

Chapter Nineteen

LIFEBRIGHT FOUNDATION FACILITY, RWANDA

KURTZ RAISED his weapon as the rear doors of the food delivery truck rattled then swung open. The smiling face of the driver appeared in the gap.

"No problems, morning delivery."

Kurtz gave a thumbs up.

The fifty-year-old Rwandan had reason to be happy. Thirty thousand US dollars had bought his services and would ensure the prosperity of his large family for years to come. He swung the doors wide open, revealing an interior loading dock and a doorway into a commercial kitchen.

"Let's go," said Kruger as he stepped out of the truck wielding his own AK.

Kurtz turned to Bianca and gave her a nod before following his partner into the large kitchen. He carried his customized AK while Bianca toted an MP7 submachine gun. All three wore dark blue coveralls, the same as the cooks who now stood terrified as the team moved past them.

Over the work-wear they'd donned camouflage body armor covered in pouches. Strapped to Kruger's back were bolt cutters and a hooligan bar for breaching doors.

As they entered the kitchen Kurtz scanned for any security cameras. On the far side Kruger was paused next to a door. Kurtz spotted the card reader and digital lock as he and Bianca joined the South African.

"You want me to pop it?" Kruger asked.

"Do it," answered Kurtz.

Bianca let out a soft cough as she leaned forward and swiped a security card she'd taken from one of the kitchen staff.

The door clicked and Kruger pushed it open, letting Kurtz through into the facility beyond. The tall German emerged into a well-lit corridor with heavy doors on either side. He immediately spotted a security camera at the far end. Raising his AK he snapped off a single suppressed round, shattering it.

"There goes the element of surprise," said Bianca as she tried her swipe card on one of the doors. The lock emitted a loud beep and an LED flashed red. She tried once more and an alarm commenced shrieking.

"Surprise?" Kruger said.

"Get the door open!" yelled Kurtz.

The burly South African shrugged the hooligan bar from his shoulder and rammed it into the door jamb. With one heave he popped the lock and shoved the door open.

Kurtz aimed his weapon into the small cell, scanning for threats. It was empty but there were signs it was recently occupied. A blanket was crumpled on a low bed on each side of the room. "Open them all."

As Kruger went to work on the next cell a doorway at the end of the corridor opened and a figure appeared.

"Who are you?" a voice yelled.

"Housekeeping," replied Kurtz as he charged down the corridor.

Like the kitchen staff the man was a local clad in blue coveralls. His eyes went wide as Kurtz approached. "Please don't shoot me."

Kurtz let his rifle hang from its sling and grabbed the man by the front of his coveralls. "Where are the girls?"

"In, in, the cells," he stammered.

"The first one is empty."

"She's in the surgery." The man whimpered.

Kurtz turned and yelled over his shoulder. "Get the girls out of the cells." He turned his attention back to the worker. "Show me where the surgery is.

"Kurtz, I don't think we should split up," Bianca transmitted over her radio as Kurtz followed the man out of the corridor of cells.

"I'll be back in a few minutes."

On the other side of the security door there was another long corridor. This one had only two doors, at the far end. One side of the corridor was wall-to-ceiling frosted glass that blocked his view into the rooms beyond.

The man swiped him into the room on the left and pointed across a high-tech laboratory to another door. "Over there."

As they crossed, Kurtz gave the equipment a once over. It looked to be a highly sophisticated setup with scanners, centrifuges and a range of machines that looked like they'd be at home in a first-world clinic. He paused before a row of fluid-filled vats the size of incubators he'd seen in the children's ward of a hospital. "What are these?" he asked.

"It's where they grow the babies," the man said.

The hairs on the back of Kurtz's neck stood on end. "Grow babies? How do they grow babies?"

"I just clean. I'm not a doctor."

Kurtz aimed his weapon at the man's face. "They'll be cleaning you off the floor if you don't answer."

"They take the parts from the girls and put them in there."

He fought the urge to pull the trigger as the reality of what he'd said sunk in. Someone was harvesting body parts from the girls to create some kind of artificial womb. "Are they taking parts now?"

He nodded.

"Where?"

"Through that door."

Kurtz snatched the swipe card from around the man's neck. "I would leave if I were you."

As he made his way to the door, his earpiece crackled.

"Kurtz, we've found the girls. What's your status?"

"RAGE!" he responded as he swiped the card reader and kicked open the heavy door.

Two masked faces looked up at him as he stepped into the room. He spotted one of the missing schoolgirls strapped to a surgical table. A robed anesthetist held a plastic mask over her face.

"Who the hell are you?" demanded an elderly male with a foreign accent.

"Wake her up," Kurtz snarled.

"How dare you barge into my surgery. You're putting my entire project at risk. Where the hell is my damn security?"

In the facility's security office Elias smirked as the intruder felled Dr. Morrison with a brutal right cross. Now the doctor would know how he felt. His neck and head still ached from his run-in with the Canadian and her girlfriend. Hopefully both of them were here so he could take his revenge.

He'd been tracking the man's progress through the medical center by CCTV and door scanners. Like every good security operative, and Elias considered himself one of the best, he had a plan to deal with this contingency.

Rather than risk a gunfight inside the lab, which he was paid handsomely to protect, he would wait for the intruders to make their exit and ambush them. The girls would die in the crossfire, but they could be replaced. The expensive equipment and Dr. Morrison's research were far more valuable.

"Have the men and drones ready at the northern exit," he ordered his second-in-command. "I'll push them out from the south with Henderson and Scott." As the man left to coordinate the ambush he punched a code into a locker and removed his body armor and pump-action shotgun. He grinned as he fed double-ought buckshot into the magazine; this was what he lived for.

Back in the surgery Kurtz tapped his foot impatiently as the anesthetist attended to the girl. She'd not yet succumbed entirely to the gasses and was coming to.

"You're going to regret this," snarled the doctor from where he lay on the floor. "You've got no idea who you're messing with."

Kurtz fought the urge to put a bullet in the man's head as he used a knife to cut the girl free from nylon restraints.

"You're going to carry her," he said to the anesthetist. He turned his weapon on the doctor. "And you're going to make sure we get out of here in one piece. Failure to comply will result in your death."

Kurtz shepherded them into the laboratory where he

shrugged out of his backpack and took a demolition charge from inside. Activating the explosive device he slid it in behind two of the artificial birthing machines.

"What is that?" asked the doctor.

Kurtz ignored him and keyed his radio. "Kruger, I've recovered one of the girls. What's your status?"

The reply was immediate. "We've got another seven. Where are you?"

He swiped the exit from the lab. "I'm coming to you now."

Back in the corridor of cells Bianca held a sobbing child in her arms as Kruger jimmied the last of the doors and peered inside.

"This one's empty."

A door creaked and she spun, putting the kid behind her as she raised her submachine gun.

"You're going to die here, bitch!" She recognized the voice and the face glaring at her over the barrel of a shotgun. It was the head of security, the man who'd killed her informant.

"Fuck you!" Her weapon spat lead a split second before he fired. .45ACP rounds slapped into his vest. The shotgun blast went wide. Dust, debris and pellets ricocheted off the wall, spraying Bianca. She winced as a chip of cement sliced her cheek.

Another weapon fired as Kruger moved up alongside her and unleashed a burst from his AK. Bullets splintered the doorframe forcing the security thug back.

"This way!" screamed Kurtz from where he'd appeared behind them. The German waved them through another door as he held an elderly man with one arm around his throat. "Get the girls out. I'll cover you."

Bianca led the line of seven girls down the corridor.

Accurate shots from her weapon destroyed the lock on the door at the other end of the hall and she shouldered it open. "This way."

Behind her, Kurtz waited for Kruger to pass with the last girl before he fired another burst along the corridor. Running the mag empty he was forced to release the doctor as he reached for a replacement in his vest.

The surgeon took the opportunity to escape. He dashed toward his guards. Kurtz felt no sympathy as the doctor ran directly into a shotgun blast. An ounce of buckshot hit him like a sledgehammer, shredding his torso. Kurtz finished his mag change as he turned and slammed the door behind him, hoping like hell it was reinforced.

As Kurtz fought a rearguard action Bianca had found the motley team a way out. She pushed through a fire exit and emerged into a parking lot. Holding the door ajar she took a quick breath of fresh air as she scanned the half dozen parked vehicles.

She turned to Kruger who was waiting with the girls and the anesthetist, carrying the semi-conscious girl. "I'll check it out," she yelled over the gunfire behind them.

She propped open the heavy fire door and dashed a few feet to the side of an SUV. Peering around the vehicle she concentrated on the tree line past a security gate. Right as she thought it was clear she saw a glint in the scrub. Narrowing her eyes she spotted the outline of a man's head and shoulders. "Damn!"

Gunfire erupted and bullets tore into the vehicle she was using as cover. Glass showered her as the distinct rattle of AKs filled the air. "Guys, they've got the drop on us."

Kurtz fired into the smoke and dust that filled the corridor they'd escaped along. He was holed up at a doorway that led into a storeroom where Kruger and the girls were seeking refuge. His magazine ran empty and he let it drop from the gun. He was down to his last. What was supposed to have been a straight-forward mission had turned into what Bishop would call a shit show. It was time to enact the contingency plan.

Bianca was hunkered down behind the engine block of the now hole-ridden SUV. Her ambushers had lowered their rate of fire now they had her pinned. Kruger had managed to fire a few bursts from the doorway, but they also had a bead on his position. The rumble of a diesel engine caught her attention and she spotted a tracked vehicle trundling out of the tree line. A machine gun chattered as the drone opened fire.

"Guys, what the hell are we going to do?" she transmitted.

"It's OK, the cavalry is on the way," replied Kurtz.

"Screw the cavalry, we need a tank battalion." More bullets slapped into the SUV and she screamed in rage. She slid sideways to the rear of the swiss-cheesed vehicle and thrust her MP7 around the tailgate.

The gun spluttered, throwing bullets into the thick scrub. At that moment there was a roar from above and the bush exploded into a wall of fire as a volley of rockets hit it. Two drones were shredded by the onslaught, their sensors shattered. Trees and shrubs disintegrated in a hail of lead as brass casings rained down on her like scorching hot hail. She glanced up at the underbelly of a helicopter, the morning sun dancing off its spinning blades as it rained down destruction.

"The cavalry!" she mouthed.

Back inside the facility Kurtz had expended his last

magazine and was down to his pistol. Picking up on the lapse in fire the head of security and his team were pressing home their attack. Shotgun blasts reverberated along the hallway, forcing Kurtz back. "Last mag," he announced.

"Chopper's on the deck and the girls are almost all onboard," reported Kruger.

A hail of gunfire announced the security team's assault. Kurtz backed into the storeroom as he fired the last of his bullets. As the slide of his pistol locked open he dropped it and pulled a remote from his pocket. Glancing at the doorway he spotted a broad-shouldered silhouette of a guard and the gaping barrel of a shotgun.

Elias realized his target was unarmed and paused. Smiling manically he snarled, "Oh you and your bitches are fucked now. You're going to die here."

Kurtz thumbed the trigger and the demolition charge he'd left in the laboratory exploded. A thunderous shock wave slammed into the guard, throwing him sideways as he fired the shotgun. The blast hit Kurtz in the chest, pitching him rearward as the building collapsed. Lumps of concrete fell from above as he fought for air. Stumbling he landed on his back, facing the crumbling roof.

Time slowed as he realized he was going to make it. Even though death was imminent, Kurtz felt strangely at peace. He'd rescued the last of the girls, made right on the debt that he had with the world.

"Wake up dip shit!"

Kurtz felt himself being dragged out of the building by the scruff of his neck. Soon he was clear of the building and beneath under the spinning rotor of Toppie's helicopter. He let out a groan as he climbed to his feet.

"Always laying about on the job!" Kruger screamed over

the chopper's engines as he gave Kurtz a solid slap on the shoulder. "Let's get the hell out of here."

He managed to climb into the back of the helicopter where Booyah and Bianca were handing blankets and juice boxes to the eight girls they'd rescued. Kurtz spotted the girl he'd recovered from the surgery at the front of the helicopter. There was no sign of the anesthetist. As he moved forward, he bumped knuckles with Booyah. "Just in the nick of time."

"Just like the time you saved my hand," said the Somali. "Now we're even, right."

Kurtz checked to make sure everyone was seated and stuck his head into the cockpit. "Toppie, good you finally got to use those rockets. Let's get the hell out of here."

The scruffy, bearded pilot gave him a nod before throttling up the powerful turbines, sending the massive helicopter skyward. Glancing out the window Kurtz noted with satisfaction that the Lifebright facility, or what was left of it, was ablaze.

He felt someone sit alongside and turned to see that it was Bianca. Despite a filthy blood-splattered face, she was grinning from ear to ear. "That was amazing," she yelled over the engine noise.

Kurtz shook his head and looked to the back of the chopper to where Kruger was sitting with Booyah. Like Bianca, both men wore broad smiles. The hulking South African shot him thumbs up and Kurtz responded with a nod. Looking past them out the back of the helicopter at the burning facility he wondered how many girls had died within its walls. How many families would never know what had happened to their daughters and sisters?

He felt Bianca's hand on his. She wore a concerned expression.

"Are you OK?" she asked.

"I'm going to find the people responsible for this."

She squeezed his hand. "Let me help."

"It will be dangerous," he replied.

"Sounds perfect. When can we get started?"

———

REQUENA, SPAIN

"That's the van," Keila said, pointing to a white Mercedes Sprinter parked alongside a drab looking apartment block. "Right where they said it would be."

Ice was sitting behind the wheel of her hire car. He'd driven them from Bishop's cottage to the address that Keila's team had passed. Her analysts had used traffic cameras to track the van across town. Daisy had remained curled up on the back seat throughout the entire four-hour drive.

"Your people are pretty good."

"They're the best. Now, all we have to do is watch the truck and someone will lead us to Bishop."

They sat in silence for a moment.

"Or," said Ice as he reached for the door handle, "we can go find him." He opened the door and made to climb out.

"Wait, what are you going to do? Knock on doors?"

He stuck his head back into the car. "What do you think I am, some kind of idiot?"

She shrugged.

Ice opened one of the rear doors. "Come on Daisy, let's find Bishop."

The dog dashed outside with her nose held high. Running across to the van she sniffed around the rear doors with her tail wagging rapidly.

"Shit!" Keila drew her pistol, checking she had a round chambered. Then she left the car and chased Ice who was following Daisy up a flight of stairs. "Wait up," she hissed.

The dog stopped in front of a door and pawed it as she whined. Ice glanced over his shoulder at Keila as he stopped short. "You good?"

"No, wait—"

Ice pulled Daisy away from the door and ordered her to sit. Then he rapped on it with his knuckles.

When there was no response, he knocked again.

A moment later the door opened a crack. "Hi. I was wondering if you'd like to buy some Girl Guide cookies," he said.

If Keila had blinked she would have missed what happened next. Ice kicked the door in, tearing the security latch from the frame. The man inside was smashed against the wall, pinned by the solid wooden door. Ice punched him in the face, knocking him out. Grabbing the pistol the man had dropped he racked the slide before hauling the unconscious man to his feet and carrying him one-handed into the living room.

There were two more men in the living room, both with weapons drawn. Ice tossed their unconscious teammate across the room at them. The body forced them back against the couch. One of the men got a shot off and the bullet punched a hole in the ceiling mere inches from Ice's head.

"Drop the guns," he barked as they struggled out from under the body.

One of the men complied, but the other raised his weapon. Ice shot him through the forearm sending the pistol flying. Then he reached down and grasped the wounded man's throat with his robotic hand. "How many?"

Keila had entered and now covered the other man.

"Just, just the three of us." The wounded man managed between gritted teeth.

"If you're lying, you're all going to die."

"Just three."

"And your prisoner?"

"In the bedroom."

He left Keila guarding them and opened the door to the bedroom, revealing a bedraggled looking Bishop cuffed to a chair. The Australian winked as Ice entered the room. "You took your sweet ass time."

Ice chuckled as he took a multitool from his pocket and used it to pick the cuffs. "Sorry, I had a few things I had to do."

A bark sounded then Daisy shot into the room, leaped into her owner's lap and licked his face.

"I see you had some help."

"Yeah, but not just Daisy."

Bishop lowered the dog to the floor and stretched his arms over his head. "Is Saneh here?"

"No, not Saneh." Ice gestured to the door.

Bishop stepped out of the bedroom and saw Keila covering the three men who'd abducted him.

"Hello, Aden," she said with a smile.

"Keila, thanks for helping Ice out. I hope he wasn't too much of a burden."

She shrugged. "He goes alright for an old guy."

"Yeah, well I really appreciate the effort." He turned to Ice. "You got a phone I can borrow?"

Ice handed him a phone and Bishop dialed the number he had for Saneh. Three times he tried and three times the number failed to connect. "Do you have another way of contacting Saneh?"

"You using her burn number?"

Bishop nodded.

"That's all I got, bud. I had contact with her yesterday. She was in Dubai, taking care of something."

Handing the phone back to Ice he turned his attention to the three men Keila was guarding. "You guys going to talk?"

The man he'd nicknamed Biceps shrugged. "We ain't got nothing to tell you. We got the contract to pick you up and hold you, that's it."

"Whose contract?" asked Keila.

"Some generic sounding firm. It'll be a cut out for someone else. That's the way it always works."

"So you're guns for hire?" She sounded disgusted.

"Hey, we gotta make a living."

"How did the bid come in?" she asked.

"Same way it always does, over the app."

"There's an app for this kind of thing?" Ice asked.

"Yeah big man, there's an app for everything," replied Biceps.

Bishop held out his hand. "Phone please."

The contractor reluctantly handed it over.

"Password?"

"0112"

He slid the device into his pocket. "Well, you guys treated me pretty good except for the part where you tried to kill my dog. But, I'm not going to get all John Wick on your asses. Although, if we cross paths again I'm going to send the big guy after you."

The two conscious men nodded, glancing at Ice who smiled.

"Let's get out of here," said Keila.

A minute later Bishop was sitting in the back of Keila's car with Daisy. Ice was back behind the wheel with Keila riding shotgun.

"I can help you find Saneh," said the Israeli operative as they weaved their way through traffic.

"If your people haven't found her already," said Bishop.

"Aden, I want you to know I had nothing to do with any of this."

"You're not with Mossad anymore?" he said sarcastically.

"Look, my team was shut out of Lascar Logistics. I'm not supposed to have any contact with you."

Bishop looked her in the eyes. "So who's after us?"

"I can't say but I think it's got something to do with your girlfriend. The organization has a black-listed file on her that I can't access."

He nodded as he patted Daisy's head and gazed out at the vine-covered hills flashing by. "I really didn't expect you to come find me. Not going to forget that anytime soon."

"You did the same for me in Iraq."

"True."

"Bish," interrupted Ice as he turned on to a highway. "We heading to the airport?"

"Yep, if Saneh is looking for me I know where she'll go."

"That works for me," said Keila. "I'll get back to work and see how I can help."

Bishop reached forward and grasped her shoulder. "I'm not going to forget this."

Keila nodded then glanced sideways at Ice. "Where you heading big guy?"

Ice shrugged. "Someone better keep an eye on these two." He tipped his chin in the direction of Daisy and Bishop.

She laughed. "Well at least we know they're in good hands."

Chapter Twenty

ABU DHABI, UAE

SANEH BACKED her hire car into the parking lot at the Lascar Logistics cargo terminal, grabbed a rucksack from the passenger seat and left the vehicle. Using her company ID she swiped through a gate and made her way between two hangars to a security door. A biometric scan granted her access and, for the first time since it had been shut down, she entered the PRIMAL hangar.

The first thing she noticed was the absence of aircraft from the cavernous space. She guessed that Tariq had moved the Priority Movements Airlift business jet and cargo plane to another location. Then she remembered that Mitch was using the highly modified Gulfstream as a part of his new business in California.

A lump formed in her throat as she remembered all the missions that the team had run from inside this structure. She pushed the thought from her head as she crossed the floor to the corner where transportable buildings and shipping containers had once formed an operating base.

As she approached she noticed that only the shipping containers remained. The planning room, accommodation and gym had all been removed.

She placed her backpack in front of a container door secured with a padlock. From her bag she took a cordless angle grinder fitted with a carbide blade. Attacking the lock with an ear-splitting shriek and shower of sparks it took her less than twenty seconds to cut it free.

Then she took a flashlight from her pack and pulled the latch on the door to Mitch's armory. The heavy steel door swung open with a creak. Inside, the confined spaced had been modified, most likely in preparation for shipment to the US. Gone was the wall of weapons, workbench and engineering equipment. Instead she saw plastic cases stacked deep on both sides of a narrow walkway.

The Pelican cases were neatly labeled and it didn't take long to find the one she wanted. Sliding the long black case out from under another crate she wheeled it from the container and cracked it open on the floor of the hangar.

The RT-20 anti-materiel rifle inside was dismantled and packed inside laser cut foam inserts. She pried each of the parts free and snapped the weapon together. Saneh had been the first and most likely the last to fire the gun after Mitch had modified it. The technician had improved the recoilless system so it could be fired indoors. Additionally, he'd shortened the barrel, making the heavy rifle easier to handle and carry. It fired 20mm armor-piercing cartridges, six of which were included in the box. During testing the bullets had penetrated carbon nanotube armor, and more importantly, inches of bulletproof glass.

Assembled, the weapon weighed over 40 pounds and

was nearly five-foot long. She tested all the components, chambered a cartridge and lay behind the gun, tucking it into her shoulder. Comfortable that everything was in order she disassembled it and placed all the parts into her backpack. The barrel of the weapon didn't fit inside so she put a sports sock over the muzzle. Once she'd returned the Pelican case to where she'd found it, she slung the heavy backpack over her shoulder and closed the container door.

On the way out of the hangar she felt an overwhelming sense of loss. There was no doubt in her mind that what she was about to do would utterly destroy what relationship she still had with the PRIMAL team. Anger replaced sadness as she focused on the betrayal she'd experienced at the hands of someone she trusted. Tariq had single-handedly destroyed the life she had built and put the man she loved in danger. For that his life was forfeit.

TEL AVIV, ISRAEL

Asher's finger hovered over the mouse and he exhaled slowly. His next move could well be career ending. By activating the query to locate Keila's target, Saneh, he was directly violating an order from the Mossad Director of Special Operations to close out all of the Lascar related tasks. He had no doubt that if Lisker got wind of what he was doing, his work at 8200 was over. However, Keila was adamant that the Director was corrupt, and Asher did hate him. More to the point he really, really liked Keila.

"Screw it," he murmured as he activated the search. Worst case he'd get booted from 8200 and accept his best friend's job offer.

The query was one of the most sophisticated he'd built and probably the most effective signals intelligence capability he'd ever employed. Powerful algorithms took a seemingly dead number and checked every possible avenue to locate the user's new device. The *piece-de-resistance* of the system was its ability to correlate historical tower data and identify trends regarding device linkages.

Locking his workstation he left his office and visited the coffee machine in the foyer of his building. It made terrible coffee but he didn't want to risk leaving the building while he was running a search.

Moments later he was back at his desk nursing a polystyrene cup filled with lukewarm caffeinated UHT milk. Unlocking his workstation he checked the application. Much to his surprise it already had a hit. He scribbled the number on a post-it note and stuck it in his pocket. Then, out of interest, he activated an alert blocking program and ran it against the 8200 databases.

His hunch paid off. The number was blacklisted, meaning that someone, most likely Manfred Lisker, didn't want anyone tracking it or listening in on it.

Ditching his coffee in a trashcan he swiped out of the secure office and collected his phone from a security locker. Once he was clear of the building he sent a text to Keila and made his way to the coffee shop. With the stress of the situation he definitely needed a decent cup.

The coffees he'd ordered were ready at almost the same time Keila appeared. As they walked around a corner together he handed her the beverage with the post-it note slipped into the cardboard sleeve.

"You're the best."

"He's watching this one. Be careful."

"Got it."

He waited as she sent a text from a phone then removed the sim card and snapped it in half.

"You do know that's not an infallible method."

She winked. "No one can hide from you, right?"

"It's not just me. Be careful."

"I will."

————

ABU DHABI, UAE

Fuelled by petrodollars and foreign investment Abu Dhabi had no shortage of construction sites near Saneh's target building. She'd chosen one a block away and overrode the security system giving her access to a loading dock. As she parked her hire car alongside stacks of construction materials a security guard approached.

"The site is closed today," he said once she'd lowered the window. It was Friday, a day of rest in the Emirates.

Saneh smiled. "I'm here to review the health and safety register."

The man looked confused. "No one told me about—" His eyes went wide as the twin barbs of Saneh's Taser thudded into his chest. Convulsing, he dropped to the ground.

"Sorry," she said as she stepped out of the car and taped his hands, feet and mouth.

Hefting her backpack from the trunk of the car she walked past the bound security guard to a freight elevator. She chose the 56th floor of the recently constructed tower, which she'd calculated as the same height as her target. According to the development company's website the level was destined to become offices.

The floor she'd selected was yet to be fitted with internal walls or windows. Hot desert air swept through the open space as she unzipped her pack and removed the components of the rifle. Her hands shook as she fitted the parts together and she fought the urge to cry. Exhaling, she managed to mount the optic and power up the thermal imager.

Lying behind the weapon she chambered one of the six-inch-long armor-piercing rounds and tucked the stock into her shoulder. Adjusting the scope she scanned her target building.

She located Tariq Ahmed exactly where she knew he'd be, sitting behind his desk in the penthouse office of Lascar Tower. The man was a workaholic who took the responsibility of running a billion-dollar corporation personally.

Saneh knew from her time in the office that the windows were made of two-inch-thick ballistic glass. She also knew that Mitch's custom 20mm ammunition would slice through them like a hot knife through butter.

The laser range finder built into her scope told her that Tariq's back was a little over eight hundred and six yards from her weapon. That meant that once she squeezed the trigger the Arab would have less than a second of life left before the massive projectile blasted him into oblivion.

Tariq was a man who Saneh had admired. The first son of an Arab extremist he'd taken a stand against his father and put an end to the hate and violence. Working with Vance, Ice and Chua, he created PRIMAL, an organization that had given Saneh a second chance at life. But, he had betrayed all of that when he'd sold her out to Mossad and subsequently put Bishop's life in danger.

She exhaled, cleared her mind and took up the slack in the trigger.

The trill of the burner phone Avi had provided almost caused her to fire the shot. Backing off the trigger she took the phone from her backpack and checked the screen. The number was blocked. It had to be the Mossad operative.

She answered it. "What do you want?"

"OK, not the response I was expecting."

"Bishop?" Her heart jumped. "Wait, how did you get this number?"

"Yeah, I'm fine babe. Ice found me, with a little help from our friend in Tel Aviv."

Saneh swallowed the lump that had formed in her throat. "Aden, I'm so sorry. I should have told you everything."

"Look, it's all good. I just wanted to let you know I'm safe. I'm on my way to our lady now."

It took Saneh a moment to realize what he was saying. "OK, I'll meet you there as soon as I can."

She felt elated as she rose from behind the weapon and ended the call. Staring at the phone for a moment she smiled and tossed it out the side of the building. Then she packed the sniper rifle and took the elevator back to the loading dock.

As she descended Saneh was filled with hope. With Bishop rescued from Lisker's clutches and the rest of the team enacting Exodus the two of them were free to run.

The elevator doors opened and she stepped out into the loading dock. First things first, she needed to free the security guard. As she approached where she'd left him she immediately sensed something was wrong. The guard's head was twisted to one side. She checked his pulse. He was dead.

"Do I always have to clean up after you?"

She spun and saw Avi leaning against a stack of drywall. He winked. "Hello, Saneh. I take it our mutual friend is deceased?" He had one hand behind his back, no doubt holding the pistol that would end her life once she confirmed mission success.

With the rifle dismantled her only weapons were the Taser and her stiletto.

Avi tipped his head ever so slightly to one side. "Is that a no?" The pistol appeared. "I'm going to enjoy this."

"Not as much as me." In one smooth movement she drew her knife and tossed it as she dove sideways, behind her car.

Avi's weapon barked and bullets punched through the car windows as she landed on her side. "You're so fucking dead!" he yelled. His rage told Saneh that her blade had found purchase.

She shrugged out of the backpack and gripped her Taser as rounds thudded into the car. Another two shots snapped past her as she sprinted to a stack of steel piping and hid behind it.

"There's nowhere you can run," he yelled.

She frantically searched for an escape route. Leaping onto a raised dock she rolled in behind a stack of electrical cable spools. Peering through a gap she saw Avi moving deliberately with his pistol held ready. Aiming her Taser she waited till he was in range and fired.

One barb struck Avi in the arm but the other sailed over his shoulder failing to complete the circuit. She immediately ejected the second cartridge as he fired a volley of shots into the spools.

Saneh felt a round tug her jacket as she dashed to the next pallet of building materials.

"You're just going to die tired!" yelled Avi as he gave chase.

She leaped through an open door into a section of the

building site that had framing and walls constructed. Ducking and weaving through the maze of offices and corridors she hunted for a way out.

Pausing behind a wall she held the Taser ready. Her heartbeat thumped in her ears as she concentrated on keeping her breathing under control. There was a noise to her right and she adjusted her grip on the weapon.

The wall alongside her exploded as a bullet punched through the sheetrock. She dove as more rounds punched through the wall. Scrambling across the concrete she lost her grip on the Taser. More gunfire thundered and she rolled sideways into a half-completed room. There was a stack of drums below a gap in the ceiling. She clambered up and squeezed through the gap.

The space was bigger than she anticipated and she found herself hunched over in the metal framing designed to hold cabling and ducting. Having moved deeper into the space she spotted a worker's toolbox alongside rolls of cabling. She took a hammer from inside and felt its weight in her hands.

As she considered moving she glanced down through a light fitting and saw Avi standing below. The Mossad operative was scanning the rooms around him.

Rage flowed through her veins like hot lava as she focused on the pain that Avi and his boss had caused her. With the hammer clenched in one hand she stepped off the metal framing onto the thin ceiling.

Saneh crashed through the roof, knocking Avi to the ground in a shower of debris. She landed sideways on top of him, her elbow smashing into the concrete. Rolling clear she swung the hammer at his gun hand. The pistol fired as she smashed his fingers against the floor and he screamed in agony. A second blow dislodged the gun and sent it skidding away.

He lashed out with his good hand and connected with the side of her head. Vision blurred, she swung the hammer again. He caught her wrist and began to twist the hammer.

Spinning away she kicked sideways and made contact with his groin. He let out a grunt and hit her with his wounded fist. The blow came with the sickening wet crunch of the broken bones in his hand. Avi bellowed and Saneh scrambled on top of him. She forced the hammer closer to his face as she slid an elbow across his throat and pushed down with all her weight.

Avi was much stronger and forced his hips up in a Krav Maga move known as bridging. Saneh managed to stay on top but knew she wouldn't be able to control him for long.

She ran with a second thrust and let him toss her over his head. Instead of fighting to stay balanced she flicked her feet skyward and rolled across the floor. Spinning her legs like a breakdancer she spun into a crouch and grabbed his pistol from the floor. Avi was almost as fast, launching toward her with his good fist cocked.

She fired a single round and the Mossad operative collapsed, skidding across the cement. The bullet had torn through his neck leaving his body limp in a spreading pool of blood.

"I'm out!" she hissed as she wiped her prints from the pistol and tossed it next to his body. "And your boss is next."

––––––

TARIQ AHMED STOOD at the window of his office and gazed down at the flashing lights on the street below. There must have been an incident at the worksite next door.

Returning to his desk he continued reading the file he'd printed. It was the work that Flash had completed before leaving the country.

The report wasn't as damning as he would have liked, but it did link payment for arms shipments to Sakkin Industries, an Israeli company with defense contracts.

What Tariq was missing was the connection between Manfred Lisker and Sakkin Industries. He was pretty sure that was a link he was never going to be able to prove. Not with hard evidence. All he could hope for was that Flash's file was enough to prompt a more detailed investigation.

He added the printed manifests from the Lascar flights to the folder and slid them into a thin black attaché case before locking it. Then he picked up his desk phone and dialed the Lascar Logistics operations room as he checked his watch.

"It's Tariq, can you please have my jet ready for a nineteen hundred departure."

"Yes sir, what is the destination?"

"Tel Aviv, Israel."

He ended the call and took the attaché case from his desk. As he left the office he passed his assistant's empty desk. Friday and Saturday were the weekend in Dubai. On Fridays he handled his own administration including driving himself to the office. Prior to his flight he would dine with his wife and children, before praying. Beyond that, there was no real certainty.

LAVRIO, GREECE

Ice unhooked a mooring line from a rusted bollard and tossed it to Bishop who was standing at the stern of his boat, *Susurro*. Striding along the floating pontoon, he did the same for the bowline then paused at the edge of the dock. "Permission to come aboard, Captain?"

Bishop threw him a mock salute. "Permission granted."

They finished stowing the mooring lines before descending the steps into the interior of the ketch.

"Damn this is nice," said Ice as they passed through the neat galley into the main living area.

"Mitch's handy work," replied Bishop as he controlled the vessel's thrusters from the tablet strung around his neck. Electric propulsion pods drew power from banks of solid-state batteries hidden along the keel. He touched an icon and high-resolution screens appeared from behind polished wooden furnishings. They displayed the feed from an array of cameras positioned around the hull and on the mast.

"That's some high tech gear."

"And that coming from the six million dollar man," said Bishop as he programmed a route for the yacht that took them out of the marina and into the Mediterranean.

"So, what's the go with Saneh and Mossad?" asked Ice when Bishop looked up. He had already updated him on the attack on the Sandpit and their narrow escape.

"Remember, Keila said her team's file on Saneh was blocked. Compartmented."

"And she implied that someone in her organization was going after her network. Us."

"Yeah, but to what end?" Bishop stepped back into the galley, opened a fridge and removed two Coopers beers. He handed one to Ice and they sat on either side of a retractable table. "Thanks for the rescue mate."

They touched bottles.

"My pleasure."

Bishop wore a frown as he drank and wiped his mouth with the back of his hand. "I think Mossad has leverage over Saneh."

"Over a former Iranian intelligence operative?"

He nodded. "Yeah, someone in the organization has been pulling her strings. You know the guy we were guarding in the Emirates?"

"The tech guy who died?"

"Someone accessed the building using her security pass. She told me she'd lost hers at the conference."

"You think she killed him?"

"God no. I think someone forced her to give them access."

"Is there a link between the tech guy and Mossad?"

Bishop took another swig as he shook his head. "Not that I can see, but then again we don't have Chua onboard to sort that out."

"You heard from him or Vance?"

"Not yet, they're following Exodus to the letter." He paused. "Ice, I think someone from Mossad kidnapped me to control Saneh."

Ice sipped his beer thoughtfully. "Yeah, and if I was Saneh, with you free I'd be looking to cut the strings controlling me."

"The question is how?"

"That part is simple. I'd kill my handler."

The realization hit them simultaneously.

"She's going to assassinate someone in Mossad," said Bishop.

"Not even Saneh is going to get out of that alive," added Ice.

Bishop leaned to his right and touched a panel, revealing a rack of rechargeable cordless headsets. "I need to contact Keila. We need to stop Saneh before it's too late."

Chapter Twenty-One

ROTOBURN, NEW ZEALAND

CHUA STARED out of the window of the Squirrel helicopter as it hammered along a narrow gorge. If it wasn't for the highway that snaked alongside the crystal blue water of a river he could have been back in Afghanistan. The mountains around them were devoid of trees and had the same craggy outcrops that the Taliban favored for observation.

The helicopter punched out of the gorge and the river expanded into a lake bounded by more mountains and a valley covered in green orchards and vineyards.

"The mountain biking here is going to be unbelievable," he said into his headset.

"The Pinot Noir is world-class," added the pilot as they climbed over a mountain range and descended toward an expansive green valley.

"How long have you had this place?" he asked Vance, who was staring out the window on the opposite side.

"Bought it sight unseen a few years back. Bishop has spent a bit of time here and said it was the ducks nuts. I think that means it's good."

"OK, that's our landing zone." The pilot gestured to a black pickup parked alongside a grass airstrip. There was a figure standing next to the truck.

The chopper flared before touching down. The pilot helped them unload their bags as the figure from the vehicle approached. Chua recognized the bald head and bushy beard of PRIMAL's former technician and head pilot, Mitch Freeman.

"Lads, welcome to Kiwi land."

Chua winced as the muscle-bound Brit hugged him.

"You OK?" he asked as he exchanged back slaps with Vance.

"He took a bullet."

"No shit."

"Just a graze," said Chua.

The chopper interrupted their conversation as it took off, whipping the grass and dust into a frenzy as Mitch tossed their bags into the back of a Volkswagen pickup. He drove them out of the field onto a sealed road that curved down into a wide valley.

"There she is."

A long white building with a raked iron roof appeared from behind a row of tall lush green trees. With its small wooden-framed windows the building looked turn of the century, a contrast to the antennas and solar panels that adorned the roof. They turned off the main road and an automatic gate set in a rock wall swung open revealing sweeping lawns and a hangar-sized garage. Mitch drove the truck inside and a roller-door closed behind them. As Chua climbed out of the pickup he noted the well-equipped gym at the opposite end, and the tool-laden pin boards and workbenches on either side. There were also a range of vehicles, including a tracked All Terrain Vehicle (ATV), dirt bikes and a Range Rover SUV. He grinned as he spotted a rack of mountain bikes hanging from the roof.

"Mitch, you've outdone yourself," said Vance as he made a beeline for the gym.

"You ain't seen nothing yet." Mitch activated a remote control and the squat rack rose a foot into the air and slid rearward revealing a set of stairs.

Chua shook his head and descended into a hidden armory.

"I took the liberty of equipping it with all your favorites," yelled Mitch from above.

The space stretched twenty feet under the garage and was eight feet wide. On one side the wall was covered with weapons. The other side had shelves stacked with black cases and boxes of equipment.

"How the hell did you get this all here?" asked Chua as he climbed back up the stairs.

"I have my ways. OK, let me show you the pub."

"The pub? You bought a pub?" Chua asked Vance.

"It used to be a pub. Now it's our safe house."

"Slash retirement home," said Mitch with a chuckle as he closed the armory and led them out of the garage into the backyard.

"Taste that air," said Vance as he inhaled deeply.

Chua took in the sweeping lawns and what looked to be a natural swimming hole. "This is amazing."

"There's a sauna and outdoor bathroom over there," said Mitch as they walked to the rear of the hundred-year-old hotel. "You've got six bedrooms in total, a bar, kitchen, dining room and an office. I've been calling it The Hub."

"We expecting a lot of guests?" said Chua.

Vance shrugged. "Hey, when you live somewhere this awesome you gotta share the love."

Mitch opened the rear door and showed them into a long hallway with white walls and dark wooden floors. Industrial bulbs hung from the ceiling.

"Love what you've done with the place," said Vance.

Chua wore a look of concern. "Vance said this place was a black hole, do we even have Wi-Fi?"

Mitch let out a snort. "You're hooked into high speed fiber. Wi-Fi repeaters cover the whole property and then some." He pressed his thumb to a biometric lock and pushed open a door revealing a well-equipped office. "You've got all the systems you need and a few extras. Flash says it's more secure than anything he's previously built. Kept banging on about the Dark Web."

"Good to know," said Vance.

"You heard from any of the others?" asked Mitch as Chua sat behind a desktop. The device registered his face and allowed him to access the operating system.

"Only Kruger and Kurtz," Chua replied. "They extracted the last of the girls they were hunting from a human trafficker in Rwanda." He opened a communication application and found a handle for Bishop. "I'm going to check in with Bish."

The application rang and a moment later it connected.

"Hey, guys." Bishop's Australian accent was particularly noticeable. "I've got Ice with me here on the *Susurro*."

"Ice, buddy I knew you'd be OK. Vance and I felt terrible about leaving."

"All good. At least this time it didn't take five years for me to surface," replied Ice referencing his time in a CIA black site. "Tariq helped me with my exfil. Hey, how you doing? That wound looked nasty."

"I'm, OK. I've got Mitch and Vance with me here in The Hub."

"The Hub, is that the name of your retirement home?" asked Bishop.

"Laugh it up asshole, we're all retired now," said Vance.

"This is true."

"Tell us about your E&E? Is Saneh with you?" asked Chua.

"Not yet. We're literally heading out to meet her right now and then we're hitting the high seas. Good to hear from you guys. Drop us a call later on."

"Will do, fair sailing." Chua ended the call and turned to face Vance. "You get the feeling that something's out of place there?"

Vance shrugged. "Everyone's in a state of flux."

"Yeah, you're probably right."

"OK guys," interrupted Mitch. "I'm going to show you the bar."

Vance cracked his knuckles. "Hell yeah, I could slay a beer."

———

MOGADISHU, SOMALIA

Jamilah's throat was dry and her heart pounded as she stepped from the rear of the helicopter that had rescued her and the others. They'd landed on the soccer pitch at the school from where they'd been kidnapped. Past the goals she could see a large crowd gathering. Tentatively she walked forward and the other girls followed her. Then, as someone in the crowd identified a loved one, there were cries of joy and names were shouted. Girls ran into the arms of their mothers, sisters, brothers and fathers.

"JAMILAH!" the voice was loud and clear over the commotion and it was one she instantly recognized.

Her younger sister, who she'd last seen when they'd been separated in a rebel camp, burst from the crowd and tore across the pitch toward her.

Kurtz stepped from the side door of the helicopter and smiled as he watched the reunion.

"That's what it's all about," said Bianca from behind him.

"*Ja*, it is." He spotted a familiar face in the crowd. Al-Mumit, the pirate king and financier of the operation, was crying as he watched a woman embracing her daughter. Kurtz hadn't realized that one of the kidnapped girls must have been a direct relative of the Somali gangster.

"That's why the money kept coming," said Kruger as he joined them.

"I'd do it for free," said Kurtz.

"Whoa, you crazy Kraut. We're not running a charity here," said Toppie as he stepped out. He tipped his head in the direction of their filthy helicopter. "That thing doesn't run on thoughts and prayers."

The team broke into laughter as Booyah joined them. "What's so funny?"

"Kurtz wants to give Al-Mumit his money back," said Kruger.

"A noble gesture," said the Somalian.

Kruger's forehead creased. "What the hell? Am I surrounded by idiot altruists?"

"That's a big word for you," said Bianca.

"I read it in a Batman comic." Kruger turned to Kurtz. "So what next?"

"I will distribute the profits. I'm happy for Bianca to have half of my share."

"No, I mean what's the next mission?"

"Next mission?" Kurtz asked.

"I'm in," said Bianca.

Kurtz shook his head. "No. I meant there is no mission. We're shut down."

"Who says?" asked Toppie. "Kurtz, you've got your own show here. We can do whatever we want."

"Yes, I am in too," added Booyah.

"If you don't have a mission in mind, I've got some ideas," said Bianca. "I've got contacts in a few areas focusing on people smuggling and exploitation."

"I like your thinking," said Kurtz. "But like Toppie said, we need funding and Al-Mumit's cash will only go so far."

Toppie laughed. "I'm taking the piss. I was an arms dealer, got plenty of cash."

Kruger snickered. "Was?"

The disheveled pilot spat in the dust. "Yeah, I've got a new occupation now, idiot altruist."

———

TEL AVIV, ISRAEL

Saneh exhaled as she slumped into the rear seat of a taxi at Ben Gurion Airport in Tel Aviv.

"Tough day?" the driver asked in Arabic.

"Sorry?" she answered with an American accent, despite understanding the man.

"You have a tough day?" he asked in English.

"Long flight."

She pulled her baseball hat a little lower as she ran over her plan. She'd flown into the country on a US passport that she'd squirreled away for such an occasion. Her research had revealed that there was an Aerospace conference in town and she'd booked herself a ticket. According to her entry visa she was an aviation consultant with a small software firm based in Seattle. The cover story was thin at best, but it had gotten her into the country.

"Don't I know you?"

The comment startled Saneh and she quickly shook her head. "No, I've never been to Israel before."

"No, not from here, on TV."

Saneh chuckled. "I don't think so."

"Are you sure?"

"Quite sure."

The driver nodded but continued to study her in the mirror, making Saneh feel uneasy.

When he dropped her at a hotel a few minutes later, she waited for the taxi to disappear before walking the few hundred yards to her actual booking. It was another precaution that was probably unnecessary but helped calm her nerves.

Checking in under a separate fake identity she carried her small suitcase into her room and immediately confirmed the view out the window. The building diagonally opposite looked unassuming, a grey office block with an entry point for sub-level parking. Saneh knew from her time in MOIS that this was where Mossad housed their analytical teams and bureaucracy. This was where Manfred Lisker would have his office.

Content that she would be able to surveil the building she unpacked. Opening the suitcase on the bed she removed two phones she'd recovered from Avi, along with a laptop modified for cell phone exploitation. Then she tore the inside lining of the suitcase to reveal what Mitch called the covert kill kit. It was a single sheet of nanotech composite that doubled as the wall of the case. However, like a children's activity set the stiff black material was pre-cut, allowing her to push pieces from it. It took her less than ten minutes to construct a dagger, compact crossbow and three razor-sharp bolts.

The equipment was rudimentary, but it met her needs. It was undetectable by airport security, yet lethal. She knew from training that the crossbow was accurate to around fifteen yards, similar to the range she would expect from a suppressed pistol. However, unlike a pistol bullet, the thin nanotech blades on the end of the pencil length shaft would slice straight through even the most advanced covert armor. What's more, the toxin Mitch had ingrained in the point was fast-acting. When she punched one of the darts into Lisker's body she'd have the pleasure of watching him die.

Chapter Twenty-Two

BEN GURION INTERNATIONAL AIRPORT, TEL AVIV

A LITTLE UNDER three miles from Saneh the man she had previously planned to kill, Tariq Ahmed, sat in his private jet staring out the window at a passenger aircraft loading at a terminal.

He wondered how many of the hundreds of people traveling had faced a decision with as far-reaching consequences as the one he had made. Glancing down at the black attaché case containing his file on Manfred Lisker he thought of his wife, children and the thousands of employees that depended on him. Exhaling he rose, adjusted his waistcoat and jacket, grasped the case and walked to the front of the plane. He opened the door and lowered the aircraft's stairs.

Stepping down onto the tarmac he spotted a black SUV parked in front of a maintenance hangar. A figure waved him over. As he got closer he identified the man as a bodyguard. Broad shoulders and an ill-fitting jacket hid what Tariq assumed was probably a small arsenal and body armor.

The man smiled politely and opened the rear door of the vehicle so that Tariq could enter.

There was a younger man inside, Tariq guessed his age at early thirties. Unlike the guard he had a slender build and wore an expensive suit over a crisp white shirt.

He offered Tariq his hand. "Mr. Ahmed, it is a pleasure to meet you. My name is Dean. I'll be your liaison while you're in Tel Aviv."

Tariq almost laughed out loud. He'd come to Israel with evidence that his company was directly involved in the smuggling of weapons into Egypt. He knew that he'd be fortunate to leave alive.

The man gestured to the attaché case. "Is that the information you promised?"

"Yes."

"May I see it?"

Tariq smiled. "Are you the director of Mossad?"

The man frowned.

"My terms were very specific. If you don't like them, then I'm happy to board my aircraft and return to Dubai."

"I think we both know that we're well past that."

"Then I suggest you take me to Director Atzmoni."

———

"OK, WHAT HAVE WE GOT?" Keila asked as she wheeled her office chair alongside Abel.

"She has to be going after Manfred Lisker," he said.

Keila shook her head. "Why would a Lascar Logistics operative go after Lisker?"

"Because he's the one who's running her. He's the one who kidnapped her boyfriend as a mechanism of control."

"You think that Lisker is trying to run her?"

He shook his head. "No, he's been running her for years. Think about it. We know Saneh is Persian and we know she's been hanging out with a bunch of paramilitary types in the Emirates. We also know her boyfriend is a former Australian Army intelligence operative with a bent for social justice."

"Not to mention she's got friends that are supposed to be dead," added Keila. "The guy that helped me rescue Bishop is former CIA. His real name is James Castle and, according to our files, he died in Abu Dhabi in 2008."

"No shit. So, we can assume she's a badass, probably MOIS."

"Double agent?"

"Yeah, that would explain why Lisker's got so much leverage over her and it would explain the sealed file." He paused. "Seriously Keila, the guy's out of control. Why don't we just let her get it done?"

"Because she won't make it out of Israel alive and we owe it to Bishop."

Abel nodded. "OK, fine. So how are we going to find her?"

"Keila." Jacinta interrupted their conversation. "You've got a message from Director Atzomi's office. He wants to see you, immediately."

Her brow rose. "Did they say why?"

"No, just that you were to report immediately."

"That's not good. You think Lisker is on to us?" asked Abel.

Keila shrugged. "I guess I'm about to find out." She rose from the chair.

"I'll go back over everything and make sure it's all above board," said Abel.

"Appreciated."

"You want me to hold off on Saneh?"

"No, get Aaron out on to it. Tell him to tail Lisker, ultra discreetly."

"Will do. Good luck."

"Yeah, thanks."

As Keila left her office she felt as if she was walking into an ambush. If Manfred Lisker had blown their activities she was probably looking at being ejected from Mossad or worse. She'd already decided that she'd take full responsibility. The others may face administrative action, but it was unlikely they would be sacked. As she made her way through the building she couldn't help but wonder if Bishop had an opening on his team.

———

MANFRED LISKER STABBED his finger at the cancel call button and tossed the phone onto the car seat next to him. He'd tried to contact Avi no less than a dozen times. It had been over six hours since they last spoke and he wanted an update on the Mantis's mission. With any luck both she and Tariq Ahmed had been terminated.

Another of his phones rang and he glanced at the screen as he answered. "Daniel, what can I do for you?"

"You can start by finding out who hit our facility in Rwanda," said the CEO of Sakkin Industries. "Someone went through the place like a fucking hurricane."

"What, who?"

"Isn't that what I'm paying you for?"

"You're paying me to establish a capability not protect your assets. Now, what exactly happened?"

"Someone broke in, killed everyone and blew the place sky high."

"Sounds like a local security problem."

"They had a god damn attack helicopter. They murdered the project lead and stole our test subjects."

Lisker's eyes narrowed. "That's specific targeting. I'll have my people look into it. Did we lose any information from the Proteus project?"

"The loss of Doctor Morrison is a setback, but Marnisha assures me that his research is backed up on a remote server."

"And you have an alternate laboratory."

"Yes, in South Africa."

"Then all is not lost."

"Do you think this is related to the Canadian we had neutralized?"

Lisker felt his Mossad phone vibrate in his pocket. "I'm not sure. Like I said, I'll have my people look into it. Daniel, I have to go. I'll call you back as soon as I find something." He killed the call and tossed the phone on the seat. Pulling a third device from his pocket, he checked the screen. Director Atzmoni wanted him in his office as soon as possible. He sighed; Caleb was getting more risk-averse by the day. Lisker was continually reporting to his office to verify that an assassination that made the news wasn't one of his. It was an inconvenience he wasn't going to have to endure for much longer. Once he was Director he wouldn't have to put up with such trivialities.

"Take me to headquarters," he told his driver as he picked up a phone and once again tried Avi's number.

———

LISKER TOOK thirty minutes to make his way to Mossad HQ. Not enough time to seem tardy, but enough to let Atzmoni know he wasn't a dog to be whistled to his side. On arrival he made directly for the door to the director's office.

"Sir, please, if you'll take a seat."

He spun and shot the assistant an icy stare. Never before had he been denied entry to Caleb's office.

"He's got someone in with him."

"Who?"

"I'm not sure."

The comment was telling. It meant that whoever was in there had entered via the private elevator. He thought to call Avi before remembering that every communication device within the building was strictly monitored. Even powering up the phone would flag it.

"The director will see you now."

Lisker didn't bother to acknowledge the assistant as he pushed through the door.

Caleb was sitting at his desk with another man to his right. Lisker immediately recognized the lean features of Benjamin Sharett, the former Director of Mossad and current Chairman of the Subcommittee for Intelligence and Secret Services, the governing body of all Israeli intelligence. "Chairman Sharett, Director Atzmoni."

"Manfred, please take a seat." Caleb gestured to the chair in front of his desk.

"What's this about?" he demanded as he sat.

"Some allegations have been made against you."

"By whom?"

"What operations are you running in Egypt?" asked Caleb.

"Excuse me?"

"I don't seem to remember approving an operation to arm dissident elements in Egypt." He lifted a manila folder from his desk and gave it a nonchalant wave. "And yet here I am reading that you've been doing exactly that."

"Sir, this is some kind of smear campaign—"

"No, I think you'll find the evidence is quite compelling," added Chairman Sharett. "What's more, I've heard the testimony of one of your own intelligence officers confirming as much."

Lisker clenched his fists. "Hearsay and speculation," he spat. "If you think for even one second that I'd work outside of my mandate, you would have to be a fool. I've been loyal to Mossad and Israel for my entire twenty-three year career."

"No, you've been a self-centered, egotistical sociopath clambering over the bodies of good officers you've stabbed in the back," the director stated. "And now you're done. Manfred Lisker, you are immediately relieved of your duties and status as a Mossad intelligence officer. From this point forward you are disavowed. All resources belonging to this agency are to be immediately surrendered, and all access control is hereby revoked."

He rose. "You can't do this to me."

"The other option is a full trial that will certainly find you guilty and result in your incarceration," added Chairman Sharett. "The choice is yours."

Lisker struggled to contain his rage as he rose from his chair. "You're going to regret this."

There was a knock at the door.

"These men will escort you to the street," said the Director.

The door opened and two burly security guards entered. Lisker turned and strode out between them.

A moment after he was gone, Chairman Sharett spoke. "That man's not going to fade away quietly."

Caleb Atzmoni sighed. "He's going to be a thorn in my side till the day he dies."

"Always an option."

———

SANEH COULDN'T BELIEVE her luck. She'd been standing on the opposite side of the Mossad building wearing a headscarf and sunglasses with a coffee in hand when Manfred Lisker had exited from the pedestrian security gate.

She'd left the crossbow in her room while she was conducting her reconnaissance, but she had the carbon dagger inside her jacket. Narrowly avoiding a minivan as she crossed the road, she dropped her coffee in a trashcan and placed her hand on the hilt of the weapon.

Lisker's pace suggested he was in a hurry and she was forced to increase her stride to close the gap. She'd only met the Israeli spy on two occasions, but every detail was burned into her memory. He was the man who'd forced her to betray her country, her friends and the man she loved.

Time slowed as she focused on the point between her enemy's shoulders. The other people on the street blurred, blending with the streetscape. Taking the razor-sharp carbon blade from her jacket, she cocked her wrist, so it was concealed against her forearm. Mentally she rehearsed the move that would drive the point through his spine, paralyzing him. That would give her enough time to whisper in his ear before a final stab at the base of his neck that would penetrate his brain and snuff out the puppet master's life.

As her body tensed, ready to strike, she felt a hand on her shoulder and the barrel of a gun in the small of her back. Panic assailed her as she realized she'd succumbed to the rookiest of errors. Fixation on her kill had given her tunnel vision and she'd missed his security detail.

She sensed there was more than one operative behind her. They'd be working in a pair with a standoff between them that meant even if she killed the one behind her the other would cut her down.

A van pulled into the curb and she shot one last glance at Lisker who was a dozen feet away, oblivious to what was happening.

"Inside," a voice ordered.

Reluctantly she ducked into the vehicle. The hand on her shoulder guided her into a chair before slamming the door shut.

"God I'm glad we found you," said Keila from the driver's seat of the van.

Saneh glanced around and saw she was alone with the Mossad agent.

"If you had have killed him you'd never have gotten out of Israel."

"How did you know where I was?"

"Aden worked out what was going on. I just joined the dots to Lisker."

"So you know who I am and what I've done?"

The two women locked eyes in the rearview mirror. Saneh thought she saw an element of respect in Keila's expression.

"I've got an inkling."

"And you're going to let me go?"

She nodded. "I'm not going to forget the debt I owe your people." She paused. "And as much as I'd like to see Manfred Lisker face down in a gutter, I promised Aden that I'd get you out alive."

"He knows?"

"Yes."

Saneh gazed out the window as they turned toward the Mediterranean coast. "How's he going to forgive me?"

"Well, if you lay it all out I'm sure he'll understand. As far as Manfred Lisker goes, tell Aden he's been disavowed from Mossad. As long as he's outside of Israel, he's fair game." Keila pulled the van into the parking lot of a large marina. "This is far as I go."

Saneh leaned forward and placed her hand on Keila's shoulder. "Thank you. Not just for this, but for helping us find Bishop."

Keila smiled. "You tell Aden we're squared and give my best to Ice."

Saneh stepped out of the van and watched as it drove away. She'd always been dubious of Keila's motivations, but it would seem that the Mossad operative had a sense of loyalty that wasn't dissimilar to her own.

The marina had an office and a small café inside the front gates. She took a punt that it was where she was going to find Bishop. He wasn't sitting under one of the umbrellas on a wooden deck, but Ice was.

The big man rose from his chair with a smile and Saneh fought the urge to cry as she hugged him. "Thank you," she said when they broke.

"No problem at all. He's waiting for you at the end of the dock."

"You're not coming with us?"

"No, I've got a few things of my own to follow up. I'll catch up with you guys soon."

"Keila said to say hello." She gave him a little nudge with his elbow. "Something going on there?"

A smile appeared on his scarred face. "Maybe."

"You promise we'll see you soon?" asked Saneh as he made to depart.

"Real soon." He winked and headed to the parking lot.

She smiled as she walked along a floating dock that ran out into wide harbor sheltered by a breakwater of grey rock. There were vessels of all sizes tied up on either side of the walkway, from small power craft to ocean-going sailing boats.

She found the vessel she was looking for at the far end. The sleek blue hull of the *Susurro* rocked gently on the swell less than thirty yards distant. There was a familiar figure on the deck of the majestic ketch.

"Permission to come aboard?" she asked with a hint of apprehension.

Bishop lifted his head from the rope he was tying and fixed her with a stern look. "That depends."

"On what?"

"Are you going to keep anything from me?"

Saneh stepped onto *Susurro's* polished teak deck and Bishop stepped toward her.

"I'll tell you everything," she managed as he wrapped his arms around her and planted his lips firmly on hers. Tension dissolved from her body as she pressed herself against him. "Everything."

It took Bishop less than three minutes to cast off the ketch's lines and program the automated navigation system that would pilot them out of Israeli waters. The latest radar and optical sensors would steer them clear of any other vessels.

Steam fogged a brass-lined porthole as Saneh soaked her tired muscles under a jet of piping hot water. The bathroom on the boat exceeded her expectations. Spacious and luxuriously furnished it already felt like home.

"Is there room for two in there?"

She turned to find Bishop standing in the bathroom wrapped in only a towel. "Always."

He dropped the towel and she opened the shower door letting him inside. He held her close, the warm water cascading over their bodies as she placed her head against his chest.

"Mossad captured me long before I met you," she said.

"I know."

"When I joined PRIMAL I thought that was all behind me. But Tariq gave me up to protect the rest of you." She felt his body tense. "He didn't have a choice, Aden. It was me or all of you."

She ran her hand from his chest down the side of his abdomen to his thigh. "Manfred Lisker is disavowed from Mossad. He can't hurt Tariq or me now."

"I'm going to find him and kill him," he whispered as her lips found his and they kissed.

She pressed her body against him and felt the passion building.

"No more secrets," he whispered.

"I'm all yours," she murmured as he slid his hands under her backside and lifted her up against the wall of the shower. "All yours."

LESS THAN A DOZEN miles from where the *Susurro* cruised out to sea an air traffic controller at Ben Gurion international airport was managing the afternoon influx of flights.

"Tower this is Lima Lima Zero Zero One, please confirm we are cleared for takeoff on runway zero three," a British-accented pilot asked.

"Zero Zero One, you are cleared for takeoff." He glanced at a screen that showed the view from a camera atop the tower. The sleek Gulfstream powered across the runway and climbed into the air like a rocket. "That's the life," he murmured before turning his attention back to the radarscope.

Tariq Ahmed's private jet passed almost directly over the *Susurro* on its track northwest toward the European continent. Powerful turbofans pushed it effortlessly skyward and within a matter of minutes it had passed ten thousand feet on its way to a cruising altitude of thirty.

Back at the Gurion tower the air traffic controller kept one eye on the scope, tracking the jet's rapid climb. The G650ER was marketed as the most advanced business jet on the market and he believed the hype. The plane climbed at almost twice the rate of any of the commercial aircraft plying the sky.

Then, as the aircraft's marker indicated it was at twelve thousand, the dot blinked twice and disappeared. He tapped the touch screen with his finger. After the indicator failed to reappear he activated another screen and queried the aircraft's transponder. It took a moment for the system to return a negative report.

He activated his headset. "Lima Lima Zero Zero One, this is Gurion control, over."

There was nothing but silence.

"Lima Lima Zero Zero One, this is Gurion control, over."

"Attention on the floor," broadcast the voice of the tower's senior watch controller. "Two separate aircraft have reported observing a large explosion approximately a hundred miles north west of us. Please confirm that all aircraft have been accounted for."

The controller stood and eleven sets of eyes turned to him. "I have an aircraft missing. Lima Lima Zero Zero One dropped off the scope. They are not responding on any channels and their transponder is offline."

The senior watch controller snapped into action. "Action plan red, we have an aircraft down."

Chapter Twenty-Three

ROTOBURN, NEW ZEALAND

VANCE FLICKED his wrist and sent a tiny lead weight flying across the lush green lawns at the back of the old pub where he and Chua were based. Fly-fishing was something he'd always wanted to try, and in a region abounding with freshwater lakes and rivers this was the place to do it. Fishing, hunting and traveling was how Vance planned to fill his days now he was on permanent hiatus from the world of vigilante justice.

Teasing out a length of line he practiced making the tiny weight dance across the manicured grass, mimicking the movement of an insect. Once he'd got the hang of the basics he was planning to replace it with an actual fly and practice his casting into the natural swimming pool that Mitch had constructed next to the expansive garage. From there it was off to a stream in the hills.

Footsteps on the gravel path from the pub hit his ear and he glanced across and spotted Chua.

"What's up?" he asked as he reeled in the weight.

"There's been an incident."

Vance's heart dropped as he turned. "What sort of incident?"

"Tariq's jet exploded over the Mediterranean. Local media are reporting that Saneh is a suspect."

Vance shook his head in disbelief. "What! How?"

"I've contacted Saneh and Bishop. They think that Mossad was blackmailing Tariq. Also, it turns out Saneh was being run as a double agent before she started a new life with us."

"She was run by Mossad? She kept that from us."

"She was trying to protect us. Bishop says she was trying to assassinate her Israeli handler until he stopped her. Bottom line is they're safe now but Tariq is gone. Saneh sent through a detailed report."

Vance wound in his line. "Do you think he's dead?"

The lack of emotion on Chua's face told him the odds weren't in his favor.

"Mossad did this?" Vance asked.

Chua shook his head. "No. Manfred Lisker did this, Saneh's old handler and the former head of the *Kidons*."

"Former?"

"According to Keila, Mossad has disavowed him."

Vance turned toward the rolling green hills and the ragged grey mountains. He said a silent prayer for the man who'd financed him and Ice start PRIMAL. He was never what Vance would call a close friend, but there was a respect between the two men that was rooted in their desire to bring justice to the world.

"Vance, what are we going to do?"

"Let's take a look at Saneh's report. Then get her and Bishop online."

———

MEDITERRANEAN SEA

Bishop and Saneh were expecting the call. They were sitting side by side in the *Susurro's* lounge when Vance and Chua appeared on a wall-mounted screen.

"Gentlemen, I wish this was on better terms," said Bishop.

Both wore grim expressions. Chua spoke first. "We're going to miss Tariq Ahmed, but he would want us to continue the work he started."

"We're going after Manfred Lisker?" asked Saneh.

"We will, but we'll play a longer game," added Vance. "Saneh, we read your report." He paused. "Mossad had you over a barrel and we can understand why you kept your past a secret. It should have died with you in the Ukraine. However, you should have told us after they re-established contact. We could have helped."

"With all due respect, Vance, this was bigger than PRIMAL. I had to try and keep you all isolated from Lisker. The man is as lethal as they come. What's more, he somehow got leverage over Tariq and forced him to give me up. We know now that he was also responsible for the attack on the Sandpit, and kidnapping Bishop."

"Do you think that Tariq knew you were a double agent?" Chua asked.

She shook her head. "No. Only Lisker and his superiors would have known. Tariq would have thought he was sacrificing me to save the rest of you."

"Both of you made the fatal decision to keep that from us," said Vance. "We could have dealt with the threat, as a team."

Bishop shook his head. "Vance, we can't be so naive to think we stood a chance against this guy. He's been leveraging Israeli intelligence assets to stay one step ahead of us the whole time."

"But not Tariq," said Chua. "He found a way out."

"Yes, but it cost him his life," Saneh said with a trembling voice. Bishop took her hand.

"Tariq knew the price of doing business with Mossad," said Vance. "He managed to neutralize Lisker without endangering the rest of us. That's the Tariq I knew, and the Tariq I will remember."

Saneh exhaled. "He offered me a new life and ultimately gave his own, so I could keep it. Now I'm going to avenge him by killing Manfred Lisker."

"I think it's best if you keep a low profile," said Vance.

"Your face is on every major media outlet in the world. We need to wait for that to blow over," added Chua. "That boat is the best place for both of you. At least for the next few months."

Bishop gave her hand a squeeze. "There's been enough killing. Let's take some time off and work out a way forward."

"Which leads directly into another issue that Chua and I wanted to cover with you both."

Bishop smiled. "The answer's yes."

Vance scowled. "You don't know the question."

"I thought you guys were going to ask if Saneh and I would come to your wedding. I mean, you've bought the farm. I'm only guessing that a dog and a minivan are next. It makes perfect sense, you're such a close-knit team." He shot the pair a wink.

"You're such a dick," said Saneh, with a sigh.

Vance shook his head. "I was going to ask if you guys

wanted to take over running PRIMAL, but I guess I need to talk to someone else. Maybe Mirza and Sonia would be interested."

"You serious? You guys are actually retiring?" asked Bishop.

"Semi-retiring," said Chua.

"Think of it more as moving from management to an advisory role," Vance continued. "We've leaned out the organization and we think it's time for us to step down."

"Are you sure?" asked Bishop.

Both men nodded.

"We're still going to be involved," said Chua. "We just think it's best if you and Saneh take the helm, so to speak." He paused. "And with any luck, it will keep Bishop out of the field."

Saneh laughed. "Fat chance of that."

"Worth a try."

Bishop ignored the jibe. "Where are we at with the rest of the team?"

"Kurtz and Kruger are wrapping up their operation in Africa, Mirza and Sonia are settled in London, Miklos and Pavel are back in Spain running their lodge."

"What about Mitch? We're still going to need tech support."

"I think you'll find he's got that covered," added Chua. "His new facility in California is pretty impressive."

Bishop frowned. "I thought that was a special effects…" His expression changed as realization dawned. "Oh that's brilliant."

Saneh shook her head. "Sharp as a brick. Chua, what about Ivan?" She directed her question to Chua. Ivan was a deep cover agent who had facilitated PRIMAL's operations in no less than a dozen separate locations.

Chua shrugged. "Your guess is as good as mine. He hasn't popped up in months. If he does, I'll let you know. In the meantime, I'll send you through the new comms protocols. You can check in with everyone yourself."

"Sounds good," said Bishop.

"Guys, we'll be in touch in a few days to sort out a detailed handover and work through how we're going to support you," said Vance. "In the meantime, smooth sailing."

Bishop and Saneh gave their farewells before disconnecting and moving to the open deck at the stern of the ketch. Bishop had grabbed two beers from the fridge on his way through and handed one to Saneh. Raising it toward the setting sun, he offered a toast. "Tariq."

Saneh mirrored the action. "He can't be dead."

Bishop's brow rose. "What makes you say that?"

"Tariq Ahmed would never let himself be outmaneuvered by a man like Manfred Lisker."

"You think he faked his death?"

She shrugged as she took a swig from the beer.

"I guess time will tell."

"Lisker still needs to die."

"No doubt about it."

She reached out and took his hand. "So what are we going to call the new PRIMAL? I was thinking of something subtler."

"To reflect our new approach."

"New approach?"

"Yeah, a smaller more nimble organization that leverages off existing networks to find bad guys and deal out a little justice."

"What about *Susurro*?" she said as they gazed at the sun setting over the calm blue waters of the Mediterranean.

For a moment Bishop was transported back to Barcelona, into the ancient bookshop where he'd found a book that spoke of an organization called *Susurro*. In Spanish, it meant 'The Whisper', a group of vigilantes who appeared from the shadows to protect and avenge innocents targeted during the inquisition. And for that very reason, it was also the name of his boat.

"Perfect."

She leaned in and kissed his cheek. "So where to, skipper?"

"I thought we could spend a few weeks cruising the Med and then down the East coast of Africa to check on the boys." He placed his beer on the deck and pulled Saneh in close. "But first we need to drop into Spain and pick up Daisy. We had to leave her at a boarding kennel when I skipped town."

———

NEGEV DESERT, ISRAEL

Sand whipped against Manfred Lisker's face as he hurried across the tarmac toward the Sakkin Industries business jet. Ginsberg's plane had touched down on the private airstrip five-minutes earlier, less than a half-mile from the Israel-Jordan border.

Glancing over his shoulder Lisker checked again that no one was watching from the cluster of weather-beaten buildings where his Uber driver had dropped him. Dressed in jeans with a battered olive drab jacket, baseball cap and a shoulder bag he in no way resembled the same man who'd run Mossad's assassination teams with an iron fist.

The aircraft's stairs lowered as he approached. Entering

the jet a stewardess took his bag before directing him into the cabin.

"There's my man." Daniel Ginsberg rose and shook his hand. "Take a seat we're getting out of here."

Lisker took the chair across from Ginsberg and strapped himself in as they began moving.

"I can't say I was sorry to hear you'd left Mossad, although I was expecting it to be on better terms."

"I still have people on the inside."

"And they're loyal?"

Lisker nodded as the jet roared and launched skyward. "Have you commenced a takeover of the specialist Lascar assets?"

"Straight to business. We need to let the dust settle before we make a move. Tariq will have a succession plan in place."

"And my role in Sakkin? Is the previously discussed position still open?"

"That depends. Are you still able to expand our operations?"

"Of course. I can help you make Sakkin the single largest security provider in the world."

Ginsberg shrugged. "I'm going to need more than that. Exactly how do you see it happening?"

"I'll create the market and Sakkin will provide the solution."

"The market?"

"Instability, turmoil, violence, destruction, whatever is required. I've got the networks and you have resources. Together we can change the global security dynamic."

Ginsberg took a moment to consider the offer. "I like it." He checked his watch. We've got ten hours until we hit

Cape Town. We can use that time to work through the details. Do you want a drink?"

"Whisky, on the rocks."

He waved over the stewardess. "Two glasses of the Laphroaig."

"Talk to me about the Proteus project," said Lisker.

"You can visit the laboratory in Cape Town. Dr. Copeland has it up and running and is anticipating the first generation within twenty-four months. You're going to be impressed."

"That project will become the backbone of Sakkin and the savior of the Israeli state."

"That may well be, but we also have other projects that will interest you. I'm particularly excited by the integration of AI into air, land and sea-based systems."

"A result of your recent acquisition of Intelligent Responsive Systems?"

Ginsberg smirked over his whisky. "Exactly." He raised his glass. "I have a feeling this is going to be a very lucrative relationship."

"We're going to change the world."

CALIFORNIA, USA

Darren Robertson parked his Tesla SUV alongside the other vehicles in the Unlimited Effects parking lot and stepped out into the dry heat of a Californian summer. A successful producer with over a dozen films to his name Robertson had driven the two hours from his office in LA to meet the director of the company professing itself to be the most advanced special effects agency the world had ever seen.

Personally, he thought the claim was likely to be total crap. However, they did have a charging point for his Tesla and that was a step in the right direction. Having plugged in the electric vehicle, he paused to take in his surroundings.

Unlimited Effects looked to be a row of rusted aircraft hangars fronted by tasteful arid landscaping. Compared to the glitzy facilities closer to Hollywood it looked industrial and not particularly inspiring.

He pushed open a sandblasted metal door with the word office stenciled on it in faded white paint and stepped into a dusty waiting area. A wooden reception desk was staffed by a woman who looked like she'd stepped straight out of a World War Two recruiting poster. Her hair was up in a bun and she wore bright red lipstick and a khaki uniform.

"Mr. Robertson, Director Freeman will be with you shortly." She gestured to a pair of leather armchairs in the corner.

He felt like he was sitting in World War Two pilots' ready room as he waited. Moments later a section of the wall opened, revealing a muscular figure dressed in coveralls.

"Darren, Mitch Freeman." The man's accent was British.

Robertson rose and took the hand he was offered. Freeman looked nothing like the film industry types he dealt with daily. With his bald head and full beard, Mitch resembled a Viking not a Hollywood executive.

"Allow me to show you around the place." Mitch gestured for him to pass through the opening in the wall.

Robertson straightened his suit jacket and stepped

through the gap into the cleanest workshop he'd ever seen. Polished concrete floors stretched for hundreds of yards with workbenches, heavy machinery, computers, and shelves stacked with materials on either side.

"This is where the magic happens. If your people visualize it, then we can make it."

Robertson watched in fascination as an autonomous robot weaved between the equipment, sucking dust from the floor.

Mitch led him between high-tech machinery, giving a brief description of what each one contributed to the fabrication process.

"Do you have any examples of your work?"

"Sure do. The vault is this way."

At the rear of the hangar was a solid-looking steel door. Mitch stared up at a camera. "Mitch Freeman," he spoke in a loud voice. The heavy door slid sideways with a hum revealing a space the size of a tennis court, crammed with military equipment. "We've primarily been focused on the action genre," he said as they entered.

Robertson scanned the shelves laden with tactical equipment and robust black cases. Seeing a strange looking robot in one corner, he made his way across to it. "What's this?" He reached out and touched the battle-scarred metal.

"Exo-suit, we used it in a scene where the lead character busted a special ops team out of a Syrian prison."

"Looks fantastic."

"Worked well, even better now I've extended the battery life."

"You mean it actually works?"

"Sure does. You can give it a spin if you want."

He laughed. "No, I'll leave that for the stunt crew."

Mitch gave him a wink as they moved into a corridor

dominated by weapons. "As you can see we've got almost anything you could want."

"Any older era stuff?"

"No, it's all pretty contemporary and we'll be updating it regularly. Now, would you like to see my pride and joy?"

"Of course."

Mitch led him through a narrow corridor that ended in an opaque sliding door. Standing before the door, he turned and grinned. "This is where I keep the real shiny kit."

The glass slid sideways and Robertson peered into what could have been the Smithsonian Institute. Aircraft and vehicles filled the cavernous space, with additional equipment hanging from the ceiling fifty feet above. Central to the exhibit was a massive four-engine transport aircraft and business jet. Under its gargantuan wingspan, like chicks beneath a mother hen, were a camouflaged dune buggy, a black Little Bird helicopter and what looked to be an array of drones.

"Do all of these work?" asked Robertson.

"Better than the day they were built, mate." Mitch pointed to the far corner of the hangar where an internal office was positioned. "Most of them, including the big girl, can be piloted remotely via satellite uplink. Takes a lot of the risk out of filming the tricky stuff."

"That's very interesting. What's the range?"

"Global, yesterday we were flying a bird on the other side of the world, today we're going to put up one of the smaller drones in the backyard."

"That's unbelievable."

"We try to impress."

"How many staff do you have here?"

"Currently there are only four of us. Myself as the chief engineer, you met Sarah at the front desk, I've got a guru IT guy named Flash, and another engineer. However, with any luck, we're going to be expanding fast. I've got another two hangars under construction and plans for a special effects lab and firing range."

"You don't think digital effects are going to make all of this redundant?"

Mitch chuckled. "No, I've got people who are always going to want their bang live."

Robertson nodded. "Yeah, you just can't beat the real stuff."

"Amen to that." Mitch gestured to the jet-black helicopter that sat under the wing of the transporter. "Now, you mentioned a complex helicopter scene in your next film? Let's get you into a flight suit and crank this girl up."

ROTOBURN, NEW ZEALAND

Almost ten thousand miles from the scorching sands of the Californian desert Vance, clad in waders and a fishing vest, stood knee-deep in a mountain stream. "Come on, jumbo," he murmured as he used deft flicks of his wrist to dance a fake insect across the crystal clear water.

His pulse quickened as a foot-long trout rose and made a beeline for his bait. Then, at the last moment, it turned and with a flick of its powerful tail, disappeared. "You little…"

"I thought this was supposed to be relaxing?" asked Chua from where he sat on the bank cradling a .22LR bolt-action CZ rifle. On the grass next to him lay two of the fattest and healthiest looking rabbits Vance had ever seen.

"It's less stressful than keeping Bishop and Ice out of a

gunfight." He climbed out of the stream and placed his rod alongside a cooler bag. Taking out two beers he handed one to Chua as he sat on a folding chair. "At least you've got dinner."

"Enough for one more?" The Russian accented voice came from above, higher up the side of the densely vegetated gorge.

Chua turned and slowly raised his rifle. Simultaneously Vance took a pistol from inside the cooler.

There was a curse from the bushes then the sound of someone pushing their way through the heavy brush. A moment later a figure wearing hiking garb burst into the clearing.

"Ivan?" said Chua.

"*Da.* Who else would be stupid enough to climb a mountain to find you assholes?"

"More to the point, how the hell did you find us?"

The Russian operative shot him a look that screamed, 'It's my job to know.'

"Yeah, fair point."

Vance slid his pistol back into the cooler and swapped it for a beer. "So what brings you to our new digs?" he asked as he threw the bottle to Ivan.

He shrugged. "I just wanted to check out the retirement home. See if there was any room for another old dog."

Vance raised his beer. "The more, the merrier." He paused. "Did you hear about Tariq?"

Ivan nodded. "I never met him, but I know how important he was to our work. He will be missed."

"Yeah, he will be."

The Russian took a swig from his beer and sat alongside Chua. "You guys aren't really retired though, are you?"

"That depends on how you define retired," answered Vance.

"Out of the business."

"In that case, I'd call us semi-retired."

"Why?" asked Chua. "What have you got?"

Ivan tipped his bottle in Chua's direction. "That's why you're the master spy. Always one step ahead."

"Look out, he's buttering you up," said Vance.

"Gentlemen, come on. When have I ever not given you the best intelligence?"

Vance and Chua looked at each other and Vance nodded. "He's got a point. So like he said, what have you got?"

Ivan tipped his head back and finished his beer. "It's a long story. I'm going to need another beer."

Vance reached into the cooler and tossed him another.

Ivan caught it and deftly twisted the top off. "OK, so I know this guy in Cambodia, great guy. Works with an organization that rescues children who've been sold into slavery. For years I have been providing him with small donations to continue his work. Recently a number of his volunteers have disappeared. Last week one of them turned up dead. He thinks they're being systematically targeted.

"By who?"

"My initial investigations indicate it's likely to be a crime syndicate known as Rogue Darkness."

Chua frowned. "I've never heard of them."

"Neither had I, but trust me when I say they're not people you want to mess with."

"And yet that's exactly what you want us to do," said Vance.

"Well, it is what PRIMAL does best. That is if we're still

in the business of doing. Or does semi-retired mean PRIMAL isn't open for business?"

Vance took a swig of his beer and glanced at Chua. "This might keep Bishop and Saneh out of trouble. South East Asia is a long way from the Middle East."

Chua nodded. "They could use Kurtz and Kruger as the action arm. But, we're not part of the executive anymore. All we can do is pass the information and make our recommendation."

"Ah, so this is semi-retirement? You fish and hunt in the mountains, make some recommendations, and others go forth and wield steel in the pursuit of justice?"

Vance and Chua looked at each other and shrugged. "Pretty much," they echoed.

Ivan grinned. "I like this semi-retirement."

Epilogue

SAKKIN HEADQUARTERS, CAPE TOWN

MARNISHA COPELAND TUCKED a stray length of hair behind her ear as she studied the results of an experiment that one of her lab technicians had been running. She'd spent the weeks since the laboratory in Rwanda had been destroyed going over Dr. Morrison's notes. They were only a month away from opening a new birthing facility in South America. He'd made some amazing progress that she was going to be hard-pressed to replicate.

As she finished with the document a phone on her desk beeped and she tapped the receive button with her finger. "Copeland here."

"Marnisha, your patient has arrived."

"Excellent, I'll be right over."

Rising from her chair she took a white lab coat from a rack in the corner of her sleek new office and stepped out into the facility that Sakkin Industries had built her.

Occupying an entire floor within the newly constructed

Sakkin Tower, the tallest building in Cape Town, the research center consisted of offices, laboratories, surgeries and a cadaver refrigerator. Marnisha had worked with the engineers to ensure it was fitted with everything she needed to further the research that would eventually provide Sakkin with a limitless supply of operatives endued with the best attributes that money could buy.

She followed the sterile corridor that looped its way around the building linking each of the individual labs, her heels ringing on the laminate flooring. The walkway was cluttered with boxes of equipment that were yet to be installed. Arriving at her personal surgical suite she swiped through an opaque glass door into the ready room where her patient was waiting.

The man, or what was left of his wasting body, sat strapped in a wheelchair with an oxygen line taped into one nostril. Drool ran from the corner of his mouth into a scooped bib.

"Hello, Avi," she said softly as a wave of pity flooded over her. She'd never met the Mossad operative, but the file Lisker had sent showed a handsome and physical man with a distinguished career. All that had ended when a bullet had shattered his neck, severing his spine.

Avi managed a grunt as he studied her through eyes still bright with life.

"Did they explain why you are here?"

He grunted again.

"Right. Well we've had some success growing the nerves, bone and tissue that we need to attempt a reconstruction of your damaged spine. We've also developed the drugs required to ensure your body doesn't reject these components. Overall I'm confident that that we can improve your situation. All I need is your consent to get started."

Avi let out a series of grunts.

"I'm going to take that as a yes. OK, I'm going to leave you in the hands of my staff, but rest assured that we're going to be seeing a lot more of each other.

Marnisha left him in the ready room and moved into the laboratory that adjoined it. Here, in a tank of chemicals was the spine that they'd grown from a sample of Avi Lerner's tissue. The mass of flesh and bone hung suspended by life giving synthetic veins that fed it the nutrients it needed.

However, Avi's spine tank wasn't the only one in the state-of-the-art lab. There were no less than six of them spaced evenly along a stainless steel table that ran from one side of the room to the other. Inside them were tissue samples that she'd grown from fabricated DNA. The irony of the whole thing was that Avi's replacement parts were being grown alongside a sample containing the DNA of the very woman that Lisker suspected had tried to kill Avi. In fact, if everything went to plan, components of Avi's genetic makeup would soon join that of Afsaneh Ebadi's in what would eventually become Sakkin's most lethal weapon.

Also from Jack Silkstone

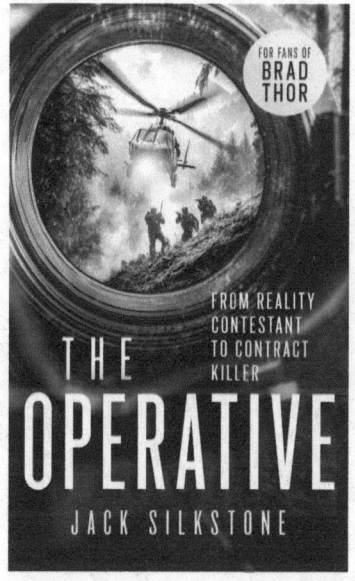

vinci-books.com/primal-operative

Fame is the perfect cover, but in this game, survival is the ultimate prize.

Turn the page for a free preview…

The Operative: Chapter One

David Martin stepped out of his rental SUV and squinted as he donned a pair of designer sunglasses. Dough-faced with curly black hair, he was an unremarkable-looking man with an unimpressive physique. At first glance, most people assumed he was an accountant or, worse, a real estate agent. In fact, he was a lawyer and fixer for a shadowy intelligence consultancy known as *The Entity*.

It wasn't his first trip to Texas, and he wasn't thrilled to be so far from the safety of the urban environment. *This place is a dusty shit hole*, he thought as he slammed the car door and surveyed his surroundings.

The Delta Ranch, such a lame name, he thought. It was smack bang in the middle of nowhere surrounded by thousands of acres of rugged, tree-covered hills. He imagined that they were crawling with rattlesnakes and spiders.

The ranch house was a short walk, but that wasn't where he'd find who he was looking for. Instead, he made for a sizeable open-ended barn, where boots poked out from under a tractor.

"X, is that you?" he asked between bursts of a rattle gun.

A leathery face appeared from under the machinery.

"Do I look like that behemoth? He's out back." The man gestured through the barn then slid back under the tractor.

"Thanks," mumbled David as he straightened his sports jacket and entered the barn, careful not to get horse shit on his loafers.

The structure had stalls on both sides and an open door at the back through which he could hear the crack of gunfire. Exiting, David made his way to an open area cleared between two low hills.

He spotted the man he was looking for crouched over a hefty tractor tire.

X, a massive lantern-jawed former CIA paramilitary officer, let out a grunt as he flipped the tire. Before it dropped, he sprinted toward a row of steel targets, unslinging the carbine that hung across his back as he moved.

Skidding to a halt, he rapidly engaged the targets in one direction, changed magazines then hit them in reverse before unloading. He slung the weapon across his back as he strode toward David.

"What's up?" his said, deep and abrupt.

David noted that despite the grey at his temples and the wrinkles on his face, the retired paramilitary officer looked as fit, if not fitter, than ever.

"Good to see you too."

"Niceties are for nice people. We ain't fucking nice!" X gestured to the barn. "I'm guessing we need to talk somewhere secure?"

"Preferably."

David had known X for nearly a decade and knew the big man wasn't one for small talk, which was OK with him. He followed him back to the barn into one of the horse stalls, lined with cupboards to hold tack. X fished a device from his pocket and waved it over a wall panel. There was a click, and a cabinet slid sideways, revealing stairs that disappeared into a basement.

"Very 007," said David as he followed him down.

Lights flickered on, illuminating a bunker. X strode across to a line of lockers, punched in a code, opened the door, and placed his carbine beside a dozen other weapons.

"Rather well equipped," said David as he sat on a Chesterfield sofa.

"Beer?"

"Why not."

X grabbed two cold bottles from a fridge, twisted off the caps, and handed one to the lawyer. Then he lowered his hulking frame on to a couch opposite. "So, what have you got?"

"We've had a compromise," said David.

"How bad?"

"Four of our best field operatives."

"And the rest?"

"In hiatus."

"That's untidy."

"To say the least. Which brings me to my next point. We're enacting the plan."

X took a swig from his beer and swallowed. "What plan are you talking about? We had a lot of plans."

David smiled. "Plan Survivor."

X frowned. "No shit! The board approved it?"

"They did, and you and I will run it."

"We got a budget?"

David reached into his jacket and withdrew a folded piece of paper. "This is your contract." He handed it over.

X inspected the document and let out a long whistle. "That's a decent lump of treasure."

The lawyer nodded. "It's a big job. You up for it?"

X finished his beer and wiped his chin. "Ain't got anything else on."

———

Jennifer Murphy sat in her cubicle on the eleventh floor of an office block in Charlotte, North Carolina. Middle-aged, she had shoulder-length curly brown hair and blue eyes. She was in reasonable shape, training three times a week at a local gym to maintain her figure. She'd described herself on a dating site as bubbly and a chronic oversharer.

Jen, to her friends, was a case manager for a multinational insurance company. A job she loathed, and subsequently, she spent a lot of time planning her holidays. Today, she was researching horse trekking in the Italian Alps.

"Jenny, have you wrapped up that O'Malley case yet?" her supervisor called across the office.

She minimized her internet browser, replacing it with a spreadsheet of her allocated cases, all of which were on schedule. "No, Neville. I'm still waiting on the photos."

Neville spoke from behind her. "Well, get onto it. I need that case cleared by the end of the week."

"They're an older couple, Neville. I'm waiting on their daughter to take better images."

"Jenny, I don't care. Get it done."

As he moved to the next cubicle, she shook her head. "What the hell am I doing?" she murmured as she scanned her case files. Forty years old and working a crappy insurance job to fund holidays, which she went on alone. Not exactly where thirty-year-old her would have hoped to be.

Glancing over her shoulder, she saw Neville had returned to his office. Reopening her browser, she turned her attention back to the horse trek.

In her imagination, she was already there. She was cantering up a flinty hillside between olive-laden trees on a beautiful mare, spurred on by her handsome Italian guide.

Her fantasy was interrupted by a gentle cough. "That doesn't look like work, darling."

Her best friend and work colleague, Ben, leaned over her shoulder. "Does look amazing, though."

"Yeah, I know, and I've almost got enough leave."

"Did you see the email I sent you? I've got a better option."

She opened her email client and found his message. Opening it, she frowned. "What's this?"

"Perfect for you, is what it is. I found it on Facebook and thought Jen has to do this."

The email was a flyer for what looked to be a reality TV show called *The Operative.* She read the Tag Line.

From Zero to Hero. We're taking the average Joe off the street and turning them into James Bond.

"They're looking for people just like you," said Ben.

"You mean ordinary?"

He laughed. "Not ordinary, normal. Come on, babe, you'd crush this. Plus, it would get you out of this boring ass office. Even if it's just for a day to try out."

She opened the application form. "Ben, it's ten pages long. I don't have time for this."

"Of course not. I mean you've got to plan your horse holiday in Italy. So, I've filled out most of it already."

She scrolled down and saw that he'd done exactly that.

"Jen, fill out the gaps and email it in. Come on, what have you got to lose?"

"Fine! But you're buying me a triple-shot caramel latte. It's the only way I will get through the afternoon."

"Deal. You finish the application, and I'll run downstairs to Starbucks. But you better have that application in by the time I return."

He left the office as she started reading the application in detail. The first question asked why she would make the ultimate operative. She took a moment to think before typing her response.

Because no one would ever suspect me.

———

"Nick, your ex-wife is on line two."

Nick Liu looked up from his laptop and saw the pained expression on his elderly assistant, Magda's, face. "What does she want?"

She shrugged. "Money?"

The American-born Chinese lawyer stared at the flashing light on his desk phone as he exhaled. He'd been divorced for over six months, but the woman wouldn't leave him alone, and he couldn't say no.

"Stop giving that leech money," grumbled his father, the managing partner of the law firm, as he entered the office and dumped an armful of case files on his desk. "I want these annotated by the end of the week."

"Dad, one of the associates can do that."

"I'm not asking one of the associates. I'm asking you."

His father shot him a withering look as he left Nick's office, leaving him with the pile of folders and the flashing phone.

He stared at the light, which seemed to pulse in time with his heartbeat. His palms were sweaty as he picked up the handset and stabbed the call button.

"About time, Nick. That's why you don't have any clients, right? You keep them waiting on the phone all day."

"Anna, what do you want?"

"Want? What do I want? Is that any way to talk to the mother of your child?"

"Anna, it's a dog, not a child. Now look, I'm swamped. Can you tell me what you want?"

"He's not just a dog. It's bad enough that I had to raise him while you were at work. Now you don't want him to get the education he deserves."

"How much?"

"Three thousand dollars."

"Three thousand for dog training," he clenched his teeth. "Fine. I'll transfer it today." He placed the phone back in the cradle and sighed as he wiped his hands on his suit pants. Anna had divorced him to run off with some asshole personal trainer, which crushed his self-esteem. Something she had no problem exploiting at every opportunity.

It wasn't like he was in bad shape. He trained most days, watched what he ate, and tried to get enough sleep. But how was he supposed to compete with a ripped fitness instructor who worked out for a living?

His elderly assistant reappeared in his doorway. "Nick, the printer is broken again."

Well, at least he still had Magda.

"I'm going to have her number blocked," she said as he went to the law firm's common area print station.

"Thanks, Magda, but that's not necessary. Now, what's going on with the printer?"

"It's got some kind of weird glitch."

Nick checked the device's error code and identified a network problem. He opened the server cupboard and inspected the interface. A moment later, he'd rectified the problem.

The printer hummed, confirming the solution.

"If only you were as good with women as you are with computers."

"Wow, thanks Magda."

"This is for you." She thrust a printed page into his hands. "I think you should consider it." He frowned, examining the page as he returned to his desk.

Magda had printed what looked to be a social media post for a reality TV show called *The Operative*. The tagline caught his eye, and he immediately pictured himself dressed in a tuxedo, casually strolling into a casino.

"I thought you might be interested," said Magda from the door.

He laughed. "Magda, it's every balding middle-aged divorcee's fantasy. From Joe Schmo to James Bond."

"Then put in your application. If you're successful, you'll have to take three months leave without a call from that evil ex-wife, which is a holiday for me too. Then, when you win, we can go halves in the five hundred grand."

Nick typed the URL on the paper into his browser and opened the ten-page entry form. "You know what, Magda. I'm going to do it, but if I win, I'm keeping all the cash. My days of handing all my money to women are over."

"So far, we've had over nine thousand entrants. Based on your provided criteria, we've narrowed those down to a base of two hundred." A smartly dressed production consultant, Fiona Yang, gestured to a digital board displaying thousands of mug shots of potential candidates. On cue, most of them faded away, and the remaining hundreds came together into two blocks titled East Coast and West Coast.

David was impressed with the consultant. Two weeks earlier, he'd presented her with the concept documents that he and X had drafted, and already she'd set the ball rolling in precisely the direction he'd envisaged.

"Looks good." He glanced at X.

The former paramilitary officer sat wedged in a sleek white office chair dressed in a fitted suit that barely contained his massive frame. "Do we get the final sign-off?" he asked gruffly.

"Of course," answered Fiona. "I've sent David a link to our secure proprietary website. You will be able to access it easily. From there, you can approve the final hundred contestants for each pre-selection location."

"Excellent," said David.

"I'm excited about this project. It's a unique idea that has the potential to develop a great following. Thanks again for choosing us to help you put it together."

"We're very pleased to have you on the team," replied David. "Now, talk us through the pre-selection."

"Certainly. Again, I've used your direction to shape the program." She gestured to the screen, and the faces were replaced with maps. "I've got east and west coast teams preparing the locations and hiring the necessary crew. We should easily meet the timeline you've put in place. Fortunately, we have a standing relationship with a company we worked with on a similar project."

"What was the project?" asked X.

"Hunt for the Ultimate Ninja. You might have seen it."

"Nah, don't think so."

David hadn't either. He didn't watch television.

"Well, they used a lot of equipment that I think we can employ during the pre-selection. They also ran a fairly comprehensive command center setup we can utilize."

"Very efficient," said David.

"Thank you, the key component we needed to discuss was the budget for each location."

"Yes, what's the number?"

"I'm sorry?"

"How much do you need?"

She chuckled. "That's not usually how it works. I was expecting you to give me a number."

David turned to X, who shrugged. He had no idea what it cost to run something like this, and the board had given him carte blanche. "Funding isn't going to be an issue. Draw up a budget and have it sent to my assistant."

"OK, that's easy." She made a note on her smart device. "Right, next item on the agenda, the selection course. I've reached out to a company in New Zealand that specializes in this style of event. They're in the middle of drafting a concept that aligns with your require-ments. I take it you would like me to negotiate the budget?"

"You got it," said David.

She made another note. "That brings us to the director. Have you had a chance to look over the names I put forward?"

David took his phone from his jacket and found Fiona's

email. His assistant had highlighted one of the five names. "Charles Chen looks good."

"I agree, he's done a lot of reality TV and will be a great fit for the project."

"Right, so that's a wrap!" exclaimed David.

"If you're happy, then I'm happy."

David rose and shook her hand before leaving the office.

"That chick's way too switched on," said X once they were in David's SUV.

"I agree. We'll part ways once the selection is over. I've had a background check run on the director. He's not going to be a problem."

"Do we need a director?"

David nodded. "It's essential that the project looks legitimate as long as possible. Don't worry; you will have complete autonomy to run the training how you see fit. Have you selected your team?"

"Yep, they're already at Camp X-Ray."

"X-Ray, isn't that the name of the prison at Guantanamo Bay?"

"Yep."

David looked sideways at the hulking operator. "We're trying to build something here, not destroy their will to live."

X shrugged. "Y'all gotta break 'em down to build 'em up."

"Come up with something more marketable."

"Fine, I'll call it The Ranch."

"Except the locals don't use that term. They call them Stations."

X rolled his eyes. "Fine, let's call it the goddamn Station."

As they left the production company, Fiona remained in

the meeting room, consolidating her notes. She was updating a to-do list for her assistant when her boss appeared.

"How did it go?"

Fiona smiled. "Client is happy."

Her boss's eyes narrowed. "And you?"

"I've never had to work with people who have no idea how television production works. David seems like a smart guy, but he's no producer, and the other guy looks like a hitman."

Her boss shrugged. "Is their money good?"

"Yes, the escrow account has over a million in it."

He clapped his hands. "Well then, let's keep them happy."

———

Jenny gently opened the door to her apartment and placed her gym bag on the floor. There was a broom leaning against the wall, and she grasped it in one hand as she hit the lights with the other.

"Buffalo, where are you, you little punk?"

Buffalo was her rescue cat, an athletic tabby whose mood was violently unpredictable. His favorite pastime was stalking her when she returned to their apartment.

She entered the living area and waited with the broom held high. The hairs on her neck rose as she heard a low growl from beneath the sofa.

"Buffalo, NO!" She braced herself for the onslaught.

He moved with lightning speed, a tiny tiger chasing down its prey. She swatted him away with the broom, and he skidded across the kitchen floor. "That's enough," she scolded, waving the broom.

He sprang onto the countertop as she opened the refrigerator and found his food. His tail lashed the marble surface, and he growled again.

Tearing the lid off a serving of fish, she slid the container across the bench. "There, happy?"

He sniffed the expensive dish, tasted it, and let out a cheerful meow.

"Bipolar little shit." She stroked his fur as he ate.

Buffalo continued eating as she took her meal from the freezer. She gave his dinner a sideways glance then scowled at hers. "Yeah, you definitely eat better than me." She threw the portion in the microwave and poured herself a glass of red wine.

Five minutes later, she sat on the couch with an average lasagna and a passable glass of wine. Before starting her dinner, she checked her phone and spotted an email reply from *The Operative*. Probably a 'thanks but no thanks.'

Sipping from her glass, she tapped on the message and was surprised to see she'd been selected for a spot at the Eastern Seaboard preliminary selection in Richmond, Virginia.

"Holy shit!" She immediately called Ben and told him the news.

"That's fantastic, babe. You have to do it," he replied.

"I don't know. What if I make it through to the next round? Who would look after Buffalo?"

"You do know that cat hates women, right? He'd be much happier chilling here with me."

She laughed. "That's true."

"So, no excuses. You're going to kick ass."

"Yeah," Jen said with trepidation. "Yeah, I guess I am."

———

Nick focused on the timer on his phone as the numbers counted down. His heart felt like it would burst from his chest and sweat ran off the Asian American's forehead like rain, hitting the treadmill's deck as his feet slapped it relentlessly.

The timer hit zero, and the belt slowed. Gasping for air, Nick grabbed a towel from the arm of the treadmill and wiped the sweat from his forehead.

Sprint training was something he did when he'd had a bad day. It was therapeutic, pushing himself till he nearly puked. Self-punishment for allowing people to walk all over him.

His pace had slowed to a fast jog when an alert popped up on his phone. It was a message from Magda. The elderly assistant so rarely messaged him that he'd forgotten she was the only person not screened by his do not disturb.

Poking his phone where it sat on the treadmill console, he unlocked the screen to see the message.

Way to go, James Bond. You got a spot.

For a split second, he had no idea what she meant. Then he remembered the reality TV show and the ten-page application he'd submitted. Excited, he grabbed the phone. Hands slick with sweat, it slipped through his fingers onto the treadmill deck. He sidestepped as it shot under him and slammed into his garage wall.

"Damn it." He punched the stop button and dismounted, recovering the device from the concrete floor. Thumbing the screen multiple times, he failed to get any response from the spider-webbed screen.

"You're kidding me."

He wandered out of the garage, through his modest

apartment and into his pokey office. Tossing the phone on his desk, he unlocked his laptop.

The alert from Magda was there too.

Opening his email account, he scrolled through the dozens of work messages, past one from his ex-wife and found the response from his application.

It was short, informing him that he'd been chosen for pre-selection for *The Operative*. While that didn't sound that impressive, it excited Nick. He hadn't won anything since college, much less been 'selected'. He pressed the accept button at the bottom of the email. It opened a webpage with the event's location and what to bring.

He'd never been to Virginia. Now all he had to do was convince his father to give him the day off. Even the thought of asking that made him nervous. Nope, he was going to call in sick. Not very James Bond, but at least he wouldn't have to deal with his father's scorn.

The Operative: Chapter Two

Vomit bubbled into Jen's mouth, but she managed to keep her lips closed and swallow it down as she dashed forward and threw herself across the line. The final siren blared, level fourteen of the beep test. Someone thrust a plastic cup of water into her hands, and she took it gratefully, using it to rinse the foul acidic taste from her mouth.

"Well done. You made it," the cheerful crew member announced. "Head over to the marquee for your next challenge."

Dragging herself to her feet, she glanced back at the contestants who hadn't been able to complete the fitness screening. The ordeal had consisted of a brutal strength circuit, Pilates session, mid-distance run, and finally, the ruthless beep test. She'd never worked so hard in her life.

Over a hundred hopefuls had turned up for the event, but over half hadn't made the grade. They now stood, pained, before a bubbly fitness instructor who thanked them for attending, while a film crew captured their anguish.

Meanwhile, those who had passed the fitness test were ushered into a large tent.

A camera and a microphone ambushed her as she entered.

"How are you feeling?" asked an interviewer.

"Exhausted," she managed. "One of the hardest physical activities I've ever done."

She contemplated pushing past but remembered this was a reality TV show selection. They would be looking for contestants who were engaging and charismatic.

"There was a point where I didn't think I would make it. So I dug deep and managed to get across the line."

"Any particular motivators?"

"Yeah, my nephews. I'm doing it for them."

"Great stuff. You better get going," said the producer. "We'll catch up with you if you pass the next phase."

The words didn't seem like much. But, the 'if' hit home. Throughout the day, Jenny noticed that many younger, fitter, better-looking contestants had been breezing through the fitness test. She'd barely scraped through, and no doubt, it would get much worse.

Tentatively, she joined the others in a briefing area and waited for instructions.

"Hopefully, that's the last of the beep tests. That nearly did me in," said the man next to her. Asian, middle-aged, and balding, he had an easy smile and friendly eyes.

"Glad I wasn't the only one," she replied.

"Not many people our age made it through. Hopefully, life experience can prevail over social media reach and rock-hard abs. My name's Nick."

"I'm Jen, a pleasure to meet you, Nick."

"You as nervous as I am?"

She nodded. "God knows what they're going to do to us next."

———

"Camera two. Zoom in on those oldies at the back. They look terrified." Charles Chen, *The Operative's* newly appointed director, issued his instructions via radio from the control center. "David, we're getting some great footage here. It's going to come together nicely."

Chen and a team of technicians were monitoring the footage from three roaming camera crews in the comfort of a purpose-built semi-trailer. David sat observing the proceedings from a plush couch opposite a wall of monitors.

The lawyer had run a full background check on Chen, and the lightly built Asian had come up clean. His family was from Taiwan; parents emigrated in the late eighties. He was born in ninety-four, attended good schools, and cut his teeth shooting action TV commercials in a top advertising firm. When he went out on his own, he achieved limited success, until he got a break directing an adventure reality TV show. Not that David cared about any of that. More importantly, Charles Chen's parents were deceased, and he had no partner or siblings. He was a loner.

"The next part may not be as interesting," said David.

Charles glanced at his run sheet. "Right, the psychological profiling and intelligence testing. We'll get some facial close-ups and chase down some interviews later. The audience will be more interested in the contestants' feelings than anything else."

"But, we can see the results live?" he asked.

"Andy?"

One of the technicians gestured to a screen where each contestant was listed. "As they input their answers on the tablets, their scores will update here. A green bar indicates success, and a red failure."

"Makes sense."

The door to the trailer swung open, and X stepped inside. The Chief Instructor wore his standard heavy-duty tan cargo pants and a T-shirt declaring *Coffee or Die*. Accordingly, he held two cups in one of his mammoth hands. He spotted David and passed him one.

"X, I want to introduce you to our director, Charles Chen," said David.

"People call me Chuck. So, your name's Ex? Like as in ex-wife?" The director offered his hand.

David snorted into his coffee.

The big man scowled, ignoring the handshake. "It's just X."

"Ah, like the letter. Right. Got it. So, how do you fit in?"

"He's a producer and the Chief Instructor. You do exactly as he says," said David.

Chuck frowned. "That's not how this works. I'm used to having full creative control."

"X isn't going to get in your way. He's here for authenticity," said David.

"Right, so you're the real deal," asked Chuck.

X smiled. "You do your thing, and I'll do mine."

"Cool, cool. Oh, and for future reference, I drink quad shot lattes." The director gave X a cheeky wink.

"Can you drink that through a straw?" X asked deadpan.

Chuck's brow rose. "Huh, straw?" He glanced at David, who clenched his fist and mimed a punch to the jaw.

Chuck swallowed and turned back to the screens. "I'll get the coffee next time."

"How are our numbers looking on the psychometrics?" asked X.

David gestured to the screen. Most of the names had green marks alongside them. "So far, so good."

"Let's see how many get through the challenge course," said X. "Then we'll know what we've got to work with."

Grab your copy...
vinci-books.com/primal-operative